I0571098

WADE BOSS

HYBRID HUNTER

MARCUS MacGREGOR

SADDLE SORE
Entertainment, LLC

SADDLE SORE
Entertainment, LLC

ISBN-13: 978-0615861746
ISBN-10: 0615861741

DEDICATED

to all those who still
believe the world needs chivalry,
whether attired in shining armor
or blue jeans.

TABLE OF CONTENTS

PROLOGUE

If a man's home is his castle, then his RV has gotta be, like... his own personal space cruiser!

So thought Forrest Babb as he sank deeper into his luxury camp chair and cracked open a third can of beer. Then, to congratulate himself on the astuteness of his analogy, he tossed back his head and took an extra-long swig. The sun dipping behind the southern California hills furnished a rosy backdrop to the scene, so that it seemed to Forrest as if Mother Nature herself were giving him a big thumbs-up.

Ever since high school, he had been telling his buddies Gary and Stu that, before he turned thirty, he was going to buy an RV and start touring the country. For roughly a decade, he had worked faithfully at a video game store, saving his pennies and living frugally in his mother's basement while his pals partied hard and scoffed at his dreams. But here they all were, a full two years before Forrest's self-imposed deadline, kicking back around a campfire and having already spent one night in the glorious vehicle.

At least it was glorious to Forrest, and as such, he had hoped it would earn him a little respect from the guys. But despite the fact that he had made good on his vow — not to mention putting on twenty pounds of muscle and clearing up his acne — Gary and Stu still saw him as an unaccomplished geek. And, as neither of them had done much maturing themselves since the old days, no praise for his recent purchase seemed forthcoming.

Forrest was beginning to wish that he had decided to spend the weekend alone.

Gary, whose only achievements as an adult were some high scores on video games Forrest had procured for him at a discount, now squirmed in his own camp chair, attempting to balance a beer on his prodigious belly. Finally succeeding in this, he spoke in calm, even tones to minimize any undulations that might spill his drink.

"You know, Forrest," he began. "I've got to hand it to you..."

Forrest perked up.

"...I don't know how you were able to get that 80s camper to pass inspection."

"It's only fifteen years old!" snapped Forrest, deflated and doubly rankled.

"Really?" replied Gary. "Then how come there's an old, Kenner action figure in one of the bedroom drawers?"

"That doesn't mean anything!" Forrest retorted. "Anyone could have put it in there anytime *since* the 80s. They could have put it in there last night!"

"Well then, they were pretty sneaky," chimed in Stu, fishing through the cooler with gangly arms in search of the last hard cider.

"It's just an expression of speech, jackass!" Forrest fired back. "And stop poking around in the flippin' drawers, Gary!"

Pleased to have gotten such a rise out of Forrest so early in the evening, Gary and Stu grinned at each other as if they were still in tenth grade.

"Take it easy," said Gary. "We're just kidding."

"Yeah, whatever," replied Forrest, and then for a few minutes no one said anything.

Finally, Gary downed the rest of his beer, belched, and with some effort rose from his chair. "I need another burrito," he said, and then he waddled over to the RV and disappeared inside.

At such moments as these, it was Stu's habit to "rebuild the dike" with Forrest by way of a friendly overture. As much as he enjoyed riding Gary's coattails when it came to teasing, in truth he was no match for Forrest, one-on-one.

Popping open the coveted cider, he sidled over to the fire and, with something bordering on sincerity, said, "This is actually a pretty nice spot, Forrest."

It wasn't the praise for which Forrest was hungering, but at least it was something. "Yeah," he replied, "as long as it's not a holiday weekend, you can usually have the place to yourself."

Just then, there was a crackling in the bushes.

"What's that?" asked Stu.

Forrest strained his eyes for a moment and then gasped, "Oh, snap! I think it's Sherry Tilton!"

"Ha, ha. You're hilarious, Forrest," Stu quipped back.

"Dang, Stu! Looks like she finally tracked you down!"

"Shut up! Seriously, didn't you hear that? I sure hope it's not a skunk..."

"No, I told you: it's a *skank!*" laughed Forrest, now fighting back tears and thoroughly convulsed by the delicacy of his own wit.

Although one of Stu's defining character traits was a decidedly thin skin — especially when it came to jokes about his psycho ex-girlfriend — his courage was thinner still. As Forrest savored his minor coup, Stu sat very uneasily with his eyes fixed on the bushes. It was only a brief moment before something stirred again — louder this time.

"Uh..." said Stu, nervously taking a step backwards.

This time Forrest had no smart remark, for he also was concerned. The two of them stared into the thicket as Gary came back from the RV, burrito in hand.

"Forrest," he said with a full mouth, "you're gonna need to wear a hazmat suit when you empty that toilet tank. These things are delicious, but man, they're messing with my bowels."

Ignoring his remark, Forrest said, "There's something in the bushes."

"Isn't that sort of the deal in the great outdoors?" replied Gary.

But he took Forrest's concern more seriously as the whatever-it-was gave a low, menacing growl.

In a hushed voice, Stu asked, "Forrest — are there bears out here?"

"I don't think so," Forrest answered. He stooped and picked up one of the smaller logs from the woodpile beside the fire. "You guys head over to the RV — slowly."

They did so, and then Stu ascended the steps into the vehicle followed quickly by Gary. Forrest, however, remained where he was, clutching his improvised club and straining to see into the thicket.

"Forrest!" called Stu. "Get over here!"

He did not need to be told twice, for just then a frightening hiss convinced him to beat a hasty retreat. As he reached the RV and backed up the steps, Gary asked, "Can you see it?"

"No!" said Forrest, curtly.

Then, just as he was grabbing hold of the door handle, the bushes exploded. Something — a creature — sprang forth, sailing over the campfire and landing in a crouch just three yards from the RV.

Forrest shouted in alarm, dropped his log, and yanked on the door handle. Even as he did, the creature's powerful hind legs again launched it into the air.

It smashed head-first into the closing door, shattering the small window above the handle. Then, to the horror of the three friends, a long, sinewy foreleg shot through the opening and began groping wildly about.

It was such a blur of motion that the only features Forrest could make out were some clumps of orange fur and a host of razor-sharp claws.

Over the panicked cries of his buddies, he hollered, "The bedroom!" He then shoved them down the hall to the back of the RV, where they dropped to the floor and huddled together beside the master bed.

"What is it?!" yelled Gary.

"I don't know!" shouted Forrest. "Just stay down!"

He glanced back at the door just in time to see the creature's foreleg retract.

Stu had by now come completely unglued and was unable to contain a staccato torrent of blubbering noises. "Shut up, Stu!" ordered Forrest, and then he rose into a half-crouch and peered out the bedroom windows.

"Can you see it?" whispered Gary.

"No!" said Forrest.

As Stu made a concerted effort to muffle his mouth with both hands, Forrest strained to hear what was going on outside.

SLAM! The creature landed on the roof and started feverishly clawing at the sheet metal. The sound was like that of fingernails scraping down a chalkboard, only much louder.

At this, both Stu and Gary started screaming. Forrest, on the other hand, was intently focused on the ceiling, mentally calculating the strength of its component materials. Then abruptly, the clawing stopped.

The roof had proved too solid a barrier, and the frustrated creature jumped back down to the ground. Again, Forrest raised himself up to look out the windows. For a moment, he saw nothing.

Then, with a crash, the men were showered with broken glass as the creature hurled itself at the bedroom's rear window. The wicked claws shot inside just as before — only this time, there was enough of an opening that the creature began to squeeze its body through.

For a brief moment, Forrest stared in wonder, just trying to make sense of what he was seeing.

The creature bore some resemblance to a tiger, but it was clearly something else. For one thing, its face was long and narrow, and wasted in a sickly fashion. For another, its body was covered not with a glossy pelt of fur, but only sparse, mangy tufts that did little to conceal a black, scaly hide.

In addition to four large fangs, its mouth was packed with scores of shorter, needle-like teeth. But most disturbing of all was its forked tongue, which lashed about like a living whip — sampling the air for chemical traces of human prey.

Still baffled at the zoological identity of the beast, Forrest looked around for anything he might use to fight it. He threw books, a lamp, and even the 1980s action figure, but none of these had any effect. He scanned the room for a more effective weapon but found none.

In desperation, he stumbled out into the hall, where at last he spotted a tool that held some promise: a fire extinguisher, mounted on the wall just past the bathroom. He tore it off its hook and raced back to the bedroom.

By now, the tiger-lizard had forced its head and one shoulder completely through the window frame. With a mighty battle cry, Forrest opened fire.

This time, he got some results. The chemicals from the fire extinguisher filled the creature's mouth and nose. Gagging and hissing, it yanked its head back outside and dropped to the ground.

"Forrest! Get us out of here!" cried Stu.

Forrest ran to the front of the vehicle. After frantically fishing his keys out of his pocket, he jumped into the driver's seat and cranked the ignition.

"Hold on!" he yelled, and then he floored the accelerator.

Outside, the tires spun freely for a second before gaining traction. Finally, with all the spectacle of a Cape Canaveral rocket launch, Forrest's "personal space cruiser" burst from a cloud of dust and sped towards the red horizon.

CHAPTER 1: HISS HISS, FANG FANG

For strength and beauty, few animals on Earth can compare with the Bengal tiger, and Ginger was an exceptional specimen. In one fluid motion, she jumped from the ground up to the top of a seven-foot platform, which creaked under the sudden burden of her three hundred pounds.

"Good girl, Ginger. Now across," said her trainer, a muscular twenty-nine-year-old with sandy hair and a boyish face. His name was Chet Hubbard, and anyone could see that he loved his job.

Four years ago, while working at a wildlife refuge on the East Coast, Chet had been toying with the idea of relocating to Southern California, where his brother lived.

While researching the opportunities in the region, he came across an employment website with an ad calling for a full-time tiger trainer at a ranch north of Los Angeles.

When he called to find out about the details, he learned that the tigers were actually *performing* tigers that worked in television and the movies. This was intimidating, since he knew nothing about show business. But he figured that it was worth a shot anyway, and that his competence with the animals ought to be the thing that mattered most.

He was right. After a cross-country flight and a two-day "tryout," he was hired as an employee of Boss Ranch. In the four years since then, he had learned virtually every aspect of the business, so that by now, he was essentially capable of running it.

With his training staff, Chet directed Ginger to walk across a ten-foot beam to the top of another tower. She crossed the span with ease, dropped to the ground, and waited expectantly.

"That's right. Good girl!" said Chet, reaching into a pouch slung across his hip. He pulled out a hunk of raw meat, stuck it onto the pointed end of his staff, and extended it to Ginger. With teeth that could easily have bitten off her trainer's arm, the great cat daintily removed the morsel and gulped it down.

Supervising all of this was Chet's mentor, the owner of the ranch. Leaning against the inside of the chain-link pen, he appeared experienced and worldly-wise — which, after many years of adventurous living, he was.

Still in his physical prime, he stood about 5'10" and dressed for comfort in a flannel shirt, blue jeans, square-toed boots, a tan leather jacket, and a light gray cowboy hat. His hazel eyes were warm and friendly, though for the moment hidden behind the mirrored lenses of his aviator sunglasses.

Such an iconic appearance begged for a name just as distinctive. As it happened, his was.

Wade Boss.

A native of Texas, Wade had first moved to Hollywood to pursue a career as a stuntman, but lately he was better known as a world-class animal trainer. He was especially qualified for the work, since his father had been one of the few remaining tiger trainers in the country attached to a traveling circus.

From a young age, Wade's parents would pull him out of school whenever tour season came around. His mother would temporarily oversee his education, and the little family of three would hit the road together.

Although Wade naturally missed his friends back in Dallas, the excitement of his father's world made up for it. Wade readily developed a close kinship with the circus animals — not only the tigers that were owned by his father, but also the performing elephants, bears, and chimpanzees.

When he was a little kid, it was all a matter of fun. But once he entered middle school, his father began teaching him the serious business of tiger training.

Wade was an apt pupil and his father a skillful teacher. By the time Wade reached adulthood, he was choreographing his own spectacular routines. He seemed destined to follow in his father's footsteps, and his future seemed assured.

Except for one thing, which was that he did not want to spend the rest of his life in the circus. With each passing year, a yearning grew inside him to venture forth into the world to see if he could make it on his own.

On his twenty-fifth birthday, he announced that the next tour would be his last. It came as a hard blow to both his parents, and Wade felt terrible to see them so hurt. But he had made up his mind, and slowly he helped them to understand why he had to leave.

Wade had expected his final tour to be full of sadness and tears, but to his surprise, it was one of the best ever — thanks to his father. The elder Boss decided that if he couldn't keep his son from leaving, then he would encourage him in every way possible.

The question now was: What did Wade want to do? This was harder to answer than Wade had anticipated. Setting out on his own was one thing, but setting out for an actual *destination* was another.

After months of thought and research, he had gotten nowhere. Then, his mother made the brilliant suggestion of stunt work for the movies. Her words were like a bugle call to Wade's heart. As soon as the circus tour ended, he moved to Southern California and enrolled in stunt school.

Though he was entering the field a little older than most, he was still plenty capable of holding his own against the younger competition. Ironically, once he graduated, his greater years became an asset that helped him to establish a reputation as a mature and level-headed stuntman.

But as much as he loved the work, after about six years, Wade began to feel like something was missing in his life. Certainly he lacked a wife, though he remained ever hopeful. But there was something else as well — something he couldn't put his finger on for some time.

Then, while randomly watching a nature program on cable T.V. one night, he finally figured it out. Animals! There were no animals in his life — not even so much as a pet goldfish.

No sooner had he arrived at this realization than his father announced that he had decided to retire from the circus.

Like a burning match to a pile of dry leaves, the news set Wade's mind afire with a new vision for the future. He quickly drew up a business plan and purchased a ranch in the Santa Monica Mountains — horses and all. He then flew to Dallas, persuaded his father to give him ownership of the two youngest tigers, and went into business for himself as an animal trainer for the entertainment industry.

Applying the skills his father had taught him, Wade got his tigers to deliver some jaw-dropping performances while the cameras were rolling. This initial success allowed him to build a state-of-the-art animal housing facility, and to subsequently adopt a grizzly bear, a lion, and a cougar.

Rubbing elbows with movie stars was all part of the job, but in his free time, Wade shunned the glitz and glamour of their world. He was quite content to spend his days at the ranch, riding and training and savoring the fruits of his labors.

With pride, he clung to his old-fashioned manners and sing-songy Texas accent. His laid-back personality actually scored him points with the Hollywood crowd, which regarded him as corny, but refreshing — like a classic black and white movie.

Today, Wade was as happy as a clam, drinking in the morning sun and providing the occasional word of encouragement to his dedicated right-hand man.

"That's good, Chet," he called out, with a Texas twang. "Go again."

Chet obediently led Ginger past a series of platforms, ramps, and hoops to the beginning of the obstacle course.

At the same time, a lovely Latino woman in her mid-twenties came riding up on horseback — the main mode of transportation around the vast property, due to the intentional lack of a road past the main office.

Chandra Delgado had been working at the ranch for nearly a year longer than Chet, though her role was slightly different than his.

In the early days of the business, Wade had needed a part-time office manager to take care of the clerical duties he didn't have time for. He posted the job opening in the local papers, and Chandra was one of the many applicants.

During her interview, she told Wade that she had just finished her undergraduate degree in zoology and hoped to become an animal trainer. She went on to say that she was not only the best candidate for the position he had advertised, but that she would also make an excellent trainer-in-training.

Wade was so impressed by her intelligence and boldness that he agreed to take her on as an apprentice — provided she remained his office manager first, and performed that job well.

Neither Wade nor Chet was blind to her beauty, but since she already had a steady boyfriend, the working atmosphere at Boss Ranch remained happy and free of interpersonal drama.

"Hey, Chandra," Wade called out to the maiden as she reined her dapple-gray mare to a halt.

"Hey, Boss!" Chandra replied cheerfully, her long black hair swishing in unison with the horse's tail. "You left this in the office again." So saying, she pulled a cell phone from her pocket and handed it down to Wade through a hole in the chain-link fence.

"Oh... thanks," said Wade, receiving the device with a sigh of chagrin. He considered it more of an annoyance than anything, and was forever misplacing it.

"Also, you've got a call on the landline," Chandra informed him.

"They won't leave a message?" asked Wade.

In a slightly more serious tone, though still with a smile, Chandra replied, "I think you need to take this one."

* * *

Wade rode his buckskin Quarter Horse, Tango, at an easy canter behind Chandra. The building at which they finally arrived was built of cedar logs and looked more like a hunter's cabin than an office. The two riders dismounted, tethered their horses to the hitching rail, and headed inside.

The front office was decorated with movie posters and framed photographs. A number of these featured Wade's father and grandfather with the family tigers. Wade felt that being a third-generation trainer gave him an edge over the competition, and he did not hesitate to advertise it.

The other photos were mostly of Wade himself, posing with famous actors — not because he was a show-off, but because actors frequently visited the ranch to receive training for upcoming productions.

The most common need was for riding lessons, though the occasional role called for a star to act with one of Wade's carnivorous animals, in which case rehearsals were required.

The choice of office decor was thus a calculated business decision: a little bit of flattery went a long way in Hollywood, and an actor who knew that his picture was hanging in the office at Boss Ranch was more likely to boast of his experience there.

Taking a seat at her desk, Chandra picked up the business phone and said, "He's right here, Officer. I'll put you through."

"Officer?" asked Wade, his nerves suddenly jangled.

"I didn't want to worry you," replied Chandra.

"Thanks," said Wade, sarcastically.

He plodded glumly into his private study, where the artwork was more reflective of his own personal tastes: bronze sculptures of cowboys on horseback, oil paintings of wide open ranges, and worn-out horse tack that testified to many happy hours spent riding for work and pleasure.

Wade sat in the leather chair behind his tidy maple desk and soberly contemplated the flashing red 'hold' button of the phone. He had never done anything criminal, so he knew he had no reason to be afraid. Yet even a blameless man may feel an involuntary chill if the Law suddenly calls him by name.

He cleared his throat, took a deep breath, and picked up the receiver. "Wade Boss," he said.

"Mr. Boss," came a gruff voice. "This is Officer Mark O'Connor, L.A.P.D."

"Mornin', Officer," replied Wade, in a tone that he hoped would convey both self-confidence and respect. "How can I help you?"

"Sir, you wouldn't happen to be missing a tiger, would you?"

Of all the questions that Wade had anticipated, this was not one of them. And even though he knew exactly where both of his tigers were at all times, he paused to recall when he had seen each of them last.

He had just left Ginger in the training pen with Chet. And right before riding out to join them, not fifteen minutes ago, he had checked in on Fred to find him lounging comfortably in his habitat.

Finally, with complete assurance, Wade told the officer, "No, sir — all present and accounted for. Why do you ask?"

"Because we have a lady who's got one trapped in her garage," explained Officer O'Connor. His matter-of-factness suggested that years on the force had made him a hard man to ruffle.

"Apparently," he continued, "it was picking through her trash, and she closed the automatic door to keep it from running loose in the neighborhood."

"Has Animal Control arrived?" asked Wade.

"No, sir. They're tied up with some chimpanzee that turned on its owner. Bloody mess, sounds like. Anyway, they said you were in the area, and the tiger might be yours."

"I see," said Wade. "So, what's your plan until they show up?"

"Well, this here is a residential area," said Officer O'Connor. "We'll try to keep the animal in the garage, but if it looks like it might get out, we're just going to have to shoot it."

"No, no!" exclaimed Wade, lurching forward in his seat. "Don't shoot it! Listen, just tell me where you're at, and I'll be right there."

* * *

Except for his soft-spoken manner, everything about Wade Boss was larger-than-life. And although at first sight one might have suspected him of being vain, in truth, he had no more of that dangerous, twisting sort of pride than the average man.

Rather, his grand sense of style was the product of two key influences: his Texas heritage and the circus. Wade was a showman, born and bred, and the image he projected was merely an expression of the cultures in which he grew up.

Hence his vehicle of choice: a colossal, extended-cab orange pickup truck with black tiger stripes, which now progressed slowly down a peaceful suburban street. In tow behind it was a black trailer with "BOSS BEASTS" printed in red on both sides. For added flair, the letters had been slashed to look as though some fierce predator had gotten at them with its claws.

The truck arrived at a two-story canary-colored house where a police cruiser was parked with its lights flashing. Wade swung his truck around to position the trailer, and then he backed into the driveway.

After parking, he hopped out of the cab and looked about for an officer. Then, from around the corner of the house, he heard a gruff voice he recognized: "Over here, Mr. Boss!"

He walked around a two-car garage to a side yard, where a burly policeman stood with a drawn handgun in front of a closed window. The fellow's big, brown mustache reminded Wade of the circus strong man he had so admired as a boy.

"I'm Officer O'Connor," the policeman introduced himself, keeping his gun aimed at the window. "Thanks for coming out."

"No problem, Officer," replied Wade. He now noticed that standing behind Officer O'Connor was a squat woman in her mid-sixties, who was anxiously wringing her hands.

"Ma'am," said Wade, tipping his hat. The woman's hair was wound tightly — and Wade imagined painfully — around pink rollers. The effect was comical, but Wade didn't want her to feel embarrassed, so he looked her directly in the eyes.

Despite his effort to protect her dignity, the woman self-consciously raised a hand to her scalp. "Hi. I'm Marjorie," she said.

With a nod and a smile, Wade turned his attention back to the officer and asked, "Is this the only window?"

"My partner's around back watching the other one," said Officer O'Connor. "So far, it looks like the animal's more interested in eating the trash than trying to escape."

"Can I take a look?" asked Wade.

By way of an answer, Officer O'Connor lowered his gun. "It's kind of dark," he explained. "Plus, the cans are all bunched together in the corner, here. Not much of a view."

Wade approached the small window, removed his sunglasses, and peered inside.

The garage itself was very ordinary. Parked beside Marjorie's silver Cadillac was a lawn tractor, and the rest of the assorted clutter was typical: yard tools, bikes, bags of mulch. And though Wade could hear the tiger rummaging through the trash, it was indeed out of sight.

"Hmmm," said Wade. "Ma'am, did you get a good look at it?"

"Good enough," answered Marjorie. "Scared the life out of me! I opened the door from the house, and there it was, picking through the garbage."

"Any sense of how big it is?" asked Wade.

Marjorie stretched out her arms. "I don't know — tiger-sized! Must be diseased, though. Looks like it has mange or something. When I opened the door, it turned and made this sort of hissing noise, like it was protecting its food."

"OK," said Wade, disturbed to hear that the animal was in such poor condition. "So, there's a door from the house that has a good view of this corner?"

"Uh-huh. Through the kitchen," said Marjorie.

"All right," Wade said to Officer O'Connor. "I think I'll just come around from inside and see if I can get a clear shot with the tranquilizer gun. It takes a couple of minutes for the drug to kick in though, so you'll probably hear the animal freakin' out for a bit before it quiets down."

"Go for it," said Officer O'Connor.

* * *

Nice place, thought Wade, as he made his way through the house.

The walls were covered with family pictures. Most of the older ones featured a handsome red-haired gentleman, but then abruptly he appeared no more, leading Wade to wonder if Marjorie was a widow. She certainly appeared to be a grandmother, several times over.

One photograph in particular caught Wade's attention: that of a young couple smiling proudly over a newborn.

Wade wondered if he would ever find himself in such a scene. He had always assumed that someday there would be little Wades running around his feet, but to his own mystification, he found himself still unmarried and childless.

He didn't know for sure whether or not his new girlfriend, Genevieve, wanted children. He suspected probably not, but was waiting for a suitable time to bring up the subject.

Anyway, there were other things to think about at the moment. After making his way through the kitchen and past the laundry room, he finally arrived at the door to the garage.

He checked his single-shot tranquilizer pistol to make sure that it was primed to fire. If he missed the first shot, he had two backup darts in a metal case, in the inside pocket of his jacket. But he hoped that he wouldn't need them, for if he did, it would mean that something had gone dangerously wrong.

He took a deep breath and eased the door open. It squeaked at the hinges, but the sound was drowned out by the crash of another garbage can.

Two small windows allowed minimal light into the garage, but the beast was in shadow, in the far corner. The Cadillac blocked Wade's view, so he crept quietly around it.

To hear the tiger so ravenous made Wade's blood boil, for this incident was not an isolated one. More and more people were buying exotic pets without any idea of what they were getting themselves into, and the consequences were tragic.

Large cats were almost always purchased as cute little cubs, but the problem was that they didn't stay that way. The usual fate of unwanted adult tigers, panthers, etc., was that their short-sighted owners stuck them in cramped, dirty living spaces.

Since these also tended to be poorly constructed, escapes were not uncommon. Wade had little doubt that the present situation was just one more ugly statistic.

He knelt down by the car's muffler, where his view was only partially obscured by the lawn tractor.

Marjorie's assessment seemed correct: the tiger was apparently suffering from some kind of disease. Not only was its fur patchy, but its skin was discolored as well. Wade wondered what could possibly account for the abnormalities, shuddering at the thought of rabies.

He slowly stood and stepped out from behind the Cadillac. Then, just as he was raising the tranquilizer pistol, a car alarm randomly went off somewhere in the neighborhood. Curious at the noise, the animal raised its head. Immediately, it saw Wade and froze.

It was Wade, however, who had the greater surprise. Despite some similarities, this was no tiger.

The feet at the ends of its crooked legs were flat and reptilian, and armed with devilish claws. Its dark hide was covered by thousands of tiny scales. It seemed to lack ears, and the eyes set into its gaunt face were black and beady.

For a fleeting instant, another animal came to Wade's mind: a Komodo dragon.

With a menacing hiss, the tiger-lizard crouched down, its lips curled back to reveal not only large fangs, but also dozens of smaller teeth, all as sharp as pins.

It suddenly dawned on Wade that in analyzing the creature he had wasted precious seconds, but the realization came too late.

The tiger-lizard pounced. With no time to take proper aim, Wade fired the pistol and dove behind the Cadillac. The tranquilizer dart missed, and the beast sailed face-first into the closed overhead door.

Wade landed on the concrete with bone-jarring force, his left hip taking the brunt of the fall. But the hardened stuntman was used to pushing through pain, and in a flash he was up on his hands and knees.

The door to the house stood open, but it was too far for him to safely reach. Scrambling around to the driver's side of the Cadillac, he yanked open the rear door and jumped into the back seat.

The tiger-lizard also rebounded quickly, lunging for Wade just as he slammed the car door shut. The creature then stood on its hind legs, planted its front feet on the door window, and with a forked tongue began slathering the glass with slimy saliva.

Seeing it face to face, Wade experienced a wave of something like nausea — except on an emotional, or perhaps spiritual, level. The thing was just so grotesque, so utterly... *wrong*.

Despite the creature's mad clawing, for a few seconds, Wade thought that the window might hold. But then, all at once, it shattered, and in came the slashing claws...

Then Wade heard the sound of more breaking glass, followed by a gunshot. It was Officer O'Connor to the rescue, now leaning into the garage through the side yard window, determined to bring the crisis to a swift conclusion.

And he would have, except that Wade was in his line of fire. The officer had no choice but to direct his first shot harmlessly off to one side, and before he could shoot again, the tiger-lizard ran into the house through the open door.

"No! No! Don't shoot!" shouted Wade, bursting from the car. Hastily, he pulled the metal dart-box from his jacket pocket and reloaded his tranquilizer pistol.

"What are you doing?!" yelled Officer O'Connor.

"Just stand back and watch the windows!" ordered Wade. "I want it alive!"

CHAPTER 2: MYSTERIES AND MOVIE STARS

For reasons never determined, ever since Wade was a boy, he had had a constant ringing in his ears, which the doctors called "tinnitus." But contrary to what one would expect, his hearing was exceptionally good — so good that his mother used to call him her little "Eagle Ears."

But as he re-entered the house from the garage, apart from his tinnitus and pounding pulse, Wade heard nothing. He paused to catch his breath. Then, taking care not to clunk the heels of his boots on the linoleum floor, he stalked forward into the kitchen.

Then something — a lamp, perhaps — crashed to the floor upstairs. Wade rushed to the foot of the central staircase and aimed his tranquilizer pistol at the landing above. He waited, but there was only silence.

Because Officer O'Connor and his partner were not likely to sit idle for long, Wade decided he had better keep moving.

He stepped on the first stair, and it creaked. Cautiously, he removed his foot and placed it on the second stair instead. He shifted his weight more slowly this time, but was rewarded with another creak, even louder than the first.

He realized that he was just going to have to go for broke. As if he were plunging into a pool of ice water, he braced himself and then rushed up the entire flight.

At the top landing, a long hallway extended to either side of him. He swung his pistol back and forth in anticipation of a swift attack. When it did not come, he dropped his eyes to the floor.

Long ago, Wade had learned the basics of tracking animals from his grandfather, who occasionally took him hunting in the Adirondack mountains. Thus he could tell from the faint depressions in the white carpet that four clawed feet had recently scurried down the hall, to the right.

At the end of the hall, the tracks disappeared through the open doorway of a bedroom, again on his right. Wade slowly followed in the creature's footsteps, and bit by bit, he could see into the room.

The walls were pink, and the centerpiece was a lovely brass bed. The rest of the decor was feminine as well: a lavender beanbag chair, a bookshelf with butterflies stenciled on it, a pretty little desk...

It was not until he was nearly inside the room that Wade at last spotted the tiger-lizard — or more accurately, its reflection.

Although he had no direct line of sight to it, a free-standing mirror in the corner opposite the doorway showed Wade the floor on the far side of the bed. There, lying on a throw rug and licking its deformed paws, was the beast — for the moment unaware that it was being observed.

Wade slowly backed into the bedroom across the hall. Here the walls were light blue, except for some yellow tape marks bearing witness to posters long-since removed.

On the windowsill of the far wall, a solitary toy soldier stood aiming a tiny rifle at nothing in particular. Wade assumed it to be the lone survivor of a once-proud plastic army.

Suddenly inspired, he walked over and plucked it from the sill — recruiting it for one final, glorious mission.

Wade gingerly stepped back into the hall until he could see the tiger-lizard in the full-length mirror. Then, raising the toy soldier to his ear, he took careful aim and threw it. The figure hit the mirror with a "clink" and then fell noiselessly onto the carpet.

The tiger-lizard looked up. Wade waved it a friendly 'hello', and immediately it charged like a bull to a red cape.

And that was the end of Wade Boss.

At least the Wade in the mirror, for the monster had mistaken the reflection for the real thing. It crashed right through the glass and then fell forward with the wooden mirror frame hanging about its neck. Only after its head had knocked a hole through the pink wall on the other side did it come to a stop.

In that moment, its right side was entirely exposed to Wade. He fired the second tranquilizer dart, and the needle sank deep into the beast's hind leg: perfect shot. Grandpa Boss would have been proud.

Part A of Wade's plan was complete, but Part B was more difficult: stay alive until the sedative took effect.

He rushed back into the blue room, hearing behind him the fury of the tiger-lizard as it first pulled its head from the wall and then thrashed the mirror frame to pieces.

No sooner had Wade shut the door than it was nearly knocked off its hinges. The pursuing tiger-lizard hurled itself at the wooden barrier again and again, threatening to reduce it to a pile of splinters at any second.

Frantically, Wade looked about for some form of protection. There was a dresser in the far corner, but he had no time to use it as a barricade. The bed was too low for him to hide under, and there was no closet that he could see.

With a loud crack, the tiger-lizard thrust one of its sinewy forelegs right through the middle of the door...

For lack of a better option, Wade grabbed the twin mattress off the bed and hoisted it upright, covers and all, to use as a shield.

The tiger-lizard finally smashed its way into the room and went straight for the mattress. It struck with terrific force, driving Wade back so that this time *his* head knocked a hole in the drywall. He swooned and fell sideways, barely managing to pull the mattress on top of himself.

Shredded padding flew up into the air, and a few metal springs were all that prevented the razor claws from slicing Wade's face to ribbons. His head buzzed like a swarm of bees, but he collected his wits enough to give the mattress a forceful kick with both feet.

The tiger-lizard fell back and the mattress landed on top of it, but inadvertently, Wade had just blocked his only path to the door.

Having to improvise yet again, he lunged for the dresser and tore out the drawers and the wooden slats that separated them.

Dropping to his knees, he curled into a tight ball, exhaled as much air as he could from his lungs, and pulled the dresser on top of himself. Feeling like a hermit crab that had outgrown its shell, he managed to squeeze into the hollow space where the drawers had been.

After finding its way out from under the tattered mattress, the tiger-lizard pounced upon the overturned dresser. It immediately began clawing, but with each swipe grew more sluggish.

Wade dug his fingers into the drawer tracks to hold the dresser on top of himself. He was beginning to fear that his nails would be ripped clean out, when finally the tranquilizer took full effect.

Groggily shaking its head, the tiger-lizard swayed from side to side and then slumped on top of the dresser, unconscious.

Once Wade was sure that it was safe to come out, he tried lifting the dresser off of himself. However, having no leverage to apply against the tiger-lizard's two hundred pounds, he had to escape in stages, wiggling out one limb at a time.

When at last he was free of his wooden shell, he lay exhausted on the floor. Staring into the monster's glazed eyes, he couldn't decide if it was more tiger than lizard, or the other way around. It was a living, breathing absurdity.

Was it some unknown species? By what process could its mismatched features have been fused together? Was this the work of Nature?

If so, Nature had gone haywire.

* * *

Wade hated parties almost as much as Genevieve loved them. Not small parties with good friends, but large parties with strangers — movers, shakers, and go-getters, all eager to "network."

Parties like this one.

As a famous leading actress, Genevieve Parker considered socializing to be the most important part of her job. And if he had wanted to, Wade could certainly have elevated his status by hobnobbing with her many industry contacts.

But for all that he was a showman, he could never quite work himself around to schmoozing. He endured evenings like this for Genevieve's sake, but did not trouble himself about being punctual.

Locating her was never hard: he just had to look for the largest cluster of bodies, and she would be at the center. Actually getting to her, however, was another matter. Usually, Wade would have to stand someplace away from the group — the higher the better — and wait patiently until he caught her eye.

Tonight that would be easier than usual, for the actor who was hosting the bash — whose name Wade couldn't remember — had installed a balcony overlooking the main room. After ordering a soda from the bar, Wade walked up an ornate spiral staircase to find a spot where he could easily be seen.

Unfortunately, the balcony also served as the dance floor. Averting his eyes from the colored lasers that flashed from the ceiling, Wade marveled to himself that no one had yet collapsed from an induced seizure.

The dancers were all too focused on busting their moves to care about the stranger who was trying to edge his way past them. After being bumped and jostled until half his drink was spilled, Wade found an opening along the bannister. Leaning his forearms upon it, he surveyed the room below.

No sooner had he begun his search than it was over.

He had guessed correctly that Genevieve would be talking, not dancing. She stood amidst a sea of couches, a martini in one hand, the other gesticulating dramatically.

Whatever story she was telling, it seemed to be a hit with her dozen or so listeners — most of whom were lesser stars trying to secure their fame by way of sucking up.

Whenever Wade reconnected with Genevieve after a day or two apart, the same phrase always popped into his head: *What a knockout!*

Before they first met, he had of course seen her on the screen — though only the television screen, since he was fed up with the ridiculous, ever-escalating prices at the theaters. And like the rest of the country, he had been wowed by her beauty and talent.

But seeing her in the flesh was something else altogether.

It all began three months ago, when Wade's grizzly bear, Hank, had been hired to bust some of his own dance moves for a movie shoot on a studio backlot.

During lunch, Genevieve had stopped by to see her actress-friend who was starring in the picture. While the two of them were gabbing, Wade was at the food table loading up his plate. He accidentally knocked a big bowl of potato chips onto the floor, and the noise caught Genevieve's attention.

At first, she was amused to see him on his knees, refusing help with a smile and insistent upon cleaning up his own mess. Then she was intrigued, for instead of throwing the chips into the trash, he picked up the bowl and walked across the set to the grizzly bear's trailer. Finally, she broke into a laugh when Wade began feeding the bear through the bars — one chip at a time — all the while speaking to it as if it were a small child.

A cowboy feeding chips to a bear. The scene was so delightful and so improbable that Genevieve could not resist playing a part in it herself — especially since the cowboy was good-looking. To the admiration of her actress-friend, she boldly walked over and introduced herself.

Wade responded to her in his usual, easygoing way, but his stomach was aflutter. To him, Genevieve seemed to glow with a radiance that no camera could hope to capture. They flirted until the director called for shooting to resume, by which time they had set a date for dinner.

Since then, Wade's life had been a whirlwind. Genevieve's "close friends" seemed to number in the thousands, and Wade quickly realized that he was expected to get to know all of them. He made a noble effort, but was soon exhausted to the point that he no longer cared.

Right now, however, it was not people who were wearing him down, but the pounding backbeat of the "music."

Because he had arrived late, it was not long before Genevieve scanned the room for him. He waved down to her, and their eyes met.

She tilted her head as if to say, *"Finally!"* Then, with fluid grace, she excused herself from the brown-nosing B-listers.

As she glided across the sofa room and ascended the spiral staircase, she turned more than a few heads. Her red dress was simple, form-fitting, and stunning. She had curled her long brown hair into ringlets, and of course her makeup was cover-model perfect.

The dancers who had shown Wade no consideration apparently had starlet-radar. As Genevieve approached, they parted automatically, giving her all the room in the world to pass by unharmed.

Wade straightened and smiled broadly as she walked up to him. Then, in a voice loud enough to be heard over the blaring speakers, he said, "You look beautiful!"

Genevieve smiled wryly, like a mother exasperated by a naughty boy who is too cute to stay mad at.

"Thank you!" she replied, also in a half-shout.

Wade shrugged sheepishly and said, "Sorry!"

By way of accepting his apology, Genevieve gave him a quick kiss. "Anything wrong?" she asked.

"No," he answered. "Just got tied up with somethin' at the ranch." Then, in a poorly disguised attempt to dodge further questions, he asked, "So, whose place is this again?"

Genevieve sighed and shook her head. "Tommy Stepp. You know, 'Best Actor'?"

"Oh, right," Wade pretended to remember. "It's nice. Never seen so many sofas."

Then abruptly, Genevieve lost all interest in the current thread of conversation and pointed down to the main room. "Oh, look!" she exclaimed. "There's James!"

"Who?" asked Wade.

"James Blakeman!" said Genevieve.

Wade followed the invisible line from her finger to an extremely short man entering through the patio door, drink in hand. He was in his fifties and wore black pants and a gray turtleneck. From his white hair and stubble-length beard, Wade recognized him as the creative genius behind some of the decade's biggest blockbusters.

"He looks taller on T.V.," remarked Wade.

Quivering with excitement, Genevieve said, "He just sent me the most fantastic script, and you won't believe this — it's set in India!"

"India," said Wade. "Wow."

"Come on, don't you get it?" asked Genevieve. *"Tigers!* We could actually work together for once."

Wade felt foolish for not making the connection, for of course his own tigers traced their lineage back to India. "Oh, yeah," he said with more enthusiasm. "That'd be fantastic."

"They want me to play the wife of a British officer who winds up getting caught by bandits in the jungle!"

"Sounds excitin'," replied Wade.

"Come on," said Genevieve, taking his arm. "I'll introduce you!"

Wade's eardrums were suddenly assaulted by a new song even louder and more annoying than the last.

"OK," he said, compliantly. At least down below he would be able to hear himself think.

But his lack of enthusiasm was obvious. Genevieve sighed, looked him in the eyes, and asked, "Hey — are you even here?"

"Yeah. This is great," said Wade, trying his best to mean it. But Genevieve wasn't about to let him off the hook so easily.

"Look," she said, "I know this isn't exactly your cup of tea, but this place is packed with people who are great contacts for you — potential clients. You need to look like you're enjoying yourself. Socialize!"

"Yeah, I know," Wade sighed.

"These are my friends," Genevieve continued. "You're only going to be seeing more of them, so you might as well get to know them. It's not hard — just ask them about themselves, and they'll do the rest."

"OK," said Wade, nodding in a way that suggested he would follow her advice.

"I'm not trying to be a nag," said Genevieve. "I just want you to have a good time."

"I know," replied Wade. And in truth, he knew she meant it.

For a few seconds, Genevieve just stared at him, trying to figure out what he was really thinking. Then she flashed him a winning smile and said, "Come on. Let's go see James!"

Wade could hardly object. And it wasn't as if he *wanted* to be a stick-in-the-mud. He returned her smile — this time a bit more honestly — and said, "Lead the way!"

* * *

The building that housed the furry residents of Boss Ranch was affectionately referred to as "the barn," though the name was misleading. It was in fact a sophisticated facility, thoughtfully designed to keep the animals safe, secure, and happy.

Entering the barn through the front door was like setting foot inside a cathedral, except that in place of a carpeted center aisle was an unpainted slab of concrete, measuring twenty feet wide and a whopping two hundred feet long.

Running down its entire length on both sides were steel bars that reached from the floor to the ceiling. The end product was a spacious corridor running between two rows of animal habitats.

There were ten habitats in all — five to a side, separated from each other by concrete walls. Currently, only four of the units were in use, with the rest being intended for future members of the ranch family.

Similar to those at a well-funded zoo, each occupied habitat was furnished with plants, rocks, logs, and a pool of constantly cycling water. Each also had a door to an outside play area where the animals would regularly find new and unusual toys for their enrichment.

Wade, Chet, and Chandra were always trying to outdo each other coming up with these items. Chet was the reigning "toy king," having recently woven an old fire hose into a large ball, which the tigers went bonkers over.

In addition to Fred and Ginger, the barn housed Hank the grizzly bear, Roland the lion, and Dolly the cougar. It was Wade's custom to check on them all just before he went to bed, and after this evening's soul-sucking party, he was especially looking forward to the ritual.

Chet had a standing order to leave on a few of the overhead lights at the end of each day, so Wade entered the barn to find it dimly lit. The hollow clunking of his boot heels echoed throughout the building as he walked over to the first habitat on the left, which belonged to the tigers.

Ginger was comfortably settled in the far right corner. Fred was taking a drink, but as soon as he saw Wade, he plodded over to greet him.

"Hey there, Fred! How you doin', boy?" asked Wade. Fred lowered his head and rested it against the wall of steel bars. Wade reached in with both hands and gave the tiger an affectionate head rub.

"You have a good night, pal," said Wade. After giving Fred a parting scratch behind the ears, he withdrew his hands and called out, "'Night, Ginger!" But Ginger was either asleep or else too contented to look up.

Next on the left came Hank. For all his five hundred pounds, he was a gentle soul and a creature of habit. He always retired early, and tonight was no exception. Wade smiled to see him nestled like a small brown mountain in amongst his favorite logs.

"Hey, Hank," said Wade. "Sleep well! I know you will." Indeed, he was already dreaming of honeycombs and berries.

Wade turned around and walked back to the first habitat on the right side, where Roland the lion was gnawing on a shank of beef.

One day, the adolescent male would be a king, but at present, his mane was still coming in. Little did he suspect that he would soon have a companion, for it was Wade's plan to acquire a young lioness within the year.

"Roland!" called Wade. The tawny prince looked up, smacking his chops. "That's all right — don't get up for me," Wade joked. "We'll catch up tomorrow."

Roland turned his attention back to his snack, and Wade moved on to say goodnight to his fifth baby, Dolly.

The two-year-old cougar was a quick learner and a delight to work with. Because she was so much smaller than the other big cats, she made location shoots easy. Being as obedient as a well-trained dog, she hardly even required a leash.

As Wade passed the wall that separated her habitat from Roland's, she descended without a sound from the top of an artificial rock formation.

"Dolly! How's my little lady?" asked Wade. She approached the bars, and he reached between them to take her face in his hands. Compared to Fred, she was delicate, and Wade caressed her with tenderness.

"I'm lookin' forward to our date, sweetheart. Don't you go makin' other plans," he said. Dolly soaked in the love until at last Wade pulled back his hands and said, "Sweet dreams, now."

Normally, at this point, Wade would head back out the front door and walk the fifty yards to his house. But tonight was different. Tonight Boss Ranch had a guest.

Wade walked slowly down the corridor between the empty habitats. As he neared the far end of the building, the hair on the back of his neck stood on end. With each step, he could see further around the wall that separated the fourth and fifth habitats on the left.

Finally, the guest came into view, pacing back and forth in the middle of the unfurnished space.

The tiger-lizard.

At the sight of Wade, it glared and hissed. Wade stopped midway down the wall of steel bars and studied the creature intently.

It walked to the rear wall of its prison, occasionally standing on its hind legs to scratch at the cement blocks, searching for any possible escape route.

Then, in a rush, it turned about and charged. Wade jumped back just as five bared claws shot between the steel bars. The tiger-lizard groped at him madly, but it had missed its chance for revenge.

Wade folded his arms and contemplated the situation. He was deeply troubled, for no avenue of thought seemed to lead to an explanation for this... abomination.

It did not seem to be the product of mere disease. And Wade had even more difficulty imagining how it could represent some as-yet undiscovered species.

Thwarted in its attempts to reach him, the tiger-lizard withdrew its foreleg and resumed its agitated pacing.

His face pinched with concern, Wade wondered aloud, "What *are* you?"

* * *

The doorbell rang. Wade roused himself and checked his alarm clock — 3:00 a.m.

Except for the animals, he lived alone at the ranch, the driveway of which was a quarter mile of dirt road. It was therefore unlikely that the person who had rung the bell was just some stranded motorist. Whoever it was almost certainly had an agenda, and Wade doubted that it would be a welcome one.

He put on his orange, tiger-striped bathrobe, shuffled to the front door, and turned on the outside light. Peering through the door window, he saw three men on his porch.

The one who had presumably rung the bell wore a beige jacket, stood about 6'3", and was clean-shaven and balding. Passing him on the street in broad daylight, Wade would have guessed him to be a decent chap, for his face was open and honest. Under the circumstances, however, his friendly appearance and fixed smile made Wade all the more suspicious.

Behind the man in beige stood two men in dark jackets. One was nearly seven feet tall, had slicked-back hair, and a long face with an unreadable expression. He reminded Wade of Abraham Lincoln.

The other was barely five feet tall with his shoes on, and was built like a tank. He had a military-style crew-cut and thick glasses with black, 1960s rims. Given his short arms, he would have made a lousy boxer. But Wade imagined that in a wrestling match anyone caught within his grasp would have little hope of breaking free.

Taken together, the trio came off as being less imposing than comical. Still, it was the middle of the night, and something about them seemed to say "official."

Wade opened the door a crack and said, "Yes?"

With a warm smile, the man in beige spoke. "Good evening, Mr. Boss," he said. "We're sorry to disturb you, but we understand that you have in your possession something of an anomaly."

CHAPTER 3: HOOK, LINE...

Thunk! A tranquilizer dart sank into the tiger-lizard's left hindquarter, and predictably, the animal went berserk.

The squat, tank-like man stepped back from the steel bars of the habitat and returned a compressed-air rifle to its case. Meanwhile, the tall man wheeled a hospital gurney into the barn.

As a matter of course, Wade always donned his hat upon leaving his house — though tonight he might have made an exception had he realized what the combined effect with his bathrobe would be.

Oblivious to the zany fashion statement he was making, he stood with crossed arms next to the man in beige, who still had not revealed anything about himself or the powers he represented.

Within five seconds of the dart hitting its mark, the tiger-lizard was overcome by the sedative and sank to the floor.

"That was fast!" Wade marveled.

"Secret formula," said the man in beige, with a wink. From his casual manner, he might just as well have been boasting of his grandmother's recipe for spaghetti sauce.

The short man opened the habitat door, which consisted of the same steel bars that lined the corridor. He then held it open for the tall man, who wheeled in the gurney.

The man in beige turned to Wade and asked, "So, none of your employees have seen the creature?"

"No," answered Wade. "I called ahead and sent 'em home before I got back."

"Good," said the man.

"So, are you gonna tell me what the heck that thing is and where it came from?" Wade asked.

"I'd like to," replied the man, "but this is a highly sensitive matter. In fact, I'm going to have to ask you not to discuss it with anyone."

"Or what?" asked Wade, testily.

"Just please don't," said the man — though there was no detectable threat in his tone. On the contrary, he seemed so pleasant that Wade began to suspect him of being some kind of con artist.

Inside the habitat, the odd couple lowered the gurney. Then, with some difficulty, they hoisted the tiger-lizard on top.

"Exactly what department are you from?" asked Wade, now almost as curious about the three men as he was about the creature they had come to collect.

"I'm not at liberty to say," said the man in beige, "but we work closely with Homeland Security." Then, smoothly changing the subject, he asked, "So, you're a wrangler for the entertainment industry?"

Annoyed at his evasiveness, Wade replied, "Trainer."

"I didn't know there was a difference."

"Wranglers work with animals you can't really teach."

"I see," said the man. "And you do stunts as well?"

"Yep."

"Horseback riding?"

"Yeah, lots of horse-work. Falls, teachin' actors how to ride."

The man in beige fell silent for a moment, as if choosing his next words very carefully. At last, he asked, "So... do you ever take time to get away from it all? Hiking, camping — the great outdoors?"

Wade wondered why he was interested in such information, but saw no harm in providing a cursory answer.

"Did a bit of campin' with my grandfather growin' up," he replied, "but not so much lately."

"Hmmm," was the man's only comment, and then he and Wade watched as the men in dark jackets wheeled the tiger-lizard out of the habitat.

"You know," said the man in beige, as if he were coming around to his true objective, "it's very impressive that you were able to bring in this animal on your own. We're uh... we're always on the lookout for capable men who are willing to lend their skills and expertise, from time to time. Might you be someone we could call upon in the future, should the need arise?"

So that's it, thought Wade. *The guy's some kind of recruiter.*

Shaking his head, Wade replied, "I'm a busy man, Mister...?"

"I'm sorry," said the man. "It's Fairfield. Paul!" And with another smile, he extended his hand.

Out of politeness, Wade shook it, though he had no desire to continue the conversation. "I'm a busy man, Mr. Fairfield," he said. "I don't have much time to spend doin' volunteer work."

"Of course not!" said Mr. Fairfield, hastily. Then, after a pause, he added, "I was only thinking in terms of an emergency — if public safety were at issue."

Wade drew a deep breath. Like anyone else, he had no desire for his life to be disrupted by unsought obligations. Still, he had never been one to turn his back on someone in genuine need.

Finally, he said, "Well, I'll put it to you like this: As long as you won't be sore if the answer is 'no', then you're free to ask."

"Understood," said Mr. Fairfield, seeming to relax ever so slightly, as if he had just checked an important item off his "to do" list.

* * *

Outside, the silent duo loaded the gurney into a white delivery-style truck. The tall man stepped up into the bay and then pulled the rear doors closed, shutting himself inside with the tiger-lizard. Meanwhile, the short man walked around to the cab and hopped into the driver's seat.

Mr. Fairfield turned to Wade and extended his hand for the

second time, as casually as if they had just finished a game of racquetball.

"Many thanks, Mr. Boss," he said. "And good luck with your business!"

Wade shook his hand warily and replied, "Thank you."

Mr. Fairfield turned towards the white truck, walked around to the cab's passenger door, and climbed in. A few seconds later, the vehicle was rumbling down the long, dusty driveway.

Wade stood where he was, watching the glowing red tail lights fade into the distance. The answers he had wanted he hadn't received. And now, in addition to the mystery of the creature itself, was the intrusion of a covert government agency.

For all Wade knew, they might already be secretly monitoring him to make sure he didn't leak any classified information.

He pondered Mr. Fairfield's question about whether or not he would be willing to lend assistance "should the need arise." He wondered if it ever would, and if so, whether he would regret having opened himself up to further involvement.

* * *

It was another beautiful morning at Boss Ranch — Wade's favorite part of the day. And in spite of being an hour or two short on sleep, he was ready for action. Armed with a mug of coffee, he stepped out onto the front porch of his log-cabin home.

The ranch office was situated between the house and the barn, and as Wade made his short walking commute, Chet's black Jeep rolled up from behind him.

"Morning, Boss!" called Chet, giving a casual wave out the window as he passed by.

"Mornin', Chet!" returned Wade, cheerfully. As usual, Chandra's old maroon Buick was already parked in front of the hitching rail. Wade smiled at the sight of it, for it meant that the black-haired beauty was taking care of all the office duties that kept the business running smoothly.

Chet parked his Jeep beside Chandra's car, hopped out, and then called over to Wade, "So, what's the plan?"

"Well," said Wade, as he drew near, "I figure we can start workin' on that bear attack for the Oregon shoot. Maybe after lunch spend some time on that soda commercial."

"Sounds good," said Chet.

Just then, Wade's cell phone rang. With a grunt of annoyance, he pulled it from his pocket and answered, "Hello?"

The voice on the other end said, "Mr. Boss! This is Paul Fairfield. We met last night."

"Uh... yeah," said Wade. "Hang on a second." He covered the phone and told Chet, "Why don't you go in and ask Chandra to spend some time with Dolly as soon as she's done on the computer."

"You got it," replied Chet, and he headed inside.

Wade resumed his phone conversation. "Mr. Fairfield, when I said you could call, I didn't think you meant the next day."

"I know," said Mr. Fairfield. "And I'm very sorry to trouble you again. But we have another situation, and it's a matter of public safety."

"Are you tellin' me another one of those things is on the loose?" asked Wade.

"Something like that," said Mr. Fairfield. "I really can't say any more over the phone, but if you wouldn't mind coming down to our main office, I can brief you in person. I wouldn't be asking, except that we need to resolve this quickly, before someone gets hurt."

At those words, Wade felt a sharp pang of conscience. He wouldn't be able to sleep thinking that, somewhere out there, someone's life was in danger just because he didn't want to be inconvenienced.

He took a deep breath and exhaled slowly. "Well, Mr. Fairfield," he said, "I won't commit to anything just yet, but I'll come down and listen to what you have to say — on one condition. I want the truth about what those creatures are, and what you people are really up to."

"Deal," said Mr. Fairfield.

"So where exactly is your office?"

* * *

Whenever Wade had to leave town, Chet would stay at the ranch in a guest room they called "the bunkhouse," which was built onto the back of the office. And on the rare occasions when both Wade and Chet were gone, Chandra would take up temporary residence and hold down the fort.

But even though his faithful employees were capable of managing just fine without him, Wade always felt guilty whenever he had to skip out on them unexpectedly.

He would not have done so this morning, except that the questions of the last twenty-four hours were itches begging to be scratched, and the chance to get some answers was irresistible — not to mention the fact that lives were apparently at stake.

With a mixture of irritability and eagerness, he followed Mr. Fairfield's directions to a semi-deserted business district on the outskirts of Los Angeles. Fearing that he had perhaps taken a wrong turn, Wade re-checked the address he had written down. After concluding that he was indeed in the right place, he pulled his truck into the pothole-ridden parking lot of a one-story brick building.

He saw only a handful of cars, which only added to the strangeness. After parking beside a boxy blue Volvo, he strode up a thoroughly cracked cement walkway to the front entrance.

He found it hard to believe that such a bland-looking structure should contain something as outlandish as the tiger-lizard. At least, he guessed that the creature was inside. In any case, the location was perfect if the goal was to keep a low profile. There wasn't even any kind of official sign.

Wade entered the lobby through a set of glass double-doors. Directly ahead of him was a half-wall that looked like a bank counter, behind which sat a receptionist, at a desk. She appeared to be reading, for only the top of her blonde head was visible.

At the sound of Wade's cowboy boots on the hard tile floor, the woman looked up.

She was cute.

Wade had never been able to decide which was better: drop dead gorgeous or outright adorable. Genevieve was definitely the former, while this receptionist was very much the latter.

"Mornin'! May I help you?" asked the woman. To Wade's surprise and delight, she spoke with a heavenly Texas accent. He was enchanted, for it was the sound of home, and it struck a bittersweet chord in his heart.

Wade imagined the woman to be in her mid-thirties, though it was difficult to tell for sure. Her eyes were blue — cornflower blue, like his mother's. She wore just enough makeup to bring out her natural beauty, and her hair fell in loose curls that stopped just below her shoulders. A quick glance at her left hand told Wade that she wasn't married or engaged.

All he could see of her outfit was a light-cream blouse embroidered with floral designs. He guessed that she was only a few inches over five feet tall, which meant that she would have to stand on tiptoe in order to drape her arms around his neck...

But suddenly he realized that he hadn't answered her question. He cleared his throat, tipped his hat, and then as smoothly as possible said, "Mornin'. I'm here to see Mr. Fairfield. The name's Boss — Wade Boss."

"Oh, yes, Mr. Boss," said the petite blonde. "Mr. Fairfield is expectin' you. You can just head right through that door behind me."

No. No he couldn't. Not just yet.

Leaning forward on the half-wall, he said, "Nice to hear someone who knows how to per-nounce things right. How long you been in town?"

"Oh, just about a month. I'm Rose."

Wade looked down at the nameplate beside his elbow, which read, "Rose Rogers."

"So I see," he said. "And how do you like L.A.?"

"Oh, it's a bit overwhelmin', I guess. 'Specially the drivin'."

"Yeah, I used to feel the same way," said Wade. "Still do! I guess we're just two fish out of water."

Rose smiled and said, "I guess so."

Wade would have liked to talk with her longer, but he figured he ought to keep moving, lest he appear too interested.

"Well, Miss Rose," he said, "it's been a pleasure to make your acquaintance. Best of luck to you."

"Thank you," she said, charmingly. "I'll buzz you in."

Wade again tipped his hat, giving her the one-sided smile that he reserved for things he found delightful or amusing. He then walked around her desk to a solid oak door.

Here, he got his first clue as to the kind of organization he was dealing with. Affixed to the door at eye level was an official seal that bore a striking symbol: a short segment of DNA underneath the crosshairs of a gun sight. Around the circumference of the seal were the words, "GENETIC ANOMALIES TASK CENTER."

Wade heard a loud buzz as Rose pressed the button beneath her desk. He turned and nodded to her by way of thanks and then opened the door.

In most respects, the next room was like any other large office. The space had been divided up with cubicles, and the main colors were tan and gray. Wade did notice, however, that there were an unusual number of flat-screen televisions hanging on the walls.

The roughly two dozen men and women in the room were all hard at work and all professionally dressed. Since Wade had seen only a few cars out in the front lot, he figured that most of these people must have parked somewhere behind the building.

Some of the workers were hunched over their desks, while others walked at a fast clip from here to there. A few were focused on the large T.V. screens, which Wade now realized were displaying satellite images of different parts of the country.

A hydraulic hinge slowly pulled the door closed behind him, and he waited to be noticed. Back in Texas, his fashion sense was more widely shared, but on the West Coast, it tended to attract attention. As usual, it was the hat that caught someone's eye.

"Sir, can I help you?"

Wade turned to his right and saw an alert young man peering over the wall of his cubicle. He was in the middle of a phone call, but had put it on hold long enough to offer his assistance.

"Oh — I hope so!" answered Wade. "I'm here to see Mr. Fairfield."

"Right here, Mr. Boss!"

Wade spun around to see Mr. Fairfield briskly approaching from the other side of the room. In addition to pressed pants and a crisp shirt and tie, he wore the same smile that had seemed so suspicious the night before. Now, in the middle of the morning, Wade realized that it was genuine.

"Thank you so much for coming out!" said Mr. Fairfield. "Welcome to the circus."

"Mr. Fairfield," returned Wade.

"No, please," said Mr. Fairfield, "call me Paul!" He gave Wade a familiar pat on the arm, and then without missing a beat, he held out a ballpoint pen and a piece of paper that was covered with fine print.

"I'm afraid I'll have to ask you to sign this confidentiality agreement," said Paul. "Everything you're about to see is classified."

"OK," said Wade, his curiosity heightened even more by the formality. He glanced down at the paper, expecting to find the same type of formulaic jargon one usually associates with contracts and legal documents.

However, when his eyes landed first on the phrase "act of treason against the United States of America," and then "maximum security prison," he started again from the top and read very carefully.

The penalties for spilling the beans regarding whatever he was about to be shown were severe — and chilling. Wade wondered what on earth could be worth the risk, but very clearly, *something* was.

Since he played his cards "close to the chest" with regards to his life in general, he saw no reason why remaining tight-lipped about one more thing should pose a problem.

Once sure that he understood every line of the confidentiality agreement, Wade signed it and handed it back to Paul.

"Thanks!" said Paul, in a jarringly light-hearted tone. "Come this way." He gestured for Wade to follow, and then led him through the maze of cubicles.

"The Task Center is young and growing," said Paul, over his shoulder. "At first we were an offshoot of Fish and Wildlife, but right before I was appointed Director we became a separate entity. Now we answer to a joint committee that includes Health & Human Services and Homeland Security.

"We've got a few satellite offices scattered across the country, but we're the hub, so to speak. Most of our funding so far has gone directly into research — as you'll see. But lately we've begun to recruit professionals from all sorts of diverse backgrounds. We're working hard to cover all of our bases, but for the time-being, we have to call on folks like yourself who have the skills and resources we lack."

"I see," said Wade.

"I thought we'd start with a little show-and-tell before we get down to business," said Paul, "just to give you an idea of the scope of our mission."

By now, they had reached the other side of the room. Paul laid his hand on the knob of a white steel door, and then he paused.

With a mischievous grin, he looked at Wade and asked, "Ever have one of those dreams where you know you're in a familiar place, but everything looks all weird?"

"Yeah," answered Wade.

"This is kind of like that," said Paul, and then he turned the doorknob.

CHAPTER 4: GRAVE NEW WORLD

Wade had spent plenty of time on movie sets, some of them very lavish and detailed. But for the first time in his life, he felt like he had just stepped into a movie.

The room on the other side of the steel door turned out to be an enormous laboratory. It was equipped with half-a-dozen ultra-sophisticated workstations, each of which was organized around a stainless steel operating table on a hydraulic lift.

Each station had a glass-doored refrigerator that contained racks upon racks of blood-filled test tubes. Computers, monitors, and high-capacity hard drives were stacked on movable carts, and scores of extension cords crisscrossed the tile floor.

A handful of stereotypical scientists in white lab coats were hunched over keyboards and microscopes, so focused on their research that they did not even notice the two men who had just entered.

Having had twenty-four hours to assimilate the idea of the tiger-lizard, Wade had begun to wonder if he had been too hasty in ruling out simple explanations.

Perhaps it was neither a tiger nor a lizard at all, but some other animal he would have recognized except for its extreme disfigurement.

And what of that? Could it not have been the result of some horrible disease? Or a random mutation? Perhaps the deformities that at first sight had seemed so diabolical signified nothing more than a simple genetic hiccup...

But as he looked past the scientific equipment and the men in white coats, a wave of that peculiar nausea he had felt in Marjorie's garage washed over him again. For not only were his initial fears confirmed, but he saw that the tiger-lizard represented only a single drop in a sea of crimes against Nature.

Along the walls to either side of him, and also on the far side of the room, were holding cells constructed of thick glass. Each one measured ten by fifteen feet, and each contained a different phantasmagoric creature.

First on Wade's left came a hateful little beast that kept hurling itself at the walls of its cell, determined to get at the scientists. Its short legs stuck out from beneath a flexible yellow shell, and its head, neck, and long tail were covered with coarse brown fur. It was obviously half armadillo, and though it would not hold still long enough for Wade to tell for certain, he concluded from its vicious temperament that it was also half wolverine.

The second cell contained what at first glance appeared to be a monkey. A small tree had been provided for it, and it swung back and forth on the branches as any ordinary monkey might do. But as Wade tracked it with his eyes, he noticed that sprouting from its ribcage were six freakish, insectoid legs. Furthermore, its tail was segmented and ended in a scorpion-like stinger the size of a baseball.

The third patchwork animal was almost a cartoon come to life. It resembled a prize-winning sow at a country fair, except that its fat, pink body was encircled by six evenly-spaced rings of gray fur. Instead of cloven hooves, it stood upon four hand-like paws, and rather than a snout, it had a fuzzy, pointed muzzle. But it was the "masked-bandit" circles around its eyes that declared it to be a pig-raccoon.

By now, Wade felt like he was on a bicycle going too fast down a steep hill — he was past the point of braking, and there was nothing he could do except hold on and ride it out. He scanned the rest of the cells more quickly, as if by reaching the end of the line he might arrive at some haven of normalcy.

After the pig-raccoon came something like a fox crossed with a chameleon. Then there was a badger-ish creature with the tusks and ears of a wild boar. This was followed by a baboon-porcupine, then a hyena-ferret, and then a kangaroo-goat. Finally, to Wade's immediate right was none other than the tiger-lizard.

By the time he was done surveying the lot, Wade felt like he had left Earth far behind. If he had been asked, he would have been completely unable to articulate his swirling thoughts.

In some indefinable way, he sensed that he had just crossed a threshold — a point of no return — and that henceforth, his life would never be the same.

The thought frightened him, but it was also exhilarating.

When he finally found his voice, he asked, "What are they?! Where did they all *come* from?"

"The short answer is, we don't know," replied Paul. "The long answer is that for some time now, we've been responding to reports of strange animals turning up in remote regions, all across the country. Each one of these specimens we've captured is entirely unique, except for one common denominator: none of them is a product of Nature.

"They're genetic hybrids, engineered by someone with tremendous resources, for reasons unknown. It's improbable that they could have all just escaped from confinement. It seems more likely that they're being deliberately set loose. The one you caught is the first we know of to have ventured into a heavily populated area, which is cause for some concern.

"So far, we've managed to keep the truth from the press, but there's only so many times we can pin these sightings on chupacabras and Bigfoot. In light of your close encounter yesterday, it could be just a matter of weeks or even days before the cat's out of the bag. At that point, people are going to want some answers, so we're kind of under the gun."

At last, Wade and Paul were noticed by one of the scientists, who approached with a smile and called out, "Morning, Paul!"

The man was in his mid-fifties and stood about 5'6". He wore wire-rimmed glasses, and his black hair looked like it had been dyed — including his goatee, which was sculpted even more precisely than Wade's. His keen, dark eyes suggested a rare intelligence, and Wade sensed that he was standing in the presence of a man for whom the staggering mysteries of DNA were all in a day's work.

"Wade, I'd like to introduce you to Dr. Jules Krennick, Head of Research. He's our resident genius," said Paul. "Jules, this is Wade Boss."

Dr. Krennick shook Wade's hand firmly. "Yes, Mr. Boss!" he said, as though he was already familiar. "Good work yesterday. We're always grateful for help bringing in the 'brids."

"'Brids?" asked Wade.

"Our nickname for the hybrids," Paul explained. "Dr. Krennick and his team are trying to figure out how such totally divergent species have been combined into viable life-forms."

"Technically," said Dr. Krennick, "it's impossible. Except..." and then he trailed off, completing his thought with a gesture to the hybrids, which were proof to the contrary.

"We have no idea how it's accomplished," Dr. Krennick continued. "We're doing the best we can to figure it out, but we're shackled by a limited budget."

More for Wade's benefit, Paul said, "We're working on that."

Then, with a sigh, Dr. Krennick said, "Well, I'm sorry I can't chat longer, but I have to prep two of these 'brids to ship out to the Zoo. I'm glad to have met you, Mr. Boss. Hope to see you around!"

"Thanks," returned Wade, somewhat bothered by the parting sentiment.

As they watched Dr. Krennick return to his lab station, Paul said, "After the hybrids are apprehended, they get a full workup here in the lab — except for the really big ones. Sooner or later, they all wind up in Nevada at our holding compound, which is an old zoo that was closed down about six years ago. We've done a little renovating, but really it's just a temporary solution until we get the funding for a proper containment facility."

"How many are there?" asked Wade.

"'Brids? Counting these, about thirty," said Paul.

For a few moments, Wade silently tried to imagine what other fantastical life forms might be populating the repurposed zoo. But finally he decided it was time to learn exactly what was going to be asked of him.

Cutting to the chase, he said, "You called me here for a specific reason."

"That's right," said Paul. "In the last seventy-two hours, we've received two separate reports of a strange creature out in the Joshua Tree National Park. Sounds like a 'brid — a pretty dangerous one. Nobody's been hurt yet, but a couple of rock climbers had a close call.

"We've made a few passes with the helicopter, but so far we've found nothing. What we really need is eyes on the ground — only it's too vast an area to cover on foot, and too overgrown with brush for a four-wheeler. It's really a job for someone on horseback, but unfortunately, the guy we would normally bring in is hunting grizzlies in Alaska — we can't reach him."

Wade drew a deep breath and then puffed out his cheeks expressively. He had no idea what he was going to say next, and spent a moment just letting his eyes roam.

They came to rest on a pair of scientists sitting on the far side of the room, facing away from him. The men concluded some sort of research-related discussion and then rose from their seats. As soon as they did, Wade recognized them as Paul's silent cronies from the previous night.

The tall one spotted Wade and then tapped the short man on the shoulder. The short man followed his friend's gaze to the front of the room. When he saw Wade, he gave an embarrassed little wave.

"What about those guys?" asked Wade, gesturing to them with a jut of his chin. "They were with you last night."

Paul looked at the pair and chuckled. "Kent and Irving? Oh, they can tranq' a 'brid that's behind bars all right, but they're no field agents!"

Wade sighed, realizing that Paul would not have called him if there was an obvious alternative. At last, he heard himself reluctantly asking, "Any idea what it looks like?"

"Sounds like a quadruped," said Paul. "Two, maybe three feet tall — hairy, with a long neck and tail. Sixty pounds, maybe. We can give you the location of the last sighting, and hopefully you can pick up a trail. If you can tag it, we'll come and haul it out."

Wade was quiet for a long moment, weighing his immediate business obligations against the guilt he would feel if this hybrid were to actually hurt somebody.

He knew that he could ask Chet to watch over the ranch for the night. Chet always said 'yes' to such requests, for not only did he have a servant's heart, but he was also always interested in overtime pay.

Having no truly compelling excuse, Wade finally told Paul, "I can get out there sometime this evenin'. But by three o'clock tomorrow, I gotta be on my way home."

Paul smiled and said, "Fantastic! In that case, let's get you a badge and a field kit."

* * *

Wade re-entered the lobby from the cubicle-office carrying an over-sized silver briefcase.

He was still disoriented from the surreal experience of the laboratory, but as he walked around the reception desk, a melodious voice brought him back to the world.

"You have a nice day now, Mr. Boss!" said the lovely receptionist.

Wade broke into an involuntary smile and turned to face her.

"You do the same, Miss Rose," he replied.

Something tugged inside his chest. He wanted to say something witty, something that might get her to laugh, or at the very least to speak again. But he couldn't come up with anything that sounded natural, so for lack of an inspiration, he turned again to the front doors.

He had only made it another step when Rose called out, "Good luck!"

Wade stopped in his tracks, racking his brains for a sparkling reply. Ultimately, he settled for a semi-suave cliché, and turning back around, he sold it as best he could.

"You, too," he said. "It's uh... it's kind of a jungle out there."

"So I've found," Rose agreed.

She had let the cliché slide, which was a clear signal that she was up for more conversation. Wade set down the silver case containing the field kit and took two easy steps towards her desk.

"You got family out here?" he asked.

"Nope," sighed Rose. "Just me, all by my lonesome. Guess you could say I'm on the lookout for some adventure."

"Is that so?" asked Wade, finally finding his rhythm. "And how is it you wound up lookin' for it out here?"

"Well, I found out about this job from my daddy — he works for

Homeland Security," answered Rose. "And since I've never lived anywhere but Texas, I figured it was time to take a chance!"

"Well, good for you," said Wade, supportively. "So, have you seen the sights?"

"The Hollywood sign, that's about it," said Rose.

"Well, L.A. is a whole lot more than just Hollywood," said Wade.

"I know," Rose agreed. "But everything's just so big and overwhelmin', I hardly know where to start." Then, for fear that the hint might be too thinly veiled, she added, "Feel like I need a tour guide or somethin'."

"Weeeeell..." said Wade, expansively. "I'm no expert on local history or nothin', but I've learnt my way around."

"Is that an offer?" asked Rose.

Suddenly Wade thought of Genevieve. He wondered what she would think if she knew he was driving all over the city with some cute little blonde.

But then, why did she have to know? After all, there was no point in upsetting her needlessly. He was just being neighborly to a fellow Texan, new to the area.

"Why not?" said Wade. "I'll even do the drivin'."

"Oh, that'd be a big relief!" said Rose.

"I'm afraid my weekend's full up, though," Wade apologized.

"Well... I'm free next weekend," Rose suggested.

"That might work," said Wade, thoughtfully scratching his chin. "Why don't we say next Friday? 6-ish?"

"That won't give us much time," Rose pointed out.

"Well, there's nothin' sayin' we have to cram it all into one evenin', is there?" asked Wade.

Rose smiled and said, "I reckon not."

"Then next Friday it is," Wade declared. "I can pick you up right here."

"OK, then," said Rose.

"OK, then," echoed Wade. Then, with a tip of his hat, he took a backwards step towards the lobby doors.

Except that, over the course of the conversation, he had forgotten all about the silver case, and suddenly found himself tripping over it. With a loud bang, it fell over onto its side, and Wade had to flail his arms wildly for a second or two in order to regain his balance.

Rose burst out laughing, but then quickly clapped a hand over her mouth.

Although he had just undone all of his efforts to appear cool and self-assured, Wade tried to salvage his dignity by carrying on as though nothing had happened.

Bending over, he grabbed the case by its handle and stood up tall. Finally, clearing his throat, he forced a smile and said, "Next Friday!"

Rose nodded wordlessly, her face as red as a beet. Then, with great care, Wade turned to the glass doors and successfully exited the lobby.

* * *

At the smell of the campfire, fond memories flooded Wade's mind.

As a boy, he had looked forward with eager anticipation to the vacations he and his parents would spend with his grandfather in the Adirondack mountains. Arriving at the cabin had always felt like stepping into some kind of European fairy tale, and wood smoke had been a big part of the magic.

Of course, the rocky desert of the Joshua Tree National Park bore little resemblance to the forests of New York. But wood smoke is wood smoke, and if Wade closed his eyes, he could almost imagine that his grandfather was still alive and sitting beside him.

In strict botanical terms, the Joshua trees that gave the park its name were not trees at all, but rather a species of Yucca plant that happened to grow to enormous size. Their trunks and branches were covered with a shaggy bark, and they were topped with bayonet-shaped leaves that grew in clusters. To Wade, they looked like frozen green explosions.

The terrain was mostly flat and covered with dry grass and scrub brush. But here and there were curious rock formations that seemed to have bubbled up out of the earth, and it was these that made the park a favorite for climbers. All in all, it was an alien landscape, but a beautiful one.

To Wade, a campfire just wasn't complete without flame-cooked hot dogs — though in an effort to be more health-conscious, tonight he was trying out a new nitrate-free variety. To his surprise, they were actually pretty good.

After polishing off his fourth, he tossed the roasting stick into the fire and rose from his collapsible camp chair. The sun had just disappeared behind the western hills, but the pastel orange sky was still bright enough for him to move about without a flashlight.

He walked over to where Tango was tethered behind his trailer, munching oats out of a bucket. At his master's approach, the horse gave a friendly snort of greeting.

Tango was a highly intelligent animal, and after four years of training with Wade, he was also a skilled performer. Whether it was pursuing a stagecoach through a hail of bullets or tumbling safely to the ground on cue, Tango always delivered the goods.

Wade patted the horse's long, soft face and then moseyed around to the passenger side of his pickup truck. As he opened the front door, the ceiling light came on and illuminated the silver case from the Task Center that was sitting on the seat.

Wade flipped open the latches and lifted the lid. Inside, the case was lined with black foam that had been cut to conform to the dimensions of several shiny silver objects.

The central item was a high-tech handgun that had an enormously fat barrel. Set into the foam above and below it were what appeared to be two additional barrels, which for some reason, lacked handgrips.

Given his extensive experience with both firearms and tranquilizer guns — and also because he had been eager to get underway — Wade had assured Paul Fairfield that as long as the weapon came with some type of manual, he would be good to go.

Excited to learn about the gun's capabilities, Wade lifted it out and looked it over. He saw that the barrel and cylinder were actually one and the same: a single rotating piece, about the size of a can of spray paint.

It had five chambers that were loaded, not with bullets, but projectiles of differing types. Labels on the outside of the barrel indicated the sort of payload each projectile would deliver.

Two of the chambers contained tranquilizer darts, as indicated by the abbreviation "TRANQ." The syringes were visible through little windows on the gun barrel, and small thumb-sliders allowed the user to adjust the amount of serum in each dart.

Two other chambers were loaded with self-contained "SHOCK" rounds designed to incapacitate a subject in much the same way as a Taser. The final chamber was filled with "OC SPRAY" — so labeled for Oleoresin Capsicum, the active ingredient in pepper spray.

Just behind the gun's trigger was a small switch labeled "EJECT." When Wade flipped it, the five-shot barrel popped off of the handgrip. He now understood that, instead of reloading the separate chambers, one simply swapped out spent barrels for fresh ones.

Finally, for improved performance under low-light conditions, the weapon was equipped with a miniature flashlight and a laser sight for precision aiming. After flicking them both on and off, Wade set the gun down and turned his attention to the inside of the case lid.

He unfastened several straps to remove a tanned-leather gun belt. Emblazoned on its circular buckle was the seal he had seen earlier that day: a segment of DNA under the crosshairs of a gun sight, encircled by the words "Genetic Anomalies Task Center."

The holster was specially fashioned to accommodate the oversized handgun. There was also a strap to hold it snug to the thigh, which had pockets on it for the storing of two backup barrels. Wade imagined that, wearing the getup, he'd look like some kind of gunslinger from space.

Last of all, he pulled a small booklet from the case lid. In capital letters on the front cover was the word *"FLEXCALIBER."* Beneath that, in smaller letters, was printed "Operator's Manual." Wade cracked open the booklet and read aloud to himself.

"The *FLEXCALIBER* Flexible Response Sidearm was developed to provide military police and peace-keeping personnel with a range of readily interchangeable, less-than-lethal technologies. The system has also been adapted for use by the newly created Genetic Anomalies Task Center."

G, A, T, C.

Suddenly Wade realized that the Task Center's name was a clever nod to the four proteins that combined to form DNA: Guanine, Adenine, Thymine, and Cytosine. He chided himself inwardly for not seeing it before, and then continued reading.

"Please review this manual carefully and completely, as misuse of the *FLEXCALIBER* may result in serious injury or death."

"Okaaaaay," said Wade, raising an eyebrow at the ominous warning.

All of a sudden, from somewhere in the distance, he heard a long, spine-chilling howl. It was vaguely canine, but with a harsh, rasping edge.

Wade knew that coyotes were numerous in the area, but this was something other.

Tango shifted nervously, snorting and bobbing his head as the mournful peal faded to silence. It seemed to have come from the northeast, which was consistent with the report from the rock climbers. Wade waited for more, but nothing came.

In the stillness, he reflected upon the fact that he really had no idea what he was up against. Though he had planned on sleeping under the stars, he now thought that inside the truck would be wiser. He would put Tango in the trailer, too — better safe than sorry.

He set the *FLEXCALIBER* Operator's Manual on the dash and then pulled the two extra barrels from the silver case. The first of these was a duplicate of the TRANQ / SHOCK / OC SPRAY combo already affixed to the gun's handgrip. The second was simply labeled "NET," which sounded to Wade like it might come in handy.

He slid the assembled gun into its holster, stuffed the two extra barrels into the pockets on the thigh strap, and tucked the whole apparatus under his left arm.

He then shut the case, rustled up a flashlight from behind the seat, and grabbed the *FLEXCALIBER* manual off the dash. It wasn't exactly a bedtime story, but Wade knew better than to go off hunting with an unfamiliar weapon.

CHAPTER 5: ROUNDUP

At just before nine in the morning, the sun reflected brightly off the light brown sand. The spiky Joshua trees stood like sentinels over the desert, where some of them had been keeping watch for centuries.

Older still were the ancient rock outcroppings, or "monadnocks," that had been slowly eroded by wind and water until at last they resembled giant, misshapen meatballs.

Paul had guessed that the critter in question weighed about sixty pounds, so before breaking camp, Wade had adjusted the thumb-sliders on the barrel of the *FLEXCALIBER* to fill each tranquilizer dart with the correct amount of serum.

He then rode Tango for a mile or so until they arrived at the rocks where the hybrid — or 'brid, to those in the know — had last been sighted. Wade figured the best strategy would be to circle the rocks and continue in an ever-widening spiral until he found something.

On his first loop, he saw nothing promising, so he steered Tango further out. After an hour of circling, he began to despair of finding any tracks at all. To the disappointment of his inner boy, it seemed less and less likely that he would have an opportunity to use the gun.

Then, like a bolt out of the blue, it appeared: a distinct trail of paw prints, headed west. They looked to have been made by a dog or coyote, but what especially caught Wade's attention was the thin, wavy line that ran between them. Apparently, the animal had a long tail that dragged behind it on the ground. Bingo.

Wade directed Tango to follow the trail. It veered occasionally, but the distance between the tracks remained consistent, suggesting that the 'brid had been loping along at an easy pace.

The size of the prints seemed to confirm Paul's hypothesis about the animal's weight. Compared to the tiger-lizard, Wade imagined that this little varmint would be a piece of cake.

Then Tango reared up so suddenly that Wade was nearly thrown from the saddle. From the thicket just ahead of him came a loud warning rattle, and although the horse had never before encountered a rattlesnake, instinctively it recognized the sound of death.

Wade pulled hard on the reins to remind Tango who was in charge. The horse trembled with nervous energy, but once reassured by the controlling hand of its master, it held its ground.

Wade squinted hard at the tangle of dry brush before him. After a long minute and no sign of the snake, he decided he would simply give it a wide berth and pick up the 'brid's trail further ahead.

Steering Tango off to the right, he arrived at what he felt was a safe distance. But when he urged the horse forward, yet again he heard the harrowing rattle.

Dang it! Where is this thing? he wondered.

After restraining Tango for the second time, he fished a quarter out of his pocket. Making a wild guess at the snake's location, he flung the coin into the bushes.

It happened so fast, Wade caught only a fleeting glimpse. As Tango reared up again, something grayish-brown darted out from the underbrush — not a rattlesnake, but the four-legged hybrid he was looking for.

Unlike the tiger-lizard, this creature was hard-wired for flight rather than fight, and it ran at breakneck speed off to his right, kicking up a trail of dust.

By the time Wade got Tango pointed in the right direction, the 'brid had established a fifty-yard lead. Even so, Tango's long strides closed the distance. Forty yards... thirty... twenty...

Suddenly the 'brid broke left.

What it lacked in speed it made up for with agility. Tango, on the other hand, had to overcome considerable momentum to change course. In the time it took for Wade to redirect the horse, the 'brid had regained its fifty-yard lead.

Wade let out the reins to allow Tango maximum range of motion, for although their quarry was a fantastic sprinter, it could not outlast a horse over distance.

As Tango closed the gap, Wade saw a monadnock looming directly ahead. He drew the *FLEXCALIBER*, but before he could properly line up his shot, the 'brid was bounding up the rocks.

Finally, Wade got a good look at it. The creature was not nearly as mangey and wretched-looking as the tiger-lizard, but it was grossly unnatural in its own right. Its body and legs resembled that of a coyote, and it was covered with dust-brown fur that was a natural camouflage in the dry sage.

But the skin underneath its fur was comprised of thousands of snake-like scales. Its neck was a foot-and-a-half long, and supported a head that was a bizarre blend of canine and serpentine features. This was counterbalanced by a three-foot tail, at the end of which was a six-inch rattle.

Tango could not follow the coyote-snake up the rounded boulders, so Wade's only hope of ending the chase was a "Hail Mary." Aiming instinctively, he fired the gun.

With a POP, a tranquilizer dart was propelled from the barrel by a blast of compressed air. There was so little recoil that Wade could easily have followed up with a second shot. However, since the first dart missed so completely, there was no point.

As the 'brid crested the rise and disappeared from sight, Wade pulled Tango to a sharp halt and jumped from the saddle. He then clambered up the mount, finally arriving at the summit out of breath.

Here, he found boulders of all sizes clustered at random, like children's blocks strewn about a family room floor. Many were taller than he was, and he knew that behind any one of them the coyote-snake might be lurking.

Like a policeman searching for a dangerous criminal, Wade moved methodically forward. Since there were no tracks on the bare granite, he kept his eyes up.

Soon the rocks funneled him into a narrow pass where there was no room at all to get out of the way of an angry animal.

On the back of the *FLEXCALIBER*, instead of a hammer, there was a thumb-operated switch labeled "ADVANCE." Wade had learned from the Operator's Manual that this would de-activate the firing pin, so he pressed it and then pulled the trigger.

The gun did not fire, but the barrel rotated so that one of the "SHOCK" projectiles was moved to the top position.

As he entered the pass, Wade became increasingly uneasy. He began to think that perhaps he should just rejoin Tango and wait for the 'brid to come back down of its own accord. After all, it had to eat and drink sooner or later.

Just then, he stopped short as a pebble crunched loudly beneath his boot. From somewhere very close, the hiding animal responded to the sound with a chilling rattle.

Not good, thought Wade.

He couldn't pinpoint where the sound had come from, and there were any number of crevasses between himself and the end of the pass. If the coyote-snake was half rattler, he reasoned that it was likely not only to be lightning fast, but also venomous. He would have zero margin for error.

Why am I doing this? Wade suddenly asked himself. For although he was no coward, he was also no fool. Certainly Paul Fairfield didn't expect him to throw his life away over this thing. He wasn't even getting paid.

He took a step in retreat...

FOOM! The coyote-snake burst from a gap just five feet in front of him. As he fell backwards, the creature covered the distance to the end of the pass and broke out into the open.

Wade scrambled to his feet and chased after it, but even as he emerged from the pass, the coyote-snake was already descending the far slope of the mount.

By the time Wade had sprinted to the edge of the summit, the 'brid was streaking across the plain.

* * *

Astride Tango once more, Wade picked up the coyote-snake's trail. Since it had fled at top speed, its tracks were initially wide apart. Gradually, they drew closer together until at last they reflected a walking gait.

Wade knew that the 'brid could be recuperating its strength beneath any one of the desert bushes just ahead, so his non-lethal gun was drawn and ready.

After a good hour, however, Tango was still plodding along. The sun was beating down hot, and constant vigilance was taking its toll on Wade.

His neck was stiff from so much looking down, so to loosen his muscles, he rolled his head around. As he did, he saw that directly in his path was another monadnock, just like the last.

He urged Tango forward again, and soon saw that the 'brid's tracks led not up to the summit, but into a cool, dark cave formed by a collection of irregular boulders propped against each other.

Wade immediately understood his two choices: either go in after the thing, or wait it out. In his mind, he quickly went over the pros and cons of each option...

If he went in after it, he could finally put an end to this game. On the other hand, if the cave was too cramped for him to wield the gun, he would be defenseless.

Of course, if he chose to wait the creature out, he wouldn't have to risk life and limb. But if it did not come out before he had to return home, it would remain dangerously at large.

For a minute, Wade wavered between his two alternatives, but as usual, his sense of duty won out. He turned Tango to the left, and then after about fifty yards, he dismounted and tied the reins to a young Joshua tree.

After removing his sunglasses, Wade drew the *FLEXCALIBER* and walked back to the mouth of the cave. There he stooped, picked a small rock up off the ground, and tossed it inside. The coyote-snake responded with a threatening rattle, but it was faint.

Great — it's way in there, thought Wade. He activated the gun's flashlight and laser sight, took a deep breath, and walked cautiously forward.

The cave was not of the dank-hole variety, like the limestone caves of the eastern United States. Rather, it consisted of a series of gaps, twists, and turns between the sand-colored rocks. Its interior was illuminated by reflected daylight, but as Wade progressed, he became gradually more dependent upon the light from his gun.

The red dot of the laser sight danced on the cave wall directly ahead of him, where the passage took a sharp right turn. He approached the bend, picked a few pebbles off the ground, and then tossed them around the corner.

The rattle sounded closer this time, but Wade estimated that he still had a little ways to go. He rounded the corner prepared to fire, but there was no need, for the cave extended for another ten feet before turning left.

Since the strategy of tossing pebbles seemed to be working, Wade picked up a few more and crept forward. Halting a foot or so from the upcoming bend, he tried to quiet his breathing.

He deduced that the coyote-snake was no more than a few feet beyond the turn, and his heart was pounding accordingly. Finally, when he was as ready as he would ever be, he quickly reached around the corner and tossed the pebbles.

This time the rattle was loud. And since it was not followed by the scampering of four padded feet, it was obvious that the 'brid had reached the end of the line and had nowhere to go.

It suddenly occurred to Wade that just popping out into plain view might not be the smartest tactic. He advanced the FLEXCALIBER barrel until the chamber labeled "OC SPRAY" rotated to the top. Then, forming a mental picture of the creature's position, he swung his arm around the bend and fired the weapon.

Bullseye. White foam blasted out of the gun, hitting the coyote-snake square in the face. Panicked, blinded, and in pain, it shot forward to defend itself.

Wade jumped back, narrowly avoiding a set of three-inch fangs that were dripping with poison. But the 'brid kept coming, lashing this way and that, smacking its head first against one cave wall and then the other.

Even though Wade had the advantage of sight, he could not get out of the animal's way. It leapt straight at him, and though he managed to deflect its snapping jaws with the barrel of his gun, he was knocked flat onto his back.

The coyote-snake came down right on top of him with its front paws planted on his stomach. Like a berserker in the heat of battle, Wade swung his gun back and forth, battering the scaly head to ward off the lethal fangs.

The coyote-snake kept trying to land a bite, but the cumulative head trauma had greatly impaired its coordination. After Wade had knocked it nearly senseless, he cracked it with one final blow that sent it rolling off to his right.

Being a reluctant fighter to begin with, and having had no success delivering its poison, the coyote-snake reverted to its only other means of self-preservation, which was running.

On account of the pepper spray in its eyes, it could not navigate its way to the cave entrance by sight. But as long as it kept moving forward, its trajectory was automatically corrected for it by the cave walls. Like a pinball, the beast bounced from one side of the passage to the other in a painful zig-zag to freedom.

Though Wade had only narrowly survived the grappling match, he knew that he could ill-afford to shrink back now. He rolled onto his belly, came up onto his hands and knees, and took off like an Olympic runner.

The daylight was so much brighter than the light from his gun that by the time he emerged from the cave, his irises were screaming for mercy. Through eyelids nearly shut, he saw the coyote-snake fifteen yards ahead of him and stumbling its way out into the desert.

Even though the sage brush kept tripping it up, the 'brid was still moving faster than Wade could run, and he did not want to risk losing it by going to fetch Tango. He changed the setting on his gun to "SHOCK," and then in mid-sprint, he took aim and pulled the trigger.

A capsule the size of a shotgun shell whizzed through the air and struck the coyote-snake's ribcage, at a tangent. Upon impact, the capsule split in two. Half of it stuck to the creature's skin, and the other half dropped almost to the ground before being jerked to a stop by a thin yellow wire.

The coyote-snake flopped over into the dust as all of its skeletal muscles contracted simultaneously. Wade knew that the paralyzing shock would soon time out, so he set the gun to "TRANQ" and did not break pace until he was standing over the twitching creature.

Looking down at it, Wade felt suddenly sad — after all, it couldn't help what it was. And even though he had done only what was necessary to bring it down, he was sorry that he had had to inflict so much pain.

He fired a tranquilizer dart at its rump, and within a few seconds, the "secret-formula" serum took effect. Shortly thereafter, the SHOCK capsule timed out, and the 'brid lay still.

Wade turned away and gazed across the lonesome landscape. Reflecting upon the last two days, he found it difficult to remember how a seemingly ordinary phone call about an escaped tiger had led to hunting down hybrid monsters for the covert Genetic Anomalies Task Center.

The whole business could scarcely have been a greater intrusion into his life — or a more dangerous one.

But then, that was partly what made it so invigorating. For although he worked with large predators for a living, the risks were calculated, and he was hardly in constant jeopardy.

Wade looked down at the *FLEXCALIBER*. There was no denying that it was the coolest piece of technology he had ever laid hands on.

He shook his head and smiled in spite of himself. Then, succumbing to a youthful impulse, he twirled the gun on his index finger like Wild Bill Hickok and dropped it cleanly into its holster.

CHAPTER 6: TUG O' WAR

After the helicopter from the Genetic Anomalies Task Center picked up the coyote-snake, Wade left Joshua Tree for home. He and Genevieve had big plans to discuss the India picture with James Blakeman over dinner, but the reservation at the restaurant wasn't until 7:00.

That gave Wade plenty of time to get Tango to the stables and then grab a quick shower — or so he had assumed. But as he pulled up the ranch driveway at 5:30 p.m., he saw Genevieve's red Ferrari parked in front of his house.

From the way she was leaning against the car with her arms crossed, Wade knew he was in trouble.

"Uh-oh," he said, tightening his grip on the steering wheel of his truck. He shook his head, assuming he must have goofed — again. Bracing himself for her displeasure, he slowly pulled in beside her.

As he opened his door and stepped out onto the ground, Genevieve peevishly asked him, "Where have you been?"

Sticking his hands in his pockets, Wade replied, "Uh... didn't we say 6:30?"

"We did, but plans changed," replied Genevieve. "Did you forget your cell phone again?"

"No," Wade replied, pulling it out of his pocket. But after repeatedly pressing the answer and power buttons, the phone failed to turn on.

"Huh," he said. "Must've run out of battery. What's the big deal, anyway?"

"James just found out he has to catch a flight first thing tomorrow, so he wanted to do dinner earlier," said Genevieve.

Wade sighed in frustration. "OK, OK," he said. "Look — just give me a few minutes."

As he spoke, he saw Chet approaching from the barn. Eager to shift attention away from himself, Wade called out, "Hey, Chet! How'd everything go?"

"Fine," replied Chet. "Is your phone on?" For some reason, he also seemed annoyed.

"Oh — sorry about that," Wade apologized. "The battery died. Why? What's goin' on?"

"Keith wants us on set at eight o'clock *tomorrow* instead of Wednesday," said Chet.

"Shoot!" said Wade, kicking at the ground. "Have you been workin' with Hank?"

"All afternoon," said Chet. "He's good to go."

"OK — good. That's good," said Wade, feeling much relieved.

"Wade!" called Genevieve, in her most nagging tone.

"Listen, Chet," said Wade, "I hate to ask you to do this, but do you think you could take care of Tango for me? You can see I'm kinda in the dog house..."

Chet sighed and looked at his watch. After a moment of hesitation, he said, "I guess so."

"I appreciate it," said Wade, clapping him on the arm. "We'll call it double-overtime."

"All right," said Chet, and he dutifully walked over to the horse trailer.

Wade turned back to Genevieve. "Chet's gonna take care of Tango," he informed her, as if they could now be on their way.

Genevieve looked at him like he had a screw loose. "Aren't you going to get washed up?" she asked.

"Oh, right!" Wade agreed. He briskly ran up the porch steps and then called over his shoulder, "Just hang on! I'll be right out!"

"Hurry!" ordered Genevieve.

Wade flashed her a smile, entered the house, and closed the front door behind himself. Slumping back against it, he recalled the old adage that no good deed goes unpunished.

"What was I *thinkin'?"* he wondered out loud.

* * *

A week later, Wade's volunteer mission for the Genetic Anomalies Task Center seemed to him almost like a dream.

For over a month, he had been looking forward to today's shoot — or "date" as he had described it to Dolly. It was a low-stress gig, partly because the cougar was easier to transport and manage than the bigger cats, and partly because there was no serious choreography involved. Not to mention that the location was in the beautiful woods of northern California.

Though Wade preferred working on feature films, T.V. commercials were his bread and butter. The end products were usually silly little ads promoting cars, clothes, or food — like today's 30-second spot for a new brand of granola bar. Nothing particularly lofty or noble, but nothing to be ashamed of either.

The director of this shoot had an innovative style of working, for he brought his editor along with him to cut the digital footage together in the field, on a laptop. In this way, any takes that didn't quite work could be quickly identified and re-shot.

After a full morning of shooting, the editor had worked through lunch to compile a rough cut of the commercial. Now, the entire cast and crew — Wade and Dolly included — were gathered around his computer to view the finished product...

Two hikers — one dressed in blue, the other in red — trudged up to the top of a hill.

"I need an energy break," said the man in red.

"Me, too," said the man in blue.

The man in red pulled a chocolate bar from his backpack. As he began to unwrap it, a cougar suddenly leaped up onto a nearby rock. The two men froze.

"Is that your snack?" asked the cougar, in a silky female voice.

Surprised, the man in red replied, "Well — yeah. I mean, everyone knows sugar gives you energy."

The cougar gave a scoffing snort and then turned to the man in blue. "And how about you?"

"Uh," said the man in blue, "I brought this." From his backpack, he produced a small package labeled, "GRANOLA TIME."

"Smart choice," said the cougar.

"I know!" exclaimed the man in blue. "It's got oats, nuts and honey — not to mention being packed with extra protein and fiber. Everything I need to keep me going until supper. Speaking of which, you're not going to like, eat us? Are you?"

"Not you," replied the cougar. "Just your buddy, there."

"Wait! Why me?" asked the terrified man in red.

"You are what you eat," said the cougar. "You chose junk. And I'm a junk food JUNKIE!"

The cougar sprang at the man in red. Then, the man in blue proceeded to munch contentedly on his granola bar as shreds of his buddy's clothing flew up into the air behind him.

Over the screams, the mellow voice of an announcer said, "GRANOLA TIME. The 'not junk' snack."

Laughter and applause filled the air.

"That's great work, everyone — good stuff!" said the director. "OK, before we break down, I'd like to grab just one more nice close-up of the cat — if that's cool with you, Mr. Boss."

"Fine by me," said Wade.

"OK, great," said the director. "Why don't we try to roll tape in five minutes so that we can wrap in about half-an-hour." He clapped his hands, and the crew dispersed to prepare for the remaining shots.

Wade squatted down and rubbed Dolly's face. "Good job, girl!" he said. "Almost done."

"Beautiful animal," the editor called over to him.

"Yeah, she is, ain't she?" replied Wade. "Good work there, by the way. Can't believe you can do all that in the middle of the woods!"

"The tools are pretty great," agreed the editor.

"So some computer animation guys are gonna go in and make her mouth look like it's talkin'?" asked Wade.

"Yup," replied the editor. "Soon as the picture's locked."

"Can't wait to see that," said Wade. Then, since it had been a few hours since his early breakfast, he asked, "Say, did somebody mention a snack table?"

"Oh, yeah," said the editor, pointing behind him. "It's right over there."

"Thanks," said Wade. He gave Dolly's leash a gentle tug and led her over to a folding table upon which various edibles had been spread.

There were a few token apples and bananas, but these were barely noticeable beside the towering pile of GRANOLA TIME granola bars. To further recommend them, a poster-board sign behind the pile read: "COMPLIMENTARY — TAKE A BUNCH!"

Wade picked up a package, opened it, and took a bite of the bar. *Yum*, he thought. Then, because he was clearly being encouraged to do so, he stuffed several more into his jacket pocket.

Just then, his phone vibrated — his brand new phone, which he hoped would keep him out of trouble better than the last.

He hadn't yet copied over his list of contacts, so when he pulled the device from his pocket, all he saw on the screen was a number. Not recognizing it, he hit the answer button and said, "Hello?"

"Hi, Wade," came a friendly voice. "This is Paul Fairfield."

Wade suddenly had a flashback to high school. He had never been considered one of the "in crowd," but he was generally well-liked by his peers. Because of this — and because they knew he wouldn't send them away — the socially awkward kids tended to gravitate to him. He was happy to be a friend to them, but there were days when they left him feeling emotionally depleted.

Hearing Paul's voice made him feel that way now.

"Oh, hello, Paul," he said, with as much goodwill as he could muster. "How are you?"

"Good, good," said Paul. "Listen, I uh... just wanted to thank you again for your help out in Joshua Tree last week. I know it was an inconvenience, but we really appreciated it."

"Well, you're welcome," said Wade. "How's the animal?"

"Doing well," replied Paul. "Doesn't like being confined, but then none of them do. Otherwise, it's fine."

"Good," replied Wade. Then, after an awkward pause, he asked, "So... you're just callin' to thank me again?"

"Well," Paul confessed, "not just. We've uh... actually got another situation, in the White Mountains of New Hampshire. Nothing bad has happened yet, but this one is a potential nightmare. It wouldn't be a solo mission, though. You'd actually be going in with a team. Good men — very competent."

Wade rolled his eyes, thinking back to his unhappy homecoming after his adventure in the desert. As interested as he had been to learn the truth about the tiger-lizard, at present, he was less curious about weird genetic experiments on animals than he was concerned about his own personal affairs.

Not that he wasn't a thinking man. It was just that, like most people, he only had room in his life for so much. The hybrid phenomenon was certainly intriguing, but so were UFOs, the Bermuda Triangle, and a dozen other mysteries he simply didn't have time to dwell on.

"Listen, Paul," he said, "I've got a lot goin' on right now. I was glad to help you out before, but I just don't have room in my schedule for much extra these days. In fact, I was plannin' on droppin' off that field kit as soon as I get the chance."

Suddenly realizing that he was at risk of losing Wade altogether, Paul said, "Oh — there's no rush!" And if he hadn't been so desperate, he would have just left it at that.

But because his need was dire, he cautiously asked, "I... don't suppose it would make any difference if we flew you on a private jet? And compensated you for your time?"

Wade felt guilty, but he reminded himself that he had to get better at saying 'no'. Finally he said, "I'm sorry, Paul. I just can't."

After a moment of silence, Paul said somewhat heavily, "OK. I understand. Well... if you change your mind, you've got my number."

"Right. Take care," said Wade, and he hung up.

He hated disappointing people, but it was better to do it up front than to take on too much and then fail to make good on his word. He wasn't Superman, he told himself, but as usual, his conscience seemed immune to reason.

To avoid a repeat of the conversation he had just had, he took a minute to enter Paul's name and number into the contacts-list of his new phone.

Just as he finished, he heard the director of the commercial call out, "OK, Mr. Boss! We're ready if you are!"

"We're ready!" Wade called back, and then he led Dolly over to the camera for her close-up.

* * *

What a good day, thought Wade, as he plunked down on the leather sofa in front of his widescreen T.V. Better still, pizza for dinner, topped with green peppers and onions.

He cracked open a can of cold soda, took a swig, and set it on the coffee table beside the pizza box. Sliding two large slices onto a paper plate, he removed his hat and said a quick blessing:

"Thank you, Father, for this, my daily bread."

He then took aim with the remote and turned on the television. A perfectly-groomed anchorman appeared on the screen, energetically recounting the newsworthy events of the day. Wade turned the volume down a notch and then pulled his phone from his pocket.

After taking a well-deserved bite of pizza, he dialed his voicemail. While he was driving home, Genevieve had called. He hadn't picked up, and he knew that there would be unpleasant consequences if he postponed listening to her message for too long.

"Hey, Babe," said her voice over the speaker. "Just calling to let you know that James says the India picture is getting a green light! I picked up a book today on the colonial period. I'm so excited! I'm determined to get another tiger scene in there, and you know me — I usually get what I want!"

"I know," said Wade, out loud.

"Anyway," the message continued, "call me when you get home. Bye!"

There were no more messages. Wade hit the call-end button and stared at the phone. It wasn't the newest model on the market, but it was still a pretty powerful little gizmo. Already he had purchased a couple of apps that he thought might help him keep better organized.

He tapped the icon for the weekly planner, and a calendar popped up. It was empty, except for one event: in the box for Friday, he had entered, "Show Rose the town."

All day long his thoughts had kept turning to her, even though it had been a week since they met at the Genetic Anomalies Task Center. Perhaps her Texas accent had simply unlocked some suppressed homesickness in him. He mused to himself that it would be kind of nice to finally have a friend in the area who shared his Lone Star sensibilities.

In any case, today was Monday, and Friday seemed like an awfully long way away.

On the television, the anchorman's tone turned somber. "Our next story," he said, "comes from the White Mountains of New Hampshire, where today a peaceful hike turned unexpectedly tragic."

Wade was suddenly brought back to the present. *White Mountains?* he thought. It was the second time that day he had heard the region mentioned. Out of curiosity, he turned up the volume on the T.V.

The anchorman continued: "Authorities say that three men are dead after a savage bear attack on one of the mountain trails."

Next came a video clip — an interview with one of the victims, a man in his early twenties. He was sitting up in a hospital bed, hooked to an I.V. His face was badly bruised, and tears were streaming down his face.

"We... we just wanted to get in one last hike before the snow," said the young man. "I was in front, and we were coming up on Eagle Crag, from North Baldface. All of a sudden, I heard screaming behind me. I turned around, and this... *thing*... just came out of nowhere.

"It was huge — like some kind of deformed bear! It charged and started tossing us around like rag-dolls. Dillon flew back and crashed into me — his head hit me in the face, and I blacked out. When I woke up, everyone was... torn to pieces!"

As the man broke down, the picture on the screen switched to a forest ranger making an official statement.

"There are definitely bears in the area," said the ranger, "but they don't tend to attack unless provoked. Plus, they should all be hibernating at this point, which makes this incident even more unusual. Right now we're just asking people to stay clear of the area while we try to track down the animal in question."

The anchorman re-appeared and concluded the story by saying, "Unfortunately, those efforts have been hindered by significant snowfall."

Wade picked up the T.V. remote, pressed the DVR rewind button, and then replayed the clip of the victim describing the creature: "It was huge — like some kind of *deformed bear!*"

Wade paused the video. As he stared at the frozen image of the grief-stricken man, Paul Fairfield's words from that morning echoed in his mind.

Just then, his cell phone rang. Though he hardly needed to, he read the caller's name on the touch screen: Paul Fairfield.

Wade pressed the answer button. Then, raising the phone to his ear, he said, "I just saw. You can count me in."

CHAPTER 7: TWO PEERS AND A RIVAL

Sixteen hours later, Wade was driving north on Route 113 through the snow-covered mountains of New Hampshire.

As Paul had promised, the Task Center had flown him privately all the way from Los Angeles. And instead of the bottom-of-the-barrel food one usually gets on an airplane, Wade had just feasted on a sumptuous waffle breakfast with coffee and a side of eggs, over-hard.

But the V.I.P. treatment only went so far. The black, mid-sized sedan that had been reserved for him at the airport was just a standard rental. Still, it handled well enough on the icy roads, and that was the main thing.

Just like in the carol of Good King Wenceslas, the snow lay round about, "deep and crisp and even." Already, Wade was glad he had decided to come, for the beauty of the mountains more than made up for any inconvenience — plus he finally had a reason to wear his beloved shearling coat again.

His *FLEXCALIBER* was already strapped to his thigh, and beside him on the passenger seat lay a silver case — but not the one for his gun. Rather, it contained barrels that had been specially modified for the cold weather, and which he had been instructed to distribute among his teammates.

Each man, Paul had told him, had already assisted in the capture of at least one 'brid. Wade could not deny that he was excited to meet some other members of the exclusive "hybrid hunter" club to which he now belonged.

The pre-arranged meeting place was a small, unpaved parking area just off the main road. Wade arrived to find it almost entirely taken up by a flatbed trailer hitched to a red pickup truck with snow chains on the tires.

The trailer was loaded with four snowmobiles, which were to be the hunters' primary mode of transportation through the woods. Straddling one of these machines was a man in dark clothing, who waited while two other men lowered a ramp from the back of the trailer to the ground.

From the descriptions Paul had given him, Wade recognized the men as being the members of his team. He parked his rental car behind the trailer, grabbed the silver case, and stepped out into the crisp morning air.

As soon as the two men on the ground had deployed the ramp, they turned to face him. The fellow on Wade's right was a healthy, clean-shaven fellow in his early thirties with blond hair, cropped short. He had striking, Nordic-blue eyes, and he wore a smile nearly as bright as his neon-green ski-parka.

In stark contrast, the man on Wade's left was dressed all in winter camouflage. His dark hair and mustache were streaked with silver, he had deep-set brown eyes, and his lips were pursed in an ironic smile that seemed less good-humored than pugnacious.

If Wade had not been able to tell from their faces that these were his teammates, the *FLEXCALIBER* holsters protruding from beneath their coats would have removed any doubt.

"Mornin'!" he called out. "I assume you gentlemen are here at the behest of a Mr. Fairfield?"

"That we are," said the man with blue eyes. "And from the looks of it, you must be Mr. Boss."

"From the looks of it?" asked Wade.

"Can't be too many Texas cowboys in these mountains!" said the man.

"I guess not," said Wade, smiling as he held out his hand. "Call me Wade."

The man shook his hand and said, "Finn Holstad. Glad to meet you."

"The Army Ranger," said Wade, remembering back to his in-flight briefing.

"Inactive," Finn clarified, "but yeah — once a Ranger, always a Ranger." He then gestured to the man in winter camouflage and said, "And this here is Bob MacArthur."

"Professional hunter," volunteered Bob, grabbing Wade's hand and shaking it a bit too tightly. "Don't suppose that'll endear me to you, though — you being an animal trainer, and all!"

From the defiant gleam in his eyes and the way he held tight to Wade's hand, Bob was making it obvious that he wanted a fight — or a verbal spat, at the least.

He knew that it was Wade who had filled in for him while he was off hunting grizzlies in Alaska. And since Wade was the owner of a tame grizzly, Bob fully expected a righteous sermon about the sanctity of animal life.

But Wade could read him like a book, and was not so easily baited.

"Oh, I got nothin' against huntin'," replied Wade, in a disarming tone. Then, once he saw that he had thrown Bob off-balance, he added, "So long as it's done with respect."

He then abruptly pulled back his hand, leaving Bob wondering how he had just been smooth-talked out of satisfaction.

In the next moment, they were joined by the man who had backed the snowmobile down the ramp. He was an Apache Indian and an expert tracker. In addition to his non-lethal sidearm, he wore black jeans, a brown wool jacket, and a matching scarf.

His long black hair was pulled into a tight ponytail, he stood ramrod-straight, and his expression was steely. But as he held out his hand to Wade, the taut skin around his eyes relaxed ever so slightly. "Kuruk Torres," he introduced himself, in a resonant voice.

Wade shook his hand warmly and said, "Wade Boss. Saw on the news last year how you tracked down that missin' girl up in Washington. That was somethin'."

At this compliment, Kuruk's face softened even more. "It's nice when there's a happy ending," he replied.

"I'll bet," said Wade. Then, addressing the group, he asked, "Well, shall we talk shop?"

The others nodded, and Wade hoisted the silver case up onto the back of the trailer. Flipping open the lid, he exposed four FLEXCALIBER barrels, one for each man. As he handed them out, he gave a rundown of the specs.

"Now, they've improved the tranquilizer serum — made it a bit safer. If the first shot don't drop the 'brid within five seconds, you can follow it up with a second, smaller dose without too much risk to the animal.

"You've got two of those, plus two shots of pepper — except instead of a spray, it blasts out in a gel, so if there's wind, you won't get hit with blowback. If this 'brid is part bear, it should be a strong deterrent."

On the barrel that he had selected for himself, Wade pointed to a small button and said, "To keep the fluids from freezin' up, just press here." He then demonstrated, and a tiny red light next to the button turned on. "That'll heat the barrel for about eight hours," he explained.

Drawing his gun, he swapped out the old barrel that was affixed to it for the new, heated one. As the others followed his example, Wade asked, "So where are things at?"

Finn Holstad spoke up and said, "Well, the bad news is that any old tracks have been covered by the snow. Good news is, it'll be real easy to find any new ones.

"The Department of Fish and Game assumes that a rogue bear is the culprit behind the attack. They're still coordinating their efforts, but there's a storm front on the way, and they won't do anything until it's passed over. That gives us a brief window to do our little thing and bug out.

"The Task Center is sending us a chopper, which ought to be here soon. But if the storm moves in too quick, it may have to bail, which would mean we'd have to call it a day, too — no point in tagging the 'brid if we can't lift it out. That is, unless we're hot on its trail, in which case we'll take it down and keep it pacified until the skies clear."

"What's the lay of the land?" asked Wade.

In answer, Bob MacArthur pulled out a topographical map that was folded to show the search area.

"The first trailhead starts right here, where we're at," said Bob. "It splits off pretty quick into four separate trails: two leading up to South Baldface, and two that come up on Eagle Crag, which are pretty close together. About a half-mile up this road, there's another trail to Mt. Meader.

"If we split up, the odds are pretty good that we'll find some tracks. If we come up empty, it probably means the 'brid has hunkered down somewhere, or else took off down the western side of the mountains."

As the men nodded in agreement, they heard the distant whump-whump of an approaching helicopter.

"Sounds like our chopper," said Finn. "I'll get the radios."

As he walked around to the driver's side of the truck, Kuruk climbed up onto the trailer to unload the other snowmobiles.

Bob, meanwhile, ambled over to the truck's passenger door, opened it, and reached behind the seat. When he finally straightened, he had a high-powered hunting rifle in his hands.

Wade suddenly bristled — but not because he secretly had a

problem with hunting. What he had told Bob just moments before had been the honest truth. Indeed, just the thought of hunting brought back happy memories of time spent with his grandfather.

Furthermore, Wade understood the universal mandate that for something to live, something else has to die — even if only an eggplant. And then, of course, there was the fact that meat was delicious, and he ate it all the time.

So Wade was no hypocrite, nor was he bothered by the killing of animals per se. On the other hand, *needless* killing bothered him quite a bit.

The bear-'brid they were after was obviously not going to wind up on anyone's dinner table. It was destined for the Task Center's repurposed zoo, and Wade saw no reason why together the four of them could not apprehend it alive.

Conscious to keep his tone flat and unemotional, Wade called over, "We're all on the same page here, right?"

But despite his dispassionate delivery, Bob regarded the mere question to be a victory. It signified that he could get a reaction out of Wade after all — even if only a measured one.

With a smirk of triumph, Bob replied, "I take calculated risks, Mr. Boss — not foolish ones. Experience tells me that we may need more than just pepper and tranquilizers to bring in this animal. Does that offend you?"

"I'm never offended by doin' what's necessary," said Wade. "I just want to make sure you're not itchin' to kill this 'brid out of preference."

Bob smiled even wider as he pulled a fully-loaded bullet clip from his coat pocket.

"You know," he said, "I think this is the beginning of a beautiful relationship!" And with those words, he forcefully slapped the clip into the rifle.

* * *

It had fallen to Wade to take the southernmost route, towards the base of South Baldface Mountain. The going was slow, however, for the trail had been obscured by a thick layer of snow, and had never been intended for snowmobiles in the first place.

It was not enough just to look for tracks along the actual trail either, for of course the bear-'brid would wander where it pleased. Wade therefore had to scan the woods to either side of him, through trees heavily laden with snow.

Three times in the course of an hour he had seen what looked like tracks in the forest, and three times he had hopped off the snowmobile to investigate.

But each trek through the knee-deep snow ended fruitlessly, for the "tracks" turned out to be either tricks of light and shadow, or else craters formed by clumps of snow that had fallen from tree limbs.

The snow was also an acoustic dampener, so that for a long time Wade heard nothing but his snowmobile, the distant drone of the search helicopter, and the occasional crunch of his own footsteps.

After another half-hour of chasing false leads, the sky grew darker and the snow began to come down heavily. Wade noticed that the sound of the helicopter was growing gradually louder, and soon it reached a crescendo over his head.

The pilot was accompanied by a spotter whose job it was to search the area with high-powered binoculars. Wade's radio crackled to life, and he heard the spotter say, "Ground team, this is the chopper. Do you read?"

Wade stopped his snowmobile and pulled the radio from his coat pocket. "Wade here," he replied. "You boys see somethin'?"

"No sign of the 'brid," said the spotter, "but Wade, it looks like you've got a couple of campers at the shelter up ahead of you."

"Roger that," said Wade. "I'll clear 'em out when I get there."

Then the spotter addressed the entire team, saying, "Gentlemen, this front's moving in awful fast. Unless you need us to stay, we should head back."

After a second or two of silence, Wade's radio crackled again, and he heard the voice of the blue-eyed ex-Ranger: "This is Finn. I'm coming up on Meader, but pretty soon I'm going to have to pull out the snowshoes — it's getting too steep."

Next, the Apache tracker reported, "This is Kuruk. I haven't found anything yet."

Last of all, the professional hunter said, "Bob, here — ditto that. I'm beginning to think this 'brid took off to the west."

"Well," said Wade, "either he's layin' low, or he ain't here. Either way, we prob'ly don't stand to gain too much by toughin' it through this storm."

"In that case," said the spotter, "we'll see you soon. Call if there's any sudden emergency."

As the helicopter veered away, Wade told the others, "All right — I'm gonna hit the shelter and try to send those campers packin'. We can talk about plan B back at the truck."

"OK — sounds good," said Finn.

"This is Kuruk. I'm heading back."

"See you there," said Bob, and then the radio fell silent.

From his memory of the topographical map, Wade guessed that he could reach the shelter in a few minutes. But he figured he might as well take it slow and enjoy himself, for he couldn't imagine how long it would be before he found himself in the winter woods again.

It was not long before his enjoyment was cut short by a fleeting sound carried on the wind. It must have been very loud at its source, for it was audible even over the whine of the snowmobile.

Wade killed the engine, wondering where the sound had come from, and what had made it. A second later, both questions were answered: just up the trail, someone was screaming.

Wade turned the ignition back on and cranked the gas. Within thirty seconds, he saw a break in the trees ahead that appeared to open up into a clearing.

Although he could not see the hybrid, he knew without a doubt that it was the reason for the screams.

Pulling out his radio, he pressed the talk-button and shouted, "This is Wade! The 'brid is at the South Baldface shelter! The campers are under attack!"

He pocketed the radio even as his teammates replied that they were on their way.

As soon as he broke through the trees, Wade applied the brakes, jumped off the snowmobile, and drew his gun.

To his right, he saw a shelter the size of a large tool shed. Its floor was rectangular, but it had only three walls, with the fourth side remaining open to a fire pit in the clearing. The entire structure rested upon risers made of rock and wood that held it up off the sloping ground.

Perched on the roof's peak were two young men who looked to Wade like college students. One wore a blue ski jacket, had unwashed hair, and a sparse brown "beard" that was nothing short of silly. The other fellow was better-groomed, though not much smarter, for he sported only a poorly insulated yellow vest overtop red long-johns.

Silly Beard and Vest Man were desperately trying to keep away from something behind the shelter that Wade could not yet see. As he raced forward, the Something slammed into the back of the structure, causing it to shudder violently.

"Down here! Jump down! Jump down!" Wade hollered.

Because the young men were screaming their heads off and facing away from him, it was a few seconds before they realized he was even there.

Finally, they glanced down at him with terrified expressions. But it was only another instant before Vest Man looked back behind the shelter and cried, "Look out!"

He and his buddy dove off opposite sides of the roof and were still in mid-air as the back wall of the shelter exploded.

Splintered boards flew through the air at Wade. Shielding his face with his arms, he staggered back and tripped over the ring of stones that encircled the fire pit.

His gun had become slippery from the falling snow, and as he landed on his back, he lost his grip on it. The weapon went sailing through the air and came down somewhere behind him.

Jerking up into a sitting position, he at last laid eyes on the man-killing hybrid. His first impression was that it resembled a grizzly bear. His second was that it looked more like a rhinoceros.

And then he realized that it was both.

At the end of its face was the soft, fleshy nose of a bear. But just behind that, sticking up at a right angle from its skull, was a two-foot-long, pointed horn.

The folds of its gray skin looked like armor plates, and bristly, brown fur sprouted from the gaps in between. Its arms and legs were as stout as tree trunks, and its paws were armed with dreadful, six-inch claws.

As the air cleared of debris, the rhino-bear locked eyes with Wade. Forgetting all about the campers, it bared its saber-like teeth at him and snarled.

Wade hastily stood up and backed away as the monster 'brid lumbered towards him on all fours. In no time at all, he had reached the edge of the clearing and was up against the woods.

He paused, wondering at his odds of survival if he took off through the trees. The rhino-bear also stopped, and from across a span of about twenty feet, the two of them stared at each other.

Then, in a spontaneous display of physical prowess, the rhino-bear reared up on its hind legs and roared. For Wade, it was as though an amplifier at a rock concert had suddenly been turned on at top volume, and he reflexively covered his ears.

Behind the rhino-bear, where the clearing met the downward trail, the two panicked campers converged on Wade's snowmobile, which he had left running.

Silly Beard hopped onto the seat and grabbed the handlebars. Jumping on behind him, Vest Man yelled, "Do you know how to drive this thing?!"

With baseless confidence, Silly Beard answered, "How hard can it be?"

In the next instant, Vest Man found himself somersaulting off the back of the snowmobile, which shot forward at full throttle and plowed into the nearest corner of the shelter.

At the sound of the collision, the rhino-bear dropped onto all fours and looked back.

Vest Man was quickly back up on his feet, none the worse for his roll in the snow. Silly Beard, however, had paid a price for his stupidity. He had flown face-first into the dashboard of the snowmobile and now staggered over to his friend holding a bloody nose.

At the first whiff of blood, the rhino-bear lost all interest in Wade and turned back to the foolhardy friends.

Wade frantically looked about for his *FLEXCALIBER*, but the far-flung fragments of the shelter had created dozens of pits in the snow. Apart from a careful search, there was no way to tell which hole contained his gun.

He glanced up again to see Vest Man and Silly Beard backing down the mountain trail. The rhino-bear encroached upon them slowly, as if it knew they had no hope of escape.

Wade risked another quick search for his gun. After a few futile seconds, he looked up to see that the rhino-bear had reached the trailhead and was looming over its two-course meal.

Wade realized that if he was going to act at all, he had to act now. Instinctively, he felt his coat pockets for anything that might be of use...

Silly Beard was openly sobbing. Vest Man was silent, but shook like a leaf. Both knew beyond all doubt that Fate had decreed for them a gruesome and painful passage to the next life.

But just then, in their moment of utter despair, Providence intervened in an old, familiar form: that of a brave man.

"HEY!" bellowed Wade, at the top of his lungs.

The rhino-bear glanced over its shoulder to see him holding up a partially unwrapped snack bar.

Fixing the colossus with a level gaze, in a voice clear and bold, Wade called out, "GRANOLA TIME!"

The rhino-bear growled.

Wade took a bite of the granola bar. "Mmm," he said, as he chewed. "Nuts and honey. This is what you want."

With a dismissive grunt, the rhino-bear turned back to the young men.

But Wade was not about to be put off. "Hey!" he yelled. "I'm talkin' to you!"

The hulking hybrid was becoming aggravated, and it glared back at him once more.

"That's right," said Wade. "You don't want to eat people. I got what you need. Come and git it! Come on!"

It was becoming evident to the rhino-bear that it must either deal with this interloper or have no peace. Reluctant to turn away from its easy meal, it opened its fearsome jaws and roared back at Wade.

Undaunted, Wade replied, "Oh, I ain't goin' nowhere! Now you leave those boys alone and come try this! Come on, now! COME ON!"

Finally irritated to the point of action, the rhino-bear heaved its titanic bulk around to face uphill.

Wade took a step back towards the wrecked shelter and dangled the granola bar in a tantalizing fashion. "That's right!" he said. "Ol' Wade knows what's good for ya!"

The rhino-bear lumbered up the trail, pausing only to let out another angry roar.

"Keep comin', keep comin'," Wade coaxed. He kept backing up until he was right next to the shelter, at which point he said, "Now... I'm just gonna toss this on over."

He gently lobbed the granola bar, and it landed between the rhino-bear's front paws. The 'brid looked down at the snack, sniffed it twice, and then looked back up at Wade.

And then it charged him.

Down on the trail, with no regard for the man who was risking his life to save theirs, Silly Beard and Vest Man turned to each other and cried, "RUN!" Without further ado, they bolted down the mountain as fast as the accumulated snow would allow.

Despite the gaping hole right through its middle, the wooden shelter still retained some of its structural integrity and rested solidly upon its risers, about a foot-and-a-half above the uneven ground.

The crawlspace underneath offered scant cover, but since there was no other to be had, Wade dove for it. His bulky coat was now a liability, but in his desperation, he managed to squeeze his entire body into the space.

As he disappeared from sight, the charging rhino-bear skidded to a halt and sniffed around the base of the shelter. Once reassured that Wade was indeed underneath, it hooked its horn under the front of the building and lifted it effortlessly into the air.

Wade felt like an ant whose protective rock had just been removed by a boy with a magnifying glass. In shock and awe, he stared up at the belly of the beast.

But the floorboards that the rhino-bear had hooked with its horn could not support the entire weight of the shelter. They suddenly snapped, and the building came crashing back down onto the risers.

Wade stared up at the underside of the shelter, incredulous that he had not just been flattened like a pancake. But he had escaped the proverbial frying pan only to land in the fire, for the rhino-bear immediately began tearing the floor apart with its claws.

Wade scooted back as far possible, but he knew his protection would soon be stripped away. Rolling over onto his stomach, he dragged himself by his elbows to the far side of the shelter. After digging through a snowdrift, he at last squirmed out into the open air.

Here the building hid him from the rhino-bear's sight. Hopping to his feet, he ran along the edge of the clearing, back to the spot where he had lost hold of his gun.

As he resumed the search for his only means of survival, the rhino-bear finished tearing up the shelter floor. Not seeing Wade, it spent a few puzzled moments picking through the rubble and then raised its head and sniffed at the air.

The fact that Wade was five yards downwind afforded him a few critical seconds. But presently the rhino-bear turned towards him, and his time was up.

For his entire career, Wade had lived with the knowledge that one of his large, carnivorous animals might someday turn on him. He had often wondered what it would be like to be eaten alive. Now he was about to find out.

Being a God-fearing man, he had long been reconciled to the inevitability of his own death. In a strange way, he was actually relieved that the waiting and wondering was finally over.

But the serenity of the moment was tinged with regret — that he had never married, that he was childless, and that the epic story of his ancestors should have reached its untimely conclusion in him.

For a fleeting second, the rhino-bear seemed to evaporate, and all Wade could see was a vision of the wife and children he might have had.

"I never had a family," he lamented softly to himself. Why hadn't he gotten around to it? He couldn't remember any good reason.

As the rhino-bear lined up for the death-charge, Wade robotically stepped backwards. He hoped that he might be trampled, rather than gored through the chest. But either way, he didn't imagine that he would suffer long.

Just then, his morbid thoughts were interrupted by the last sound in the world he expected to hear: CLINK!

He glanced down to see that the heel of his boot had tapped the barrel of his lost gun, half-buried in the snow.

Instantly, the calm acceptance of death was overthrown by an electrifying surge of adrenaline. Here at his feet lay one last chance at life, and with it, the possibility that he might yet add another chapter to the Boss family saga. And as long as there was the faintest hope of that glorious future, he was going to fight for it with everything he had.

In a flash, Wade snatched up the *FLEXCALIBER* and leveled it at the rhino-bear.

As if sensing that the gun posed a threat, the rhino-bear snorted and pawed at the ground, but it did not charge. Then, hoping to wither Wade's defiance, it rose up again on its hind legs and roared.

Wade aimed the laser sight at the giant's chest and fired a tranquilizer dart. He watched it sail towards its mark, knowing that if he could just survive the next five seconds, the top-secret serum would take effect. All that would then remain would be to wait for the airlift — job well done.

Except that, upon striking its target, the dart did something Wade had not expected: it bounced off.

The hypodermic needle at its tip had been designed to puncture skin. But in the case of the rhino-bear, "skin" meant thick folds of natural armor. The needle was simply no match, and the dart bounced off the 'brid's chest and landed harmlessly in the snow.

Emboldened by the failure of Wade's pitiful counterpunch, the rhino-bear snorted, dropped to all fours, and charged.

Though he disliked his final option, Wade wasted no time employing it. Pressing the gun's "ADVANCE" button with his thumb, he pulled the trigger so that a round of pepper rotated into place.

With only a split-second to aim, he pulled the trigger again. A clump of gel blasted out of the barrel, whizzed through the air, and struck the rhino-bear right on the end of its snout.

Though it had the armor and power of a rhinoceros, its nose was all bear, and thousands of times more sensitive than a human's. The Oleoresin Capsicum caused the 'brid instant and overwhelming pain, stopping it dead in its tracks.

It thrashed its head back and forth, howling piteously. Then it thrust its nose into the snow, which did nothing to quench the chemical burn. Finally, having lost all its appetite, it took off down the mountain trail with astonishing speed.

Wade ran over to his snowmobile, which fortunately had suffered only cosmetic damage from its crash into the shelter. Even as he landed on the seat, he hit the reverse button and spun the machine around to face downhill.

From his coat pocket, he heard a crackling voice: "Wade, this is Finn! Have you tagged the 'brid?!"

There was no risk of losing it now, given the deep furrow it had left in its wake. Wade figured he had a second to respond, so he yanked the radio out.

"This is Wade! I shot it, but the dart just bounced off! It's part rhino — has skin like armor! I gave it a faceful of pepper, and I'm in pursuit down the mountain!"

Then came another voice over the radio: "Wade, this is Bob! I'll be there in a couple minutes! Just keep it in sight, and I'll take care of it!"

Remembering Bob's high-powered rifle, Wade did not bother to respond, but simply stuffed the radio back into his pocket. "Oh, no, you won't!" he swore aloud, and then he sped down the mountain.

The last thing the rhino-bear wanted to do was to try negotiating its way through the dense woods. It therefore kept to the trail, which meant that it was quickly overtaking the two unhappy campers on whom it had so recently intended to feast.

Silly Beard and Vest Man, still running flat out, could hear their own pulses pounding in their ears. They could hear the whipping of the wind and the heaving of their frostbitten lungs.

But what they could not hear, due to the snow's dampening effect, were the footfalls of the rhino-bear closing in behind them.

Only at the last second did they perceive that they were about to be trampled, at which point they glanced back, screamed in unison, and dove headlong into the woods on opposite sides of the trail.

The 'brid barreled on past, kicking up a flurry of fresh powder and leaving the overgrown boys astonished at their survival for the second time that day.

Moments later, Wade came hurtling down the slope on his snowmobile. If he had had time to give the cowards a piece of his mind, they would have wished that the rhino-bear had gotten them first. As it was, all he could spare them was a fleeting reproach.

"JERKS!" he shouted, and then he raced on by.

Through the heavily falling snow, he could see the 'brid up ahead. As long as it did not veer off into the woods, he would be able to catch up to it in short order.

Not that he knew what he was going to do at that point. He was counting on having some sort of brilliant inspiration when the time came. If he didn't, he knew that Bob's more permanent solution might be the only option left.

Though the rhino-bear was temporarily smell-impaired, its ears still worked fine, and it could hear the whine of the snowmobile getting louder and louder. Finally, handicapped though it was, it felt that it had no choice but to meet the danger.

As the monster wheeled about, Wade hit the snowmobile's brakes and stopped a mere thirty yards up the trail. He drew his gun, thinking to himself that, in order to tranquilize the 'brid, he would have to hit some muscle that was not protected by armor.

As far as he could tell, that left just the mucous-dripping nose. But he had little hope of nailing such a small target while it was in motion, and the rhino-bear kept pawing at the ground and tossing its head.

Wade's chances would have been much better if the pepper-gel had gotten into the animal's eyes. But because they had been shielded by the thick base of its horn, the rhino-bear was still fully capable of running him down.

He feared that if he risked a long shot he would just be wasting the dart. But in his mind's eye, all he could see was Bob speeding up the path with his rifle.

Tracking the 'brid's elusive nose with his gun, Wade yelled out, "Hold still!"

Instead, the rhino-bear charged.

Gun still in hand, Wade took hold of the snowmobile's handlebars and punched the reverse button. He made backwards progress up the slope, but not nearly fast enough. The rhino-bear gained quickly on him and lowered its head for impact.

Wade had no alternative but to abandon ship. Holding tight to his gun, he hopped up onto the seat and leaped into the woods off to his left.

He did not see the actual collision, but the sound of shattering fiberglass and shredding metal told the story. With a sideways swing of its head, the rhino-bear impaled the front of the snowmobile and tossed it like a child's toy.

The vehicle came crashing down into the woods on the opposite side of the trail from Wade. The rhino-bear halted and looked around to see if any threat remained. It spotted Wade jumping to his feet, and charged him again.

Wade ran into a stand of evergreens that were spaced just far enough apart for him to proceed in a straight line. The rhino-bear, however, was slowed down by its size, having to weave its way more slowly between the trees.

Because Wade could not sustain a flat-out sprint for long, he looked for a suitable tree to climb. Settling upon a fifty-foot hemlock, he holstered his gun and jumped up to grab the lowest branch.

By the time the rhino-bear caught up, Wade was out of reach but hardly out of danger. Too big to climb up after him, the 'brid instead used its front paws to pump the tree, CPR-style.

The tree rocked crazily back and forth, and Wade hugged it with all his strength to keep from being flung into the air. Then, with a loud CRACK, the trunk snapped just above the roots.

Wade felt himself falling backwards and braced for a hard landing. He only prayed that the snow would provide enough cushioning to protect him from a spinal injury.

But rather than falling to his doom, he was jerked to a sudden stop. The upper half of his tree had mercifully gotten hung up on the branches of its neighbors, which supported it at a forty-five degree angle to the forest floor.

Wade's arms held fast, but his feet slipped and dangled out into the air. The rhino-bear rushed over and swiped at his boots, just grazing them before he swung his legs up and hooked them on a branch.

With the beast directly beneath him, Wade thought that he might finally be able to take another shot with the *FLEXCALIBER*. Holding tight to the tree with his left arm, he drew the gun and twisted his torso so that he could look down.

The rhino-bear, however, perceived that a little more effort was required to achieve its goal. Therefore, it shuffled back to the trunk and gave it three additional pumps.

The tree broke free of the branches of its neighbors, and Wade felt himself falling backwards again. A heartbeat later, he was jerked to another stop as the tree got snagged for the second time.

The rhino-bear ran back over to stand underneath Wade on its hind legs. It swiped at the air, but he remained just out of reach. Still, with gravity as its ally, the 'brid would not have to wait long for retribution.

For Wade, it was now do or die. Once more, he twisted his body downward and tried to take aim.

Each time the rhino-bear swatted at the gun, Wade retracted his arm. Finally, in utter frustration, the 'brid threw back its head and roared up at him.

It was a critical mistake, for in that instant, its muzzle became stationary. Feeling as though he was moving in slow motion, Wade brought the gun into alignment. As soon as he saw the red dot of the laser sight dancing on the end of the moist, glistening nose, he knew the ordeal was over.

"There!" he said, and he pulled the trigger.

The projectile's hypodermic needle sank into the unprotected tip of the rhino-bear's nose. The animal howled and swiped at the dart, sending it flying off into the woods. But the tranquilizer serum had already been injected.

As Wade's tree continued to sag towards the earth, the rhino-bear rubbed its face in the snow, moaning in pain and confusion. It succumbed quickly to the drug, first leaning forward onto its elbows, then sinking to its knees, and finally collapsing altogether.

Wade stared down at the behemoth in relief and amazement — and then his tree dropped for the last time.

Having been twice halted on its downward journey, the tree lacked sufficient momentum to carry it all the way to the ground. Its branches became permanently tangled in the pressing forest, which slowed it gradually until it stopped at a thirty degree angle to the ground.

When Wade finally looked down again, he saw that he was hovering just a few inches above the insensible rhino-bear.

Letting go of the tree, he landed on top of his vanquished foe and lay back upon its stupendous, steaming body. Then, as the falling snowflakes melted upon his face, he listened with carefree satisfaction to the approach of Bob's snowmobile.

CHAPTER 9: FALLOUT

Despite the worsening weather, the helicopter returned to South Baldface Mountain to execute a daring airlift of the rhino-bear. Then, since the lab in Los Angeles was not equipped to deal with such a large animal, the hybrid was transported by truck directly to "the Zoo," in Nevada.

The storm ultimately evolved into a blizzard that buried the entire Northeast under several feet of snow. Consequently, Wade was stranded at the airport in Portland, Maine for all of Wednesday and the better part of Thursday.

So technically, it wasn't his fault that he had to miss Thursday's movie shoot featuring his tiger, Fred. Still, it had been a substantial imposition upon Chet to ask him to fill in at the last moment.

When at last Wade pulled up to his log house late Friday morning, he knew the time had come to face the music.

As he hopped out of his truck and grabbed his suitcase, he was glad to see Chandra's maroon Buick rolling towards him from the direction of the office. He figured he could at least get a quick report about Chet's frame of mind and then tailor his apology accordingly.

He set down his suitcase, and Chandra slowed her car to a stop. Then she rolled down her passenger side window and leaned across the seat to look up.

"Hey, Boss," she said, in her usual, happy voice. "Welcome back!"

Wade laid a hand on the roof of her car. Trying to sound natural, he said, "Thanks, Chandra. Where are you off to?"

"Dentist," said Chandra. "I'll be back in an hour."

"Oh. OK," said Wade. Then tentatively, he asked, "So, how big did I goof?"

"Big," answered Chandra, still smiling.

Wade just nodded. Then, at the sound of approaching hoofbeats, he looked up. Chet was riding towards them from the stables.

Chandra spied him in her rear-view mirror and then told Wade, "He did a great job with Fred on that shoot yesterday. You seriously owe him."

"Yeah, I know," said Wade, with a sigh.

Then, not wanting to get caught in the middle of anything unpleasant, Chandra said, "Well — good luck. See you soon!"

As she drove off, Wade straightened and turned towards Chet with an expression that was friendly, yet contrite.

"Hey there, Chet!" he called out.

"Hey, Boss," answered Chet, flatly. He reined his chestnut-brown horse to a halt and then dismounted as Wade ambled over.

"How was the trip?" asked Chet, more out of courtesy than genuine interest.

"Oh — all right, I guess. Kinda long," said Wade. After an awkward pause, he tried to lighten things up by saying, "Chandra tells me you did a great job fillin' in yesterday."

"Yeah, it went OK," said Chet. He had been debating all morning about how much emotion he wanted to show, but in the end, he let it all out.

"Except the director was ticked that you didn't show up in person, and said next time he'd use someone else. And then they wound up changing the schedule all around, so I missed the beginning of my niece's birthday party."

"Listen, Chet, I'm really sorry," said Wade, emphatically. "I never expected to get stranded at the airport for two days. That blizzard must've dumped three feet of snow. It was crazy!"

"What were you even *doing* out there?" asked Chet. "You never even gave us a real explanation."

This was true. But for the same reasons he couldn't give any specifics then, Wade couldn't give any now. The confidentiality agreement he had signed for Paul stipulated that any breach of silence with regards to the hybrids would result in life-altering penalties — including, but not limited to, time in a federal prison.

Drawing a deep breath, Wade tried to come up with a vague, yet satisfactory reply to Chet's very reasonable question. Finally, he said, "Someone needed my help, and I couldn't say no."

Chet made no reply, but simply looked down at the ground. Then, suddenly remembering the rest of his news, he said, "Oh — and Ginger's sick."

"Sick?" asked Wade, his guilt becoming heavier by the second.

"She was kind of mopey when we got back yesterday," Chet told him, "but I figured it was just because Fred had been gone so long. Then this morning I found she'd thrown up overnight."

"Wonderful," said Wade, shaking his head.

"I called Doc Swanson," Chet continued. "He said he'd stop by around three o'clock."

"OK," said Wade. "Thanks for bein' on top of it."

"You're welcome," said Chet. Then his tone changed, and he became less frustrated than earnest.

"Listen, Boss," he began. "You know I'm always ready to pull double duty when you need me to. And I actually enjoyed handling yesterday's shoot on my own. But this makes twice now in the last month that you've just taken off without warning, and I'm starting to get the feeling that, mentally, you're just not all here."

Convicted, Wade dropped his eyes and said, "I know."

Chet continued: "This is what I want to do for the rest of my life, and I want to work with you because I know you're the best. But it really sets me on edge when I don't know what's going to be expected of me when I come in each day. And I'm not meaning any disrespect, it's just..."

"No, you're right," said Wade. "It's not fair. I apologize, and it won't happen again."

At those words, Chet's posture became visibly more relaxed.

"Listen," said Wade, "I gotta meet Genevieve for lunch, but I'll be back around one-thirty. We can go over the schedule then for the next couple of weeks and lock it down so there won't be any more surprises."

"OK. Sounds good," said Chet. Wade offered his hand, and Chet shook it gladly.

The reconciliation complete, Wade picked up his suitcase and turned towards the house. Chet was about to mount up, but then he paused and said, "I'd never want to work anywhere else, you know."

Wade turned back around to face him and said, "I know. And I don't take that for granted."

Chet smiled and swung up into the saddle. As Wade watched him ride off, he vowed to himself that he would not be donating any more time to Paul Fairfield and the Genetic Anomalies Task Center.

* * *

"Is there someone else?" asked Genevieve from across the two-person dining table. Her expression was angry, but also wounded and worried.

The upscale French deli where she and Wade had agreed to have lunch was one of her favorite restaurants. The small, overpriced portions always left Wade hungry, but it was easy enough to grab some drive-through afterwards if he felt particularly famished.

Taken aback by her question, Wade asked, "What?"

"New England, Wade? What could you possibly have had to do in New England that was so incredibly urgent?"

Wade shifted uncomfortably in his seat. "It's... hard to explain," he said.

"What's *that* supposed to mean?" demanded Genevieve. "Did somebody die? Some old flame or something?"

"No!" said Wade, forcefully. "I mean, not an old flame. But yes, somebody died, and that's why I left."

"Really?" asked Genevieve. She was surprised that her sardonic accusation had actually hit the mark, and it did something to calm her fears. Softening her tone, she asked, "Well, why didn't you just say that?"

"Like I said, it's complicated," was all that Wade replied.

Sensing that she stood to gain more by being sympathetic, Genevieve said, "Well, I'm sorry for... whoever it was. Are you OK?"

"Yeah, I'm OK."

"Do you want to talk about it?"

Wade shook his head and said, "No, not really."

Thankfully for Wade, at that moment, the waiter arrived. "Here we are, folks!" he said, setting their 'gourmet' meals before them.

Wade by now had forgotten what he had ordered, and looking at the food, he still couldn't remember. Nonetheless, he very politely said, "Looks good. Thank you."

Genevieve, on the other hand, rolled her eyes and said, "Finally! I'm starving!"

As she dove right in, the waiter meekly asked, "Is there... anything else I can get for you?"

"I think we're good for now," said Wade, and he smiled extra-nice to make up for Genevieve's sharpness.

The waiter quietly walked off. As Genevieve chowed down, Wade tried to think of what to say next. She beat him to the punch, however, and said condescendingly, "I heard you missed a shoot."

Wade suddenly felt hot. "Who told you that?" he asked.

"Never mind who. Is it true?"

"Kind of. But it's OK — Chet filled in."

"Is it Chet's name on your business card?" Genevieve asked. "Wade, it doesn't take much to ruin a reputation in this town. A couple of mistakes, and you're through. Plus, it makes me look bad."

"You?" asked Wade, rankled at the additional charge.

"We're together now, Wade. People naturally make the connection. What one of us does reflects on the other, like it or not."

Wade did *not* like it, but neither did he protest. Then, without any forethought, he suddenly blurted out, "Do you want to have kids?"

Nothing could have caught Genevieve more off-guard. "W-what?" she stammered.

"You know — have a family," said Wade. He was almost as surprised as she was that he had raised the issue, but now that it was on the table, he figured he might as well get some answers.

Genevieve's agenda for lunch had been to cross-examine Wade and then give him a talking to. The last thing she expected was that he would turn the tables on her.

The fact was, she had secretly been dreading this conversation, having already guessed that she did not share Wade's feelings when it came to domesticity. She had hoped that, given enough time, she would be able to talk him around to her point of view. But here they were, having "the talk," and not on her terms. She decided that her best bet now was to stall and redirect.

Staring Wade directly in the eyes so as not to seem evasive, she asked, "What brought that up?"

Her unflinching gaze and seeming sincerity made Wade self-conscious. This was not how he had wanted to bring up the subject of children. He began to question his motives, and to feel that in his irritation he had just been lashing back.

He slumped in his seat and said apologetically, "Oh, I don't know. I guess I've just been realizin' how short life is. You never know when your time will be up, and I don't want the story of my family to end with me. I mean, don't you ever think about leavin' behind more than just a bunch of movies?"

The question hit home. For the first time since Wade had known her, Genevieve was at a total loss.

Looking as dazed as if she had taken a punch, she swallowed hard and said, "Listen — you obviously have a lot on your mind. Let's... let's go out tonight."

But by now, Wade was too drained for any more serious discussions, so he simply shook his head and said, "I gotta get back to the ranch. Ginger's sick."

"I could come over," Genevieve suggested.

As soon as she said that, Wade's phone vibrated in his pocket. He casually pulled it out just enough to read the screen, and then gulped as he saw an alert from his calendar app: "Show Rose the town."

He had temporarily forgotten about the commitment, and the last thing he needed right now was for Genevieve to suspect that he had a specific reason for putting her off.

As innocently as possible, he replied, "I wouldn't want you to be bored. Tomorrow's better."

Genevieve nodded, thinking that she could probably use some time to re-strategize, anyway. "OK," she agreed. "Tomorrow."

Then, reaching across the table, she took Wade's hand and said, "Listen — we've got a good thing going. But the only way we're going to make it as a couple is if we keep communicating. I want this to work."

Disarmed by her vulnerability, Wade smiled and gave her hand a little squeeze. "Me, too," he said, wondering at the same time what kind of mother she would make.

CHAPTER 10: PEAS IN A POD

"Thanks for pickin' up supper," said Wade from behind the front office desk. "Sorry to make you wait on that tour of the city!"

"Oh, no — this is great," answered the adorable Rose Rogers from across the room.

Checking email on a Friday night was something Wade almost never did. But finding himself in the front office, he figured he might as well see if there were any updates pertaining to next week's movie shoot in New Orleans. It was going to be a long trip, and if there were to be any last minute changes to the schedule, he wanted to know right away.

With Ginger being sick, Wade did not feel comfortable leaving the ranch to gallivant about town with Rose. And though he could have offered her a rain check, he hated the thought of her sitting at home alone on a Friday night.

Happily, the Texas cutie-pie had jumped at his suggestion to have dinner at the ranch.

Since the setting was informal, she had dressed casually in jeans, a button-down blouse, and a short suede jacket. But her makeup was flawless, and she had styled her hair beautifully.

It was effort well-spent, for tonight she had an especially appreciative audience. Wade's mother had always been a classy lady, and it was never lost on him when a woman took care of herself.

As Rose pulled several boxes of Chinese food out of a paper bag, she asked, "So how's your tiger feelin'?"

"Oh, she's perkin' up," said Wade. "It's just a cold or somethin', but I don't like to leave any of 'em alone when they're sick."

Seeing that there were no important emails, Wade began shutting down the computer. "Just give me one second, and I'll be done with this," he said.

"Oh, no hurry," said Rose. After arranging the food on a coffee table, she casually strolled about the room looking at the many posters and pictures.

"OK — all done!" Wade announced as he stood up and pushed in the desk chair.

Rose had paused before an especially dramatic poster featuring an army of sword-wielding men, all dressed in togas and sandals. The title was one she was familiar with, for the film had cleaned up at the box office the previous year.

"10,000 Gladiators!" she exclaimed. "Wow, that must have been fun!"

"Yeah," said Wade, modestly. "It was."

"Looks like you've worked on a lot of big pictures. Must know a lot of movie stars."

"A few," said Wade, thinking guiltily of one in particular.

Moving on to the next poster, Rose asked, "So what's it like, workin' with the rich and famous?"

"Oh, they're just people," replied Wade as he moseyed over to stand behind her.

Rose paused in front of a framed black and white photograph. The subject was a handsome man wearing a pith helmet and armed with a chair and whip.

"Is this your father?" Rose asked.

"No, that's Grandpa Boss," said Wade. "He's the one that got us started in the circus business."

"You were in the circus?" asked Rose.

"Before I moved out here, yeah," answered Wade. "My dad taught me everything I know. That's him in the next picture."

Rose took another step to get a closer look at the glossy, full color print of Wade's father. He was posed with three Bengal tigers, and he wore an over-the-top, gold-sequined costume. But what struck

Rose the most was how closely he resembled his son.

Rose glanced at Wade over her shoulder and said, "So — good looks run in the family?"

For the second time since they had met, she elicited Wade's one-sided smile. "Now, Miss Rose," he said, "you wouldn't want to make me blush, would you?"

She answered with a coy little tilt of the head and then turned back to the wall. The next photo was one of Wade with his arm around a lovely silver-haired woman in her mid-sixties.

"This your mom?" asked Rose.

"Yep. Wonderful woman," said Wade, with affection.

"Any siblings?"

Wade shook his head. "Mom got sick after I was born. She's OK now, but it kind of messed up their plans." Then, after a pause, he asked, "How 'bout you?"

"Three brothers, three sisters," replied Rose. "I'm the baby, so I kind of left behind an empty nest."

She moved on to another movie poster, the subject of which happened to be a cowboy Western. Looking it over, she asked, "So, what made you decide to move to L.A.?"

Wade drew a deep breath. "Oh, the circus is all right, I guess. But it was kind of my life growin' up, so I wanted to try somethin' different. I did stunt work for six or seven years, but when Dad decided to retire, I figured I'd bring Fred and Ginger out here and start my own business. We do a lot of stuff for T.V., but I like workin' on movies the best."

"I love movies," said Rose. Then she turned and stared Wade directly in the eyes. "Guess we got that in common, too."

Wade suddenly felt flustered. Then, as if to broadcast the fact, his voice cracked when he spoke: "U-uh... are you hungry?"

Savvy to her effect upon him, Rose smiled and said, "I could eat."

Wade cleared his throat and hastily walked over to the coffee table. Rose followed, and they sat opposite each other in the leather chairs that had been furnished for waiting clients.

Wade peeled apart the paper plates and set two places at the table. As he opened up the first of the food boxes, in her musical voice, Rose said, "We always say a blessin' at home. It's kind of a habit I carry with me. Will it bother you?"

Pleasantly surprised, Wade replied, "You just go right ahead."

He removed his hat and bowed his head, and then Rose prayed, "Thank you, Father, for this our daily bread — and for my new friend Wade, who has shown me hospitality for which I'm grateful. In Jesus' Name, Amen."

"Amen," echoed Wade.

When he opened his eyes, he felt as though he was waking from a good night's sleep. It took him a second to formulate his next sentence, but finally he managed to ask, "Pork-fried rice?"

"Please," answered Rose.

Wade began dishing out the meal. By now, he had recuperated enough from his voice-cracking flub to try easing back into his man-of-the-world persona.

"So," he said, exercising rigid control over his vocal cords, "what's a delicate Texas belle like you doin' so far from home?"

Rose's face lit up, and she said, "Oh, I guess I just felt like it was time to do somethin' a little risky! Life is so short, and you never know when your time will be up."

This response aroused mixed feelings in Wade. Though he had said the very same thing earlier that day, he feared that such a free spirit would balk at the idea of having a family.

Then he checked himself: Why should it matter to him what Rose wanted to do with her life? Heck, they had only just met, and were barely even friends.

Nevertheless, he suddenly heard himself saying, "Don't imagine you'd have much use for anything that might slow you down, then. You know — kids and such?"

But to his surprise, Rose answered, "Oh, I adore children. I hope to have three or four at least."

"You do?" asked Wade, excitedly.

"Oh, absolutely," said Rose. "I'm afraid it's taken me longer than I'd hoped to get around to the more important things in life. I guess I never..." Then she stopped and sighed, and for the first time that evening, Wade detected some inner sadness.

But after a beat, she smiled again and said, "Well, there's no use cryin' over spilt milk, is there? Anyway, here I am, and I have every intention of makin' a genuine life for myself. Soon as I can find a man who's as family-minded as I am!" Then she dropped her eyes and added, "But I suppose that must sound pretty silly to someone with a life as glamorous as yours."

"Silly? No!" said Wade. "I've always kind of felt that the 'quiet life' at home was the best sort of life, myself. 'Cept nowadays it seems harder and harder to find women who agree."

"Well," said Rose, raising her eyebrows, "I won't deny that most of the good women get snatched up awful fast. Any man lucky enough to find one who's still available would be well-advised to do somethin' about it double-quick."

Wade felt flustered again. He had never realized how quiet the front office could get, and he made a mental note to purchase some kind of ambient noise machine.

Avoiding eye contact with Rose, he opened up another box of Chinese food.

"Orange chicken?" he offered.

"Yes, please," answered Rose, and she held out her plate.

As Wade scooped out a serving, he tried to steer the conversation in a less perilous direction. "So, you said your father works for Homeland Security?" he asked.

"That's right," said Rose. "He was with Army Intelligence when I was growin' up. He retired for about a year, but then he got kind of bored. One day, one of his old buddies phoned him up about the job he's got now, and he jumped at the chance. He loves bein' in the thick of things."

"Sounds pretty well connected," said Wade.

"Oh, yes — Daddy knows everybody," said Rose. "If you ever find yourself in real trouble, he's the one to call."

"I'll remember that," said Wade with a smile, thinking how improbable it was that he'd ever need help of that caliber. He finally took a bite of his orange chicken, which turned out to be delicious.

"Mmm. That's good!" he said.

Rose swallowed her first bite and nodded in agreement. "I know, isn't it? It's from this little place just down the road from my apartment called *Yum Wang's*. When I found it, I couldn't believe my good luck!"

After a pause, she asked, "So how do you like moonlightin' for the Genetic Anomalies Task Center?" She said the name half-mockingly to show that she knew how ridiculous it sounded.

Wade grinned and then drew a deep breath. "Well," he said, "I have to admit I'm feelin' a bit torn. I don't like to tell anybody 'no', and I hate to think of people bein' in harm's way, but somethin's gotta give. I got employees countin' on me for their livelihood, and that's a big responsibility."

Slightly crestfallen, Rose said, "Well, I guess I can understand that. Still, I have to admit I'll miss seein' your smilin' face comin' through those lobby doors every now and again."

As soon as she said that, it struck Wade how much he'd miss seeing *her* smiling face, as well. Thereupon, he rashly broke his promise to himself to stop donating time to the Task Center, and said, "Well, I didn't mean I'd *never* lend a hand. I guess I just... need to scale back, is all."

Immediately, Rose brightened and said, "Oh. Well, that's not so bad, then."

"You know — moderation in all things," explained Wade, sounding very sensible indeed.

"Don't throw the baby out with the bath water," Rose wisely observed.

"It's just common sense!" declared Wade.

Then, in a tone that begged for him to read between the lines, Rose said, "Nice to find a man who still has it."

As she gazed at him with unflinching eyes, Wade felt like a prison escapee caught in the beam of a searchlight.

He swallowed hard and looked down at the paper bag from the Chinese restaurant, which stood open on the coffee table. Even though he figured it was empty, as a stalling measure, he pulled it towards himself with one finger.

To his great relief, when he peered inside, he found his excuse for changing the subject.

"Egg rolls!" he exclaimed, as excitedly as if he had just won a free vacation.

* * *

After Wade's disproportionate delight over the egg rolls, Rose mercifully toned down her flirting. She encouraged him to share his life's story, and by the time he was through telling it, he was at ease once more.

Wade, in turn, was eager to hear Rose's story, which she recounted with such drama and humor that by the time she was done, his cheeks hurt from smiling. After basking in her wonderfulness for close to an hour, he showed her the barn and introduced her to the animals.

It was a magical experience for Rose, whose favorite animal had always been the tiger. Like most people, she had never touched a real one, and although Ginger was still recuperating from her illness, Fred was very warm and welcoming.

After the barn, Wade brought Rose back to the front office for coffee and ice cream. He purposefully steered clear of his house, however, for fear that if he invited her in, she might misconstrue it as a romantic overture.

After a good deal more conversation, Wade at last decided that he should bring the evening to a close — again, lest Rose misinterpret his friendliness. He used the excuse of having to get up early to tend the horses, and Rose wisely decided not to overplay her hand by protesting.

Still, she wanted to make sure that things ended on a fun note in order to increase the likelihood of another such evening. To that end, as she took her purse down from the coat-rack, she asked Wade if he knew any good jokes.

Glad for another chance to shine, Wade reached for the joke he had rehearsed the most. Just as they were stepping outside, he dropped the punch-line:

"So then the second tiger says, 'I swear, I ain't *lion!*'"

It was a groaner, but much to Wade's gratification, Rose burst out laughing. After a minute, she gasped, "Because he's *not* a lion, he's a *tiger!*"

"And he's tellin' the truth, so it's kind of a double meanin'," explained Wade.

"That is so funny!" Rose complimented him. "Did you make that up?"

"No," Wade confessed. "That was Dad's. Must've heard it about a million times growin' up."

"Well," said Rose, regaining her composure, "you do a good job of tellin' it."

Just a few steps away, her boxy blue Volvo was parked in front of the hitching rail. As they reached it, Rose said, "I have to thank you for a lovely evenin', Mr. Boss."

"Sorry it wasn't what we had planned on," Wade apologized.

"Oh, that's all right," said Rose. "Not many people can say they've gotten to pet a tiger, a grizzly bear, a lion, and a cougar — especially not all in one night. And I've even got the pictures to prove it!"

"Sure do!" said Wade. "And if you'd still like a tour of the town sometime, the offer stands."

"You're very generous," said Rose. Then she heaved an exaggerated sigh and said, "Well... I guess I'd better be on my way."

With those words, she stared up at Wade with her cornflower blue eyes, and his heart skipped a beat.

Wow, he thought. The way the moonlight danced in her eyes and shimmered on her golden hair made her so very... what was the word?

Kissable.

Suddenly Wade remembered Genevieve. He had just told her earlier that day that he wanted things to work out between them. And didn't he? She was beautiful, intelligent, vibrant — everything he was looking for in a woman...

Or was she? Thinking back to their conversation at lunch, he remembered that Genevieve hadn't given him a clear answer to the children-question.

To be fair, she hadn't tried to dodge it either — it was Wade who had dropped the issue. But she hadn't responded with immediate and unambiguous enthusiasm, and by now, Wade was beginning to have his suspicions as to what her feelings might be.

Nonetheless, Genevieve did have many good qualities. And despite a slightly bumpy road so far, surely it would be premature to throw the last three-and-a-half months under the bus.

And yet, that was exactly what he was at risk of doing right now, standing alone in the moonlight with Rose, who was presently gazing up at him with unmistakable expectation.

Wade chastised himself inwardly. He should have seen this coming. For of course he hadn't — had he?

But regardless of how he had gotten himself into the predicament, the only thing for it now was to appear indifferent to Rose's charm and beauty, and bring the night to a close.

Putting on a plastic smile, he cleared his throat and said, "Then I guess I'll see you soon."

"Oh..." said Rose, and for the first time that evening, it was *she* who was self-conscious. More than that: embarrassed.

Cruel is the blow that makes a woman feel undesirable, and to see the look on Rose's face was almost more than Wade could bear. All he wanted to do was to speak comfort to her. But to reach out to her now, even for pity's sake, would only make things worse.

"All right, then," said Rose, almost as an apology for asking something of Wade that he obviously did not want to give. Struggling to maintain her dignity in the face of rejection, she said, "Well... good night."

"Good night," said Wade, maintaining his phony smile. *Dang it!* he thought. A wonderful evening ruined. Some friend he had turned out to be.

Rose waited for another moment, still hoping for some sign of reciprocated feeling. But when none came, she turned to her car, opened the door, and slowly sank into the driver's seat.

She closed the door and turned on the ignition, and then for several seconds just sat staring at the dash with the engine idling.

By this point in her life, she had learned from painful experience that despite what all the love songs say, nobody really wants to be wanted — at least not too much, and not too soon. She knew that clingy-ness is a major turn-off, and that success in romance is much more likely after you have demonstrated that you do not *need* the person whose affection you so desperately desire.

Rose had tried to present herself to Wade as being strong and independent — which indeed, she was. But it was also true that Wade had quite swept her off her feet. Not to mention that, after their hours of conversation, it was apparent that he shared her values — or at the very least professed them.

Thus, in spite of herself, Rose had not been able to refrain from dropping a few hints. At first, she feared they had been too obvious. Now, it seemed they had been too subtle.

Unless, of course, they *had* been obvious, and were being purposefully ignored — in which case, if she pushed Wade any harder, she would likely turn him off forever. She wavered, debating whether or not a relationship with him was worth the risk of making a total fool of herself.

At last she decided that since she had probably already blown it, she could hardly make things worse. In a dramatic show of frustration, she suddenly threw her hands up in the air and then slapped them down hard on the steering wheel.

Immediately concerned, Wade stepped forward and knocked on the driver's window. "What's wrong?!" he asked.

Rose rolled the window down and cut the engine. "I don't know how I could've been so stupid!" she said. "Would you believe I'm plum out of gas?"

Wade's heart leaped within his chest.

"I think there's somethin' wrong with this gauge," said Rose, shaking her head. "The needle keeps sayin' there's a quarter-tank, when really it's *bone dry!*" Then quickly she added, "I hate to impose, but there's no way I can make it to the gas station."

Wade quickly reminded himself that he was dating Genevieve, and there was nothing more to it.

And yet... he could hardly refuse aid to a friend in need. How else was Rose to make it home, if not with his help? Yes — common decency required that he do anything and everything to make sure that her journey was a safe one. Even if it took hours...

In a very understanding tone, he said, "Oh... no need to beat yourself up. Just a simple oversight — could happen to anybody! Anyway, it won't take but a little ride in my truck for us to go fill up a can." Then, adopting a thoughtful attitude, he added, "Matter o' fact — I think I got an empty one in the garage!"

"But what about your sick tiger?" asked Rose. At last she felt she was getting somewhere, but she wanted to test Wade's sincerity before she got her hopes up.

"Ginger? Oh, I'm sure she'll be fine for just a little while!" answered Wade, with an air of supreme confidence. "You just hold on a minute, and I'll go find that can."

Then, with strides a little longer than his usual, he marched over to the garage, which was halfway between his house and the office.

As he pulled open the overhead door, he was greeted by a mostly-empty bay, since he seldom parked inside. After turning on a light, he began his "search" for the plastic, five-gallon can — though in point of fact, he knew its location fairly precisely. For that matter, he also suspected that it was nearly full.

Rose, meanwhile, had gotten out of her car and was excitedly pacing back and forth under the moon.

By all accounts, she was a very fine and trustworthy woman. However, she also knew that honesty sometimes needs a little "plus."

When she had told Wade that she could not make it to "the" gas station, in her mind, she had naturally been visualizing the gas station near her apartment, across town. Of course, if Wade had inferred that she meant *any* gas station...

Well, that was simply a wild assumption that she felt no obligation to correct.

Concerned that he was taking rather a long time, she called over, "You find that can?"

In the back of the garage, Wade was trying hard not to splash any gasoline onto his jeans as he emptied the five-gallon can into a metal bucket.

"Yeah!" he shouted over his shoulder. "I think I see it! You just hop in the truck, and I'll be right over!"

Feeling reassured, Rose smiled and proceeded to do just that. She walked over to the tiger-striped pickup, thinking what a high step she would have to take to get into the cab. With a little bit of 'oomph', she pulled open the passenger door and then hoisted herself up.

Nothing could have prepared her for the horror that awaited.

At the sound of her scream, Wade dropped the gas can and rushed outside. He saw Rose backing away from his truck, covering her mouth with both hands. In a flash, he was beside her, wrapping her protectively in his arms.

"What is it? What happened?!" he asked.

Shaking uncontrollably, Rose buried her head in his chest and cried, "In the truck!"

Wade took hold of her shoulders and positioned her behind himself. Then, warily, he approached the vehicle, took hold of the half-open door, and flung it wide.

CHAPTER 11: BIG EASY, BIGGER PROBLEMS

Wade's first concern was to help Rose calm down, which wasn't the sort of thing that could be rushed. Since she obviously felt safer in his arms, he held her until she felt better — and then for just a bit longer, as a precaution against a relapse.

Then, very conveniently, he "discovered" some gasoline in the garage that he had previously "overlooked." After pouring it into the not-so-empty-sounding tank of Rose's car, he made sure that she had his number on speed dial — in case of another emergency — and sent her home.

At last he turned his attention to Rose's grisly discovery: a dead hybrid, half-butchered and splayed out across the front seats of his truck.

The carcass was so bloody and torn that Wade couldn't tell what combination of species it represented. He guessed that when it was alive, it had probably been about the size of a German Shepherd.

After donning a pair of leather work gloves, he grabbed a blue plastic tarp from his garage and spread it out on the ground, on the truck's passenger side. Then he half-lifted, half-slid the wet, hairy mess out of the cab and onto the tarp. Finally, he wrapped up the dead meat and hoisted the vile, oversized burrito into the truck bed.

Happily, the truck's interior was leather and could eventually be scrubbed clean of the blood and bile. Even so, Wade knew that he would be in a race against the morning sun if he wanted to prevent the foul odor from cooking into an unimaginable stench.

After informing Paul Fairfield of the situation, Wade covered the driver's seat of his truck with a few trash bags, rolled down all the windows, and then speedily drove to the Task Center.

Upon receiving Wade's news, Paul had jumped out of bed, thrown on some clothes, and then sped down to the Task Center himself — placing a quick call to Dr. Jules Krennick, Head of Research, on the way.

Paul arrived at the building just before Wade, and the two of them carried the squishy blue bundle into the laboratory. Then they laid it on one of the stainless steel operating tables, and Wade pulled open the tarp to expose the ghastly atrocity.

"Why the heck would somebody stick a mutilated 'brid in the cab of my truck?!" he demanded. He knew it wasn't fair, but at the moment, he held Paul partially responsible on account of having dragged him into the whole business in the first place.

Paul made no answer, both because he had no idea what to say, and because he was struggling not to puke. The only dead animals he had ever seen came shrink-wrapped from the grocery store, and were not nearly as aromatic as the one now lying before him.

Just then, the white steel door opened, and Dr. Krennick rushed into the lab.

"I got here as fast as I could!" he said, quite out of breath. "What's going on?"

The first and only other time that Wade had seen him, the brilliant scientist had been composed and immaculately groomed. But now, his precisely sculpted goatee was surrounded by dark stubble, and his dyed hair stuck out at crazy angles from his scalp. Underneath his overcoat, his shirt was completely untucked, suggesting that he also had just hopped out of bed.

"Jules!" said Paul, relieved to have an excuse to look away from the operating table. "Sorry to interrupt your weekend, but I need you to have a look at this."

Dr. Krennick removed his coat and tossed it over the back of a metal chair. "Oh — hello, Wade," he said as he approached the operating table. "This involve you, too?"

"Kind of," replied Wade, grumpily.

As soon as Dr. Krennick saw the mangled beast, he was overcome with dismay.

"Oh, no!" he said. Then, adjusting his wire-rimmed glasses, he looked the body over with a clinical eye. After a few seconds, he said, "Looks like a wolf-lynx hybrid... or bobcat, maybe? Where did it come from?"

"Someone put it in Wade's truck a few hours ago," Paul said grimly. After a moment's hesitation, he added, "Same thing happened to all the other field agents."

This was news to Wade, and he looked at Paul in surprise.

Guiltily avoiding eye contact, Paul continued: "Whoever is behind the hybrids apparently isn't happy that we're locking them away. This must be an attempt to scare our hunters into quitting so that we'll be cut off at the knees, and the 'brids will remain at large."

Tersely, Wade asked, "How the heck do they even know who we are?"

"I don't know," said Paul, shaking his head.

"Tonight was just a threat," said Wade, "but next time it might be worse. You've got people to think about, Paul! Poor Rose is scared half to death..."

"Rose?" Paul interrupted him. "Rose Rogers? From the front desk?"

Wade suddenly realized that he had just divulged more than he had intended. "Uh... yeah," he replied.

"How does she know about all this?" asked Paul.

Hastily downplaying his slip, Wade said, "She was, uh... she mentioned she loves tigers, so I invited her over to meet Fred and Ginger. But we're just friends!"

"Oh. OK," said Paul. He was clearly dubious, but had enough sense not to press the matter.

Quickly, Wade moved on. "Anyway," he said, "she found the

'brid first, and I calmed her down as best I could. I told her I didn't think Whoever-It-Is would have it out for the receptionist, but regardless, you need to beef up security around this place, *stat.*"

"I can see that," said Paul, sagging under the weight of the added burden. Imploringly, he looked at Wade and asked, "Wade — you're not going to bail on us, are you?"

Wade drew a deep breath. He could see that Paul was hurting bad, and despite his own anger, he truly sympathized. Still, he reminded himself that he couldn't save the world. Neither could he afford another screw-up, either professionally or in his personal life.

Although he had just told Rose that he was not cutting ties with the Task Center, over the course of the last hour he had revised his thinking yet again. The gosh-awful stink now permeating his truck had re-convinced him that there was simply no room in his life for this kind of chaos, and that he had to concentrate on getting his life back on track.

Heavily, he said, "Listen, Paul — I told you before, I haven't got time for this. Plus, I have the safety of my employees and my animals to think about. What if these psychopaths showed up at the ranch one day and tried somethin' violent?"

Paul flinched, as though the suggestion somehow made the possibility more likely. Wade softened his tone, trying to be as gentle as possible without mincing words.

"Look," he said. "I don't like the thought of people gettin' hurt by these 'brids, but I got other responsibilities. As it is, I'm gonna have to waste the day tomorrow cleanin' the inside of my truck so I can drive to New Orleans on Monday."

"You're *driving* to New Orleans?" asked Dr. Krennick.

"My tiger don't like to fly," said Wade, "and I don't make him if I don't have to."

"I'm sorry, Wade," said Paul, sounding like he was at the end of his rope. "And I completely understand why you feel the way you do. But please — you don't have to decide anything right this second. Just give me a few days. Let me make a few calls and try to get some law enforcement working on this new threat-thing."

"You're not hearin' me, Paul," said Wade, struggling to maintain his own resolve.

Paul looked at the floor, pursing his lips as though he was holding in some sensitive bit of information. At last, he sighed and confessed, "Finn Holstad and Kuruk Torres just told me they're through."

Now utterly transparent, Paul looked Wade in the eyes and said, "I'm doing the best I can with limited resources. And as of right now, you're my Number One."

He paused to let that sink in, and then said, "Please, don't call it quits until I've had a few days. Go to New Orleans — get away from all this for a while. Give me a chance to recruit some more help. After you get back, we'll see where things are at. If you still feel you have to back out... I won't argue."

Wade felt awful. But as much as he wanted to just wash his hands of the whole business, he could see that the last few hours had knocked Paul hard to the ground. And kicking a man while he was down was something Wade just couldn't bring himself to do.

In his mind, he reaffirmed to himself that he had made his final decision and that there was nothing that could dissuade him. But if waiting a few days to make the break would give Paul a chance to get his wind back... then so be it.

After a long silence, Wade said, "I'll be back in a week."

The look of relief in Paul's eyes told Wade that he had done the right thing.

"Thank you, Wade," said Paul, and Dr. Krennick nodded approvingly.

* * *

In 2005, at the tail end of August, Hurricane Katrina made brief landfall along the southeastern coast of Florida. During those few hours, it weakened and was reclassified as a tropical storm. Few could have imagined at that time how quickly it would regain strength in the Gulf of Mexico. Fewer still could have conceived how profoundly it would shape the destiny of New Orleans, Louisiana.

In the wake of the devastation, efforts were made to renovate much of the city and its environs. Even so, certain neighborhoods were simply beyond hope, and thus abandoned. In time, some of these areas were opened to Hollywood film crews to use as movie locations, particularly for films of the post-apocalyptic genre. For just such a production, Wade and Chet had made the tedious, thirty-hour drive from Los Angeles.

Such long road trips were the exception for the Boss Beasts, since most of them handled flying fairly well. Fred, however, did not. Wade had chosen him for the New Orleans shoot because a choreographed tiger attack was called for, and he was better suited to those than Ginger.

Despite the hassle of the driving, Wade had agreed to the journey because he had been recommended for the job by James Blakeman — the man at the helm of the India picture to star Genevieve.

Wade figured it would be bad form to turn up his nose at the favor, so for three days, he and Chet took turns behind the wheel, making regular stops to interact with Fred and get some proper rest.

Finally, at nine o'clock on a sunny Thursday morning, shooting was about to commence. After a refreshing night's sleep for all, Wade felt that the decision to take the job had been the right one.

The area where the "attack" was to be filmed had seen extreme flood damage. Few, if any, of the houses were safe to re-inhabit without a massive investment of money and labor, and so they had languished in disrepair.

Many of the hardest-hit neighborhoods had become literal dumps, where unscrupulous individuals and businesses alike haphazardly disposed of all manner of waste, non-toxic and otherwise. In such places vegetation grew out of control, so that with each passing year, what once was classified as 'suburb' looked increasingly like jungle.

The movie production's cast and crew had been instructed to park their vehicles out of sight, several blocks away from where the scene was being shot. After parking his truck and trailer at the end of a long line of cars, Wade put a leash on Fred and led him over to the set, accompanied by Chet.

It was not often that Wade's face appeared on the silver screen, but it did happen on occasion. Today, for instance, he was playing the part of an unfortunate soul who had survived the end of the world only to be eaten alive by a tiger.

After putting on his costume, which consisted mostly of tattered rags, Wade reported to a matronly make-up specialist whose job it was to apply his "wounds." He underwent the procedure patiently, sitting on a stool with his cowboy hat in his hands.

Chet, meanwhile, waited on the sidelines, holding Fred's leash and soaking in the human energy that one finds on a movie set. For although his love of animal training had not diminished in the slightest since he started working at Boss Ranch, he had slowly but surely developed a secondary passion for show business.

"OK, good morning, folks!" said a loud voice over a megaphone.

All eyes turned to the speaker, who was a bearded fellow dressed in khakis, a light jacket, sneakers and a red baseball cap. It was none other than Lucas Stevens, the director of the picture and a legend in his own time. Those lucky enough to work for him were well aware of their good fortune, for he treated his cast and crew like family, and got his results by using praise instead of fear.

"Just a word before we get started," Mr. Stevens continued. "First off, I just want to reiterate my thanks to the New Orleans Film Commission for such a warm welcome — you guys have been great! The scene we'll be shooting today is set after the Apocalypse, and the idea is that some of the animals have gotten out of the zoos and are wandering free. We're fortunate to have with us Mr. Wade Boss, who is going to be 'attacked' by his trained tiger, Fred. I really appreciate them coming all the way out here from L.A."

All eyes turned to Wade, who nodded humbly.

"So," finished Mr. Stevens, "let's get set up for the stunt and try to be rolling in about twenty minutes. Thank you all very much!"

As soon as the megaphone clicked off, activity resumed. The make-up lady added a final touch to Wade's face and then said, "All done! You're a bloody mess."

Wade glanced at his reflection in a small mirror on the makeup table. The fake lacerations were quite convincing. He smiled and told the makeup-lady, "That's the gentlest beatin' I ever took."

"Mr. Boss!" said a voice behind him. "Ready to get eaten?"

It was the famous director himself. Wade rose to his feet, unconsciously placing his hat back on his head. "I reckon so," he replied, shaking Mr. Stevens's hand. "Thanks for havin' me."

"No, thank *you* for making the trip," said Mr. Stevens. "Hope you're not too tired."

"Nah," Wade assured him. "We got plenty o' sleep last night." Then, with a sweep of his arm, he said, "This here is my assistant, Chet."

"Hi! I'm Lucas," said Mr. Stevens, walking over to Chet and extending his hand.

Shaking it, and trying not to sound star-struck, Chet replied, "It's an honor to meet you, sir!"

"And this must be Fred," Mr. Stevens observed. "Wow — gorgeous animal!"

"Yeah, he is," said Wade.

"I'm excited to see what he can do," said Mr. Stevens. "James told me I wouldn't regret paying a little extra to get you down here. He also mentioned that India project you're doing with Genevieve — sounds fun."

"Ought to be," returned Wade, wondering if "fun" would prove to be an accurate descriptor.

"Well," said the famous director, "as soon as you're all finished here, come on over and we'll walk through the sequence."

"Will do," said Wade, and then Mr. Stevens departed with a smile.

Wade turned to the hair stylist, who was a middle-aged lady who reminded him of his mother. As he approached her, she asked, "Ready for your hair, sweetheart?"

"Yes, Ma'am," said Wade.

"Is that, uh... part of your costume?" asked the lady, pointing to his head.

Wade reached up and felt his hat. "Oh!" he said, removing it and feeling a little embarrassed. "Force of habit, I guess! Say — do you mind if I drop it off at my truck, real quick?"

"Sure thing, honey," replied the lady.

On his way, Wade made a slight detour to the wardrobe tent to grab his cell phone from his jeans-pocket. Then, before leaving the set, he swung over to the spot where Chet was waiting with Fred.

"I've gotta run back to the truck," said Wade. "Why don't you take Fred for a little walk — keep him from gettin' bored."

"You got it, Boss," answered Chet. Wade gave his tiger a quick face-rub, and then Chet tugged the leash and said, "Come on, Fred!"

Wade watched them go, feeling pleased that things were back on track again. With a sigh of satisfaction, he headed for the street several blocks away where he had parked.

Little did he know that he was being watched...

Halfway across the abandoned neighborhood and crouched on the roof of a decaying house was a man in a dark jumpsuit. As he spied on Wade with a pair of high-powered binoculars, he spoke softly into a headset microphone.

"He's heading back to his truck," said the spy.

Two blocks past Wade's truck, an eighteen-wheeled semi was parked on another deserted street. The tractor unit was painted black, and the trailer hitched behind it was a flat gray. Nothing about either suggested the nature of the cargo being hauled.

However, if one watched the trailer for long enough, one would have noticed that every few minutes it swayed back and forth as though something heavy were being shifted about inside.

Behind the wheel of the rig sat a man dressed all in black, from his button-down shirt and designer jeans to his cattleman's hat and cowboy boots. Like the velvet of a jeweler's case, his clothing served to showcase an array of silver accents: sterling cufflinks, a custom belt buckle, expensive sunglasses, and a hat band of silver links.

In contrast to the man's flawless ensemble — and partly the reason for it — was his disfigured face. Deep scars on the left side suggested that, once upon a time, it had been raked by terrible claws.

Each aspect of the man's striking appearance seemed to underscore the others, and the combined effect was a palpable aura of danger.

The Dangerous Man raised a walkie-talkie to his lips, and in a rasping voice he replied to the rooftop spy: "Roger that." Then he hopped out of the cab and walked around to the back of the trailer.

He deployed and walked up the loading ramp, finally hoisting open the trailer's rolling cargo door. In response to the sudden flood of daylight, the Thing inside began to throw its weight about, causing the entire trailer to rock on its wheelbase.

Though the Dangerous Man's stony heart was seldom moved to anything other than cruelty, he was momentarily struck with awe. Indeed, the only thing in the world for which he still had respect was physical power, and the creature before him had that in spades.

It was also growing more agitated by the second. Quickly, the Dangerous Man jumped to the ground, ran back to the cab, and climbed into his seat.

With his walkie-talkie, he called the spy and said, "Let's see how he deals with this!" Then, from one pocket of his wrinkle-free black shirt, he pulled out a small radio transmitter and pressed a red button labeled "UP."

Through the rear wall of the cab, he could hear the cage inside the trailer being opened by powerful hydraulics. The captive beast, sensing that it was about to be released, thrashed about with increasing violence.

Finally, the Dangerous Man heard the stomping of four heavy feet down the loading ramp, and then the truck became still...

Meanwhile, Wade was slouched in the driver's seat of his pickup with the door wide open. Setting his hat beside him, he pulled out his cell phone.

Whenever he was away from the ranch, he worried that something might go wrong in his absence. So it was only natural that, while he had a second, he should touch base with Chandra.

Having worked for Wade for five years now in the capacity of both office manager and apprentice trainer, there was hardly any aspect of running Boss Ranch that Chandra Delgado did not understand, at least in part. So for her, making sure that everything ran smoothly while Wade and Chet were away was more a matter of physical rigor than mental stress.

Luckily for Wade, Chandra was a sensitive young woman with a great amount of "emotional intelligence." Aware of his tendency to worry about the ranch when he was on the road, she considered it one of her unspoken job requirements to set his mind at ease.

Even though she had already taken care of all the Thursday morning office chores, she had remained at her desk for the sole purpose of taking Wade's inevitable call.

When the business phone rang, Chandra checked the caller I.D. just to be on the safe side. Seeing the name she expected to see, she tucked a wisp of her long black hair behind one ear and picked up the receiver.

"Morning, Boss," she said, in a knowing voice.

"Mornin', Chandra!" said Wade. "How's everything?"

"Everything's great," she replied. "Ginger's a little lonesome, but that's par for the course. How's New Orleans?"

"Great so far," answered Wade, feeling very much comforted. Then he said, "Listen — we'll be tied up all mornin', but I'll be checkin' my messages at lunch if you need to reach me..."

"Boss," began Chandra, in a motherly tone.

"Yeah?"

"I got it under control. No worrying, OK?"

Wade heaved a sigh and said, "OK. I promise."

"Now go do a good job," Chandra encouraged him.

"I will," said Wade.

"And say hi to Chet for me."

"Will do. Bye."

Wade hung up and smiled. It was at times like this that he appreciated how indispensable to the business Chandra really was. Spontaneously, he decided that when he got back to Los Angeles he would give her a raise.

Just then, a text message with an attached photo came through on his phone. As soon as Wade saw it, he burst out laughing.

The picture was already familiar to him, for he himself had taken it with Rose's cell phone. It was of Rose, standing with puckered lips next to Hank the grizzly bear, as if she was about to give the gentle giant a smooch on the cheek. Since the taking of the picture, she had added a graphic of a pink heart to frame their faces.

To reassure himself that Rose was not suffering any post traumatic stress from her discovery of the mutilated hybrid, Wade had texted her from the road several times already. Her replies had not only been instantaneous, but also sparkling, witty, and ineffably charming.

Genevieve also had texted him a few times, mostly asking his opinion about stuff she was buying. She was being sweet enough to him, but even so, Wade's knee-jerk sighs of annoyance upon seeing her name were beginning to concern him.

On top of it all, in his head, he kept hearing's his father's voice, reminding him, "Life is a long time to be married to the wrong woman, son. And since a man lives by his word, you need to be darn sure before you give it to her at the altar."

Lest he become distracted to the point of being unable to do his job, Wade set his phone in one of the truck's many cup-holders and then adjusted the rearview mirror to check out his bloody makeup.

As he did, something outside caught his eye.

From around the corner of a house, about fifty yards in front of his truck, an elephant lumbered into view.

Wade didn't remember seeing anything on the schedule about elephants, but then, there were often last minute changes on location shoots. For a fleeting second, he mused that it would be kind of fun to swap stories with a fellow trainer.

But as the animal slowly emerged from behind the house, its body seemed to grow longer, and longer... and longer. And then Wade realized that he was not looking at an elephant — not exactly.

The hybrid stood eight feet tall at the hips and shoulders. It had four broad, webbed feet, and a fleshy, ten-foot tail. Its legs were mighty pillars that bowed sharply outwards. Thick green scales covered its back, and its underbelly was soft and yellow.

From its large, bulbous head dangled a short, prehensile trunk. Two massive tusks protruded from its mouth, which was otherwise lined with sharp, carnivorous teeth. Its glassy yellow eyes rode high in the skull and were almost level with two gaping holes that begged for proper ears.

In disbelief, Wade stared at the thirty-foot-long elephant-crocodile, which against all conceivable odds just happened to have turned up in the very same city, in the very same neighborhood, and on the very same street as he.

"You gotta be *kiddin'* me!" he said out loud.

The elephant-croc followed its nose to a car belonging to someone on the movie crew. The front window was rolled down, and sitting on the dash was a partially-eaten breakfast sandwich. With its stubby trunk, the 'brid reached inside, deftly picked up the remainder of the sandwich, and stuffed it in its mouth.

Suddenly, from two blocks away, the megaphone-amplified voice of Lucas Stevens rang out: "That was perfect! Do it again!"

Alarmed at the noise, the elephant-croc bolted. It followed the line of cars to the end of the block, and then at the first intersection it turned to the right and disappeared behind the houses.

Dumbfounded as he was, Wade knew that he had to make a decision fast before someone was hurt or killed.

He could call the police, but they would undoubtedly shoot the poor animal dead. He could call Paul, but the Task Center could not respond in any immediate way.

Or he could do the unthinkable.

In his mind, two mutually exclusive obligations threatened to tear him apart. On the one hand was his responsibility to Chet, Chandra, Genevieve, Lucas Stevens, James Blakeman, and himself to fulfill his contractual commitment to the movie. On the other hand was his moral duty to stand in the gap between innocent people and mortal danger.

Just as his life was getting back on track, here he was, being forced to choose between the colleagues and loved ones who were counting on him, and total strangers who had no idea their lives were even in jeopardy.

The emotional strain was so great that Wade broke into a sweat. Then, for fear that in thinking any longer he might make the wrong choice, he jumped out of his truck and ran back to the trailer hitch.

At that moment, Chet and Fred walked up from behind.

"Hey, Boss!" called Chet. "Mr. Stevens wants to know if... Boss? What are you doing?"

"Ruinin' my life!" Wade blurted out, as he yanked Fred's trailer off the ball-hitch and dropped the tow bar to the ground.

"What?" asked Chet, in bewilderment. He watched as Wade opened the truck's tailgate and pulled an oversized silver briefcase from the bed.

"Wait, wait, wait!" said Chet, in sudden earnest. "You're not *leaving?!*"

Without a word, Wade marched back to the cab, tossed the case inside, and jumped behind the wheel.

Leading Fred by the leash, Chet followed Wade and yelled, "Are you insane?! We just drove all the way from L.A. to perform for *Lucas Stevens* and suddenly you're LEAVING?!"

Wade pulled the driver's door shut and cranked the truck's engine to life. Through the open window, Chet desperately implored him,

"Boss, please! Don't DO this to me!"

It was almost more than Wade could bear. He clenched his jaw and squeezed his eyes shut. This was the last thing in the world he wanted, but there was no escape.

Finally, against a deluge of guilt and sadness, he steeled his heart... and then broke Chet's.

"I'm sorry," he whispered, and then he opened his eyes and floored the gas.

CHAPTER 12: NEW 'BRID ON THE BLOCK

When he had dropped off the mutilated hybrid at the Task Center lab, Wade had intended to turn in the silver case as well. But then his compassion for Paul had gotten the better of him, and so he had left it in the bed of his truck.

Then he had forgotten to leave it at his house before setting out for New Orleans, and so, for the last few days, the case had sat under the truck's hardcover, out of sight and out of mind.

Until sixty seconds ago.

As Chet and Fred grew smaller in his rearview mirror, Wade donned his hat and pulled out the *FLEXCALIBER*. With one eye on the road, he primed each of the tranquilizer darts to deliver its maximum dose.

From his days with the traveling circus, Wade knew that African bush elephants weighed between four and eight tons. Based on its size, he guessed that the elephant-croc tipped the scales at about ten.

A single dart filled with the Task Center's super-serum could subdue an animal of up to two-thousand pounds. As he did the math, Wade realized that he would have to nail the elephant-croc five times before it went down for the count.

It had fled in the opposite direction from the movie shoot, which was Wade's only stroke of good luck. But as the seconds ticked by, he became more and more desperate to reestablish visual contact.

Then, while speeding through an intersection, he glimpsed the 'brid out of the corner of his eye — off to his right, and still running at full tilt through the uninhabited neighborhood. He slammed on the brakes and quickly changed course.

For its part, the distraught elephant-croc was merely trying to survive, with only blind instinct to guide it. But despite the strangeness of its new environment, any freedom was preferable to the confinement of the trailer cage.

At present, the hapless beast ran with no particular destination in mind except *away* from the amplified voice of Lucas Stevens.

Sadly, its troubles were far from over.

As it thundered down the street at thirty miles per hour, Wade quickly caught up. But the closer he drew, the more difficult he realized the confrontation was likely to be.

After his near-fatal encounter with the rhino-bear, he was all too familiar with the limitations of his weapon, and it was clear that the elephant-croc's scaly hide would afford him few soft targets.

He veered to the left and slowly moved into flanking position. As he came up on the 'brid's left side, he could see just a sliver of its vulnerable underbelly.

On closer inspection, he also noticed that the scales covering the lower third of its abdomen were much smaller than those along its back. He wondered if they might be thin enough for a dart to penetrate...

But as he wondered, the elephant-croc detected the truck with its peripheral vision. Whipping its muscular tail sideways, it shattered the passenger side windows. Wade averted his face from the flying shards of glass, took his foot off the gas, and retreated to the creature's blind spot.

The elephant-croc arrived at a three-way intersection and turned right, its considerable momentum carrying it in a wide arc around the bend. Wade, however, had the benefit of the truck's brakes, and was able to slow down enough to cut the corner across a yard overgrown with tall grass.

After a few seconds, the elephant-croc completed the turn and got itself going straight on the new street. But no sooner had it done so than the truck shot out of the corner yard.

The vehicle sailed over the curb and landed on the pavement right next to the 'brid. Wade cranked hard on the steering wheel, narrowly averting a bloody collision. The rubber tires squealed in protest, but with a few corrective swerves he maintained control of the vehicle.

Now that he was on the beast's left side, Wade had a better angle on its belly-meat. Reaching his right arm across his body, he stuck the muzzle of his gun out the driver's window.

The awkwardness of the position required him to focus all of his attention on the moving target area. This rendered him temporarily oblivious to his environment, but just as he was about to pull the trigger, for safety's sake, he threw the road a quick glance.

All thoughts of the elephant-croc instantly flew out of Wade's brain. Sitting in his lane, directly ahead, was a pile of rotting construction materials that included drywall, two-by-fours, insulation foam, PVC piping, and nail-ridden plywood.

Wade swerved to the left and missed the pile by an inch, but the unintended consequence was that he sideswiped the elephant-croc.

The creature was too gigantic to be injured by the glancing blow, but it faltered enough so that the truck pulled even with its bobbing head. Wade looked out his window to find himself staring into a yellow, reptilian eye the size of a softball.

Like a dog curious at an unfamiliar sound, the elephant-croc cocked its head to one side and then thrashed it at the truck. Its left tusk did no damage at all, but jutted harmlessly into the air in front of the windshield. Its right tusk, however, came in through the open driver's window.

Wade flattened back against his seat, a hair's breadth from being skewered like a piece of shish kabob. The tusk passed through the open circle of the steering wheel and impaled the dashboard, destroying the speedometer and all the surrounding gauges.

Wade tried to turn the wheel, but the mighty tusk locked it in place like an anti-theft club. Effortlessly, the elephant-croc shoved the truck to the right until it rocked up over the curb, dealing Wade a sharp jolt to the spine that made him cry out in pain.

The 'brid did not relent in the slightest for being off-road, but kept pushing the truck diagonally across another yard gone to seed.

Wade saw that he was headed for a massive tree — an old oak that had withstood perhaps a century of hurricanes, and which was certainly not going to budge for his truck.

Since the airbag was locked inside the steering column by the 'brid's tusk, Wade knew that the full force of the impact with the tree would be transferred directly to his body. He fought the panic rising in his chest and asked himself: *Where's the wiggle room, Wade?*

When preparing for a dangerous movie stunt, part of his job was to determine how he could bail out if things started to go wrong. But even after the most careful planning, a sudden, unforeseen variable could turn a relatively straightforward gag into a life-threatening situation.

The key to survival was to keep a cool head, identify the 'wiggle room', and then go for it.

You can't steer, Wade thought to himself. *So what control have you got?*

BRAKES!

With both feet, he stomped on the brake pedal.

Immediately, the wheels locked up, and the vehicle slowed down a bit. However, it still continued to slide forward, its tires now carving deep ruts in the soft turf.

The elephant-croc's head, being connected to the dashboard by its right tusk, was forcibly slowed down along with the truck. But the rest of its giant body, being left unchecked, swung out to the side.

Caught in the clutches of a running fall, the 'brid now had to push against the truck simply to remain upright.

Wade's quick thinking had yielded some results, but he was still headed for the tree. Realizing that his inspiration had come too late, he wrapped his arms protectively around his head.

Then, quite unexpectedly, he felt himself sliding forward in his seat — not at thirty miles an hour, but much more slowly.

The reason for this was that the elephant-croc had finally found its feet and had stopped pushing against the truck. In the absence of thrust, friction held sway, and the truck's tires went from carving ruts to creating drag.

Finally, the immobilized wheels jerked the vehicle to a kinder, gentler halt than the one Wade had feared. When he opened his eyes, he saw that his truck had stopped short of the old oak without so much as a ding to the bumper.

Not that he would be allowed to enjoy the moment, for the elephant-croc promptly yanked its tusk out of the dash, doing almost as much damage on the way out as in.

Wade raised his gun to take a shot out the window, but before he could follow through, the 'brid rammed its head into the driver's door with tectonic force.

The door caved in, sending Wade flying across the cab. The back of his head struck the passenger door so hard that he nearly blacked out, and the silver *FLEXCALIBER* case hit him hard in the kidneys.

He lost his grip on the gun, and it fell to the floor. Then, all at once, he experienced a strange tipping sensation...

The elephant-croc had hooked its tusks under the driver's side of the truck and was tipping it up onto its passenger side wheels. After achieving a maximum tilt of forty degrees, the 'brid dropped the truck sharply to the ground.

The crash-landing sent Wade sailing across the cab. He slammed into the driver's door, but then immediately felt himself falling backwards again into the passenger seat.

For a second time, the elephant-croc lifted and then dropped the truck. This time as Wade flew across the cab, the rim of the steering wheel caught him in the sternum.

The excruciating pain brought him partially back to his senses, and ironically was his first saving grace. The second was that the elephant-croc did not realize that it was winning. After lifting and dropping the truck for a third time, it grew insecure about its strategy and decided to try biting instead.

Wade scrambled back into the passenger seat as the monster's lower jaw came in through the driver's window, stopping just inches from his face.

CHOMP, CHOMP, CHOMP!

The elephant-croc's bottom teeth shredded the ceiling of the cab to ribbons, while its top teeth punched dozens of holes in the metal roof.

After inflicting what would have been mortal wounds to any flesh and blood opponent, the 'brid tried to execute a 'death roll' — a crocodilian technique of twisting around in the water to drown captive prey.

But even if they had been in the water, the elephant-croc would not have had enough leverage to flip the truck. Sensing that the death roll was a bust, the animal gave up, tucked tail, and ran.

Wade scooted back over to the driver's seat — as much as the caved-in door would allow. Then he watched as the 'brid crossed the road, tromped through another yard, and tore down yet another street.

By now, Wade had no shortage of reasons to call for help — but again, he knew that doing so would spell death for the hybrid. If only he could sedate it, he could save its life. And since there were no civilians in the immediate vicinity, he still had a small window of opportunity.

In agony, he leaned over and grabbed the *FLEXCALIBER* off the floor. Then, with a throbbing chest and a spinning head, he backed his truck out of the yard and reengaged pursuit.

Remembering that powerful whipping tail, Wade decided not to repeat his mistake of trying to sneak up on the elephant-croc from behind. He figured his next best hope was to attack from the side using the only real advantage he had: speed.

In his mind's eye, Wade pictured the neighborhood from above. Because it was laid out in block fashion, he knew that the elephant-croc was running in a straight line. Imagining that line to be one side of a rectangle, he figured that if he traveled fast enough along the other three sides, he could cut the animal off and spring an ambush.

Burning rubber all the way, Wade drove several blocks and then turned left. Then he repeated the maneuver so that he was on a theoretical collision course with the 'brid.

As long as it had not changed direction — and provided he got lucky with the timing — Wade knew that they would meet at the intersection just ahead of him.

Because the elephant-croc only wanted to escape danger, in the absence of obstacles it had no reason to deviate from a straight flight path. Thus it arrived at the intersection precisely as Wade had predicted, and was completely surprised when its tiger-striped nemesis appeared from out of nowhere on its right side. Wade's gamble had paid off.

Almost. The devil, as they say, was in the details.

Since he was coming at it from the right, and since it could not stop on a dime, Wade had anticipated that the elephant-croc would veer to the left — which it did.

But what he had not counted on was that his own street would abruptly come to an end. The appointed intersection was not a four-way as he had assumed it would be, but rather a three-way T.

If he just kept going straight, Wade would shortly find himself plowing into a chain-link fence, which surrounded some kind of junkyard. In order not to hit the fence, he hit the brakes instead, and as a result his shot was ruined.

The elephant-croc met with better luck. As it veered left to avoid the truck, it also found itself headed for the chain-link fence — or more specifically, the fence's open gate. Without breaking stride, the creature passed right on through and into the junkyard.

Swearing under his breath, Wade backed up, swung the truck around, and sped through the gate.

It turned out that the junkyard was not a public dump, but rather a private lot that had been forsaken like all the rest. Most of the property was occupied by rusting cars and broken-down heavy machinery — forklifts, backhoes, etc., which were only good for scrap.

The cars were the main problem, however, being stacked several high, so that Wade's view was obscured in all directions. Having lost sight of the 'brid for the second time now, he sped recklessly through the maze.

Several twists and turns ahead of him, the bewildered elephant-croc followed a course that had been predetermined for it by all the junk. Whenever the animal's path was obstructed, it was forced to make a turn. In this way, it was funneled into a narrow alley formed by two, sixty-foot-long utility buildings running parallel to each other and spaced about fifteen feet apart.

When the elephant-croc arrived at the far end of the alley, it found that a huge bulldozer completely blocked its way forward. Quite naturally, it panicked and turned back around to retrace its steps...

Wade was not far behind as the crow flies, but he had no way of knowing this. What he did know was that, if he kept going straight, he would soon be crashing into a pile of dilapidated cars.

The obvious solution to his problem was to cut a sharp left and turn into a narrow alley formed by two, sixty-foot-long utility buildings running parallel to each other and spaced about fifteen feet apart. With barely a tap to the brakes and absolutely no idea what lay around the corner of the first building, he spun the wheel and entered the alley.

WHAM!

It happened so fast, Wade hardly saw it coming. Running at full speed on its way back out of the alley and with no room to dodge the truck, the elephant-croc had simply lowered its head and rammed the front grill.

The truck came to a dead stop, and with a stinging smack to the face, Wade's entire field of view was obscured by the airbag. Simultaneously, the cab was filled with a thick haze of smoke and powder produced by the exploding chemicals that deployed the bag.

Then Wade felt himself tipping backwards.

Hooking both of its tusks under the front bumper this time, the elephant-croc lifted the nose of the truck five feet into the air and then dropped it.

The now-deflated airbag did nothing to lessen Wade's punishment as he was tossed about like a rag-doll. In no mood to be merciful, the elephant-croc dealt him two more 'upsy-daisies' in rapid succession.

But as much as the animal wanted to destroy its hated foe, it also wanted to get the heck out of the alley. To that end, it backed up a few steps to take stock of its situation.

Strictly speaking, the beast was incapable of critical thinking. But it was not without intelligence, and after a few seconds, it perceived that there was an alternative to plowing *through* the truck, which was to run *over* it.

The next thing Wade knew, four feet the size of manhole covers were tromping the crap out of his pickup truck.

CHAPTER 13: HOTTER WATER

The elephant-croc retraced its steps back to the street and then continued on its less-than-merry way.

Wade, however, had entered into that peculiar frame of mind in which a man no longer remembers why he must continue on, but only that he must.

Eyes stinging, ears ringing, lungs burning, back aching, chest throbbing, he was sure of only one thing — that since he was not dead, he was not yet released from his moral duty.

The airbag made things difficult, but now that it was deflated, the steering wheel could be turned halfway around in either direction. The bigger problem was that there was almost no room in which to do it.

During its brief jaunt up and over the truck, the elephant-croc had done a respectable job of mashing down the roof, with the side effect of exploding the windshield. Taken together with the bashed-in driver's door, this made for rather cramped conditions.

But as long as Wade scrunched down like a little old lady and operated the pedals with his left foot, he found that he could still technically drive. In defiance of all his handicaps, he threw the gearshift into reverse.

As he backed his way out of the junkyard, the horrible grinding noises coming from the engine and undercarriage told him that his truck was probably good for only another mile or so, if that. But since it could still move faster than he could run, he had no choice but to drive it into the ground.

Once he backed out onto the road, he could see the elephant-croc seventy yards off and continuing in its previous course. For the second time, Wade snatched his gun off the floor and stomped on the gas.

Slowly but surely, the failing vehicle brought him closer to his object, but by the time he was within twenty yards of it, the engine started spewing smoke.

Wade knew that unless he stopped soon, he would have a fire on his hands. Desperate to land at least one dart before that happened, he veered to the right to make one more attempt at flanking the 'brid.

As he did, he saw that the street they were on was coming to an end, at another three-way intersection. Unless they turned left or right at the T, they would find themselves cutting across a swath of long grass and passing between two widely-spaced trees.

Then, Wade perceived that just beyond the trees there was something else — something that glistened with the reflected glory of the morning sun.

To his dismay, he realized that it was water. Even at a distance, he could tell that it was not the ocean, and in New Orleans, there was only one other thing it could be.

The bayou.

"No, no, no, no, no!" cried Wade. "Not the swamp, *not the swamp!*"

A radical change of plans was called for, and he looked frantically about the cab for inspiration. His eyes landed on the silver case, which had fallen to the floor in front of the passenger seat. Wincing at his injuries, he reached down, hoisted it up, and flipped it open.

The gun belt was strapped to the inside of the lid, and since Wade had not bothered to remove the backup barrels from the thigh pockets after Joshua Tree, the case appeared to contain nothing else besides the black foam lining.

But by now Wade knew better. Grabbing hold of the lining, he yanked it out to expose a second tray that cradled six additional barrels. One of these was labeled "TRACER," and he quickly pried it out and swapped it onto the gun's handgrip.

The truck could make no more gains on the 'brid, but Wade was able to maintain a following distance of twenty yards. Steering with his right hand and holding the *FLEXCALIBER* in his left, he reached out the window, took aim, and fired.

A pellet the size of a paintball whizzed through the air and struck the elephant-croc on the rump. The pellet burst, releasing a gluey gel that stuck to the animal's hide.

Suspended within the gel was a miniaturized tracking device that activated upon impact, as evidenced by a blinking red light.

Wade had almost run out of road, so he let up on the gas. However, the elephant-croc did not slow down in the slightest. Instead, it ran straight through the intersection, passed between the trees, plunged into the brackish water, and disappeared from sight.

As Wade came up on the intersection, he saw that the connecting perpendicular road ran along the edge of the swamp. His only hope of continuing the pursuit was to find a boat of some kind — though the smoke pouring from his truck told him that he would be conducting his search on foot.

A hundred yards down the swamp road to Wade's left, a much more tranquil scene was playing out. A local shrimp-fisherman, or "shrimper," was sitting in his pickup truck and humming a happy tune. His name was Gerald Nolan.

After twenty years spent reaping the bounty of the ocean, his skin was darkly tanned and leathery. Since shrimp was out of season and he had some time on his hands, he was preparing for a day's recreation cruising the bayou in his airboat.

Because the great hurricane had permanently driven away the former residents of the area, the swamp road no longer saw much traffic. In Gerald's eyes, that made it the ideal place from which to launch his boat, since he was by nature a private person.

He was also a traditionalist and tended to regard new technologies as being frivolous. However, he did enjoy his music, and any time he went boating for pleasure, he made sure to bring along his portable player.

His personal policy was to ease very gradually into the waters of progress, and true to form, he had just made the switch from audio cassettes to CDs. To date, he had purchased only three, so when his favorite one fell onto the floor of his truck, its recovery was a matter of some urgency.

Just as the elephant-croc was emerging from the deserted neighborhood, Gerald was bending over to look for the CD. Since the disc was wedged beneath a floor mat, it took him a few seconds to locate it.

When he did, in a thick Cajun accent he exclaimed, "'Dere you are!" By the time he sat up straight again, the elephant-croc had vanished into the bayou.

Gerald resumed his humming, popped the CD into his portable player, and got out of his truck. That's when his day started to get interesting.

Just a stone's throw down the road from the boat launch, a smoking, half-demolished, tiger-striped pickup truck suddenly shot out from among the vacant houses and screeched to a stop.

Even though Gerald was philosophically opposed to curiosity, it struck him that this development might hold some entertainment value.

Nor was he disappointed, for out of the battered truck jumped some kind of cowboy who spent the next thirty seconds strapping a gun belt around his waist.

Gerald's interest grew as the man started running along the side of the swamp road, straight for him.

The stranger's wardrobe — all except for his hat — looked like it had been picked off a trash heap. As he drew closer, Gerald also noticed that the man's face was badly lacerated, and that he was covered in a fine white powder.

Finally, the Bloody Cowboy of the Apocalypse skidded to a halt just a few feet from the New Orleans native.

"Wud 'appened tuh *yoo?*" asked Gerald, in a fine exhibition of the local dialect.

Breathing hard and wincing at the pain in his sternum, Wade said, "Listen! You're not gonna like this, but I'm a federal agent, and I need to use your boat!"

So saying, he flashed a glance over at Gerald's single-seat airboat, which was moored at the water's edge.

The shrimper looked at his boat and then back at Wade. With a distrustful frown, he asked, "Fed'rul agen'? 'Ave you godda badge?"

Wade did in fact have an official badge, but it was in the silver case, back at his truck. Having no time to run and get it, he showed Gerald the next best thing.

"Look here!" said Wade, grasping the buckle of his gun belt and angling it upwards.

Gerald leaned over and studied the Task Center seal. He didn't see anything he recognized, and the letters running around the buckle's circumference were so small that he had to squint just to read them.

"Genedic *wud?*" he asked.

"Oh, never mind!" snapped Wade. "I need that boat!"

Gerald took another look at his boat and then told Wade, "Ah don' tink so."

It was contrary to Wade's nature to impose his will by force, but given the circumstances, he broke form. Drawing his honking-huge gun and pointing it at the water's edge, he shouted, "I NEED THAT BOAT!"

The shrimper was suddenly compliant to the point of being helpful. Holding up his hands, he said, "OK — sher! De keys're in id!"

"Thanks!" replied Wade, and the two men ran over to the airboat.

The specialized craft had a shallow, flat-bottomed hull that allowed it to negotiate even the most inaccessible parts of the bayou. Instead of a motor that hung down into the water, it had a four-foot plane propeller mounted in the back. The pilot's seat was situated high above the floor, with the only controls being a gas pedal and a rudder stick.

Although Wade had precious little experience piloting motorboats of any kind, he clambered up into the seat hoping that his skill with automobiles would be at least partially transferrable.

"Now how do you drive this thing?" he asked.

Gerald set one foot in the boat, turned on the ignition, and cranked the key for the engine. Immediately, the plane propeller started to spin at a high rate of speed, and over the subsequent noise, Gerald gave Wade an extremely brief introduction to airboating.

"Well, deez two big flap on de fan are de rudder. Dey won' do nuddin' dough, 'less yooz actually movin' forward. Dat handle on de left turn yooz from side 'd side. Dat peda on de floor is de 'celerator."

Gerald's accent was so thick that Wade could only understand about half the words. But since he was eager to get moving, he nodded as if he had understood them all.

"Accelerator!" he repeated. "Got it!"

"Now 'member," Gerald continued, "don' make no fas' turn. An' if yooz headin' raht fer somedin', give youself plenny o' tahm tuh slow dow', 'cuz dere ain' no brake!"

But at this point, Wade wasn't listening.

Hinged to the side of the TRACER barrel was a small view screen, like that of a video camcorder. Flipping it open, Wade saw a digital display consisting of several concentric circles with a small green triangle at the epicenter.

The triangle represented the location of the gun, and therefore remained stationary. The other symbol of importance was a flashing red dot that showed the tracer's location, relative to the gun.

To his distress, Wade saw that the dot was fast approaching the top edge of the screen. Clearly the 'brid was not having any difficulty in the water on account of being half-elephant — which only stood to reason, since elephants were natural swimmers.

In response to Gerald's final instructions, Wade off-handedly replied, "Uh-huh — got it." He then grabbed the rudder stick with his left hand, and Gerald took a few steps back.

Just before stepping on the accelerator, Wade looked down and asked, "Hey — what's your name?"

"Geral' Nolan," the shrimper replied.

"Well, Gerald Nolan, if I'm not back soon, you just write down your address and stick it in my truck. I promise you, if I damage this boat, I'll see to it you get a new one!"

"If yoo say so," said Gerald, doubtfully. Then, without another word, Wade hit the gas and sped off.

At a ridiculous speed for someone so inexperienced, he skimmed along a channel that was roughly thirty feet wide. The inky black water was bordered on both sides by lush, green swamp dominated by cypress trees with their distinctive, swollen trunks. Every branch was laden with hanging Spanish moss that seemed to bind the bayou together like an endless, living cobweb.

Under other circumstances, Wade would have been able to appreciate the beauty of the place, but at present, it only seemed oppressive and suffocating.

Since the airboat was not equipped with any controls for the right hand, he was able to hold his gun and check the view screen every few seconds.

He was heartened to see that the blinking red dot was creeping back towards the green triangle — not because the 'brid was slowing down, of course, but rather because he was catching up to it.

What he needed desperately was a new game plan. As long as the 'brid was submerged, it was invulnerable. He could track it all day long, but unless it breached the surface, there was nothing he could do.

And then the full weight of the truth settled on Wade: despite all his best efforts, he had failed. The situation was completely out of control, and the time for trying to capture the beast unharmed was over. Now, it simply had to be stopped by whatever means possible.

Suddenly, an image popped into his mind of Bob MacArthur, laughing his head off. But even if it meant eating some humble pie, Wade knew that it was time to make a call.

Since the gun's tracking system utilized GPS, at this point, there wasn't any real risk of losing the 'brid. That is, unless the miniaturized tracer somehow got knocked off, or the adhesive lost its stickiness in the water...

But assuming that the device did *not* fall off, all Wade really had to do was shadow the animal and make sure that it did not leave the bayou. Even if it took six or seven hours for help to arrive, as long as no civilians were in immediate danger, it would be worth the wait.

Yes, Wade decided — he would call Paul Fairfield at the Genetic Anomalies Task Center in Los Angeles and then simply keep the elephant-croc under surveillance. Feeling some relief at the thought, he reached into his pocket for his phone... only it wasn't there.

And then he remembered why: after calling Chandra and checking the text that Rose had sent him, he had placed the phone in one of his truck's cup-holders so that he could check out his makeup in the rear-view mirror. And provided the phone had not flown out the window during all the recent slamming and crashing, it was still somewhere in the cab.

Great! thought Wade to himself. He was now up a creek both figuratively and literally. Unless he turned the airboat around and physically went to get help, he was on his own.

But as he was lamenting his predicament, the red dot on the view screen suddenly changed its behavior. Instead of approaching the green triangle at a slow creep, it began moving towards it at an alarming rate.

At first, Wade wondered if the 'brid had simply stopped moving, while he continued to speed towards it. But looking at the surface of the water up ahead, he saw the distinct V-shape of a wake, pointed not away from him, but towards.

It didn't make sense! Since he had first started pursuing it, the elephant-croc had only wanted to get away from him. And now, suddenly it was coming straight for him, almost as if it had a vendetta. But that wasn't possible — was it?

And then the old saying popped into his head: *An elephant never forgets.*

Wade knew that elephants as a species were intelligent and emotionally sensitive. He also knew that if a man shot and killed a wild elephant in the bush, then that man might soon find *himself* being hunted down by the surviving members of the herd.

No — there could be no more doubt: the tables had been turned. The elephant-croc had obviously heard the airboat closing in from behind. And feeling emboldened for being in the water, it had finally decided that enough was enough, and that it was payback time.

Wade quickly moved his right foot from the accelerator to the non-existent brake pedal.

"Brakes? *Brakes!*" he cried.

In the absence of a pedal, he sought an equivalent lever, but there was none.

Dang it, Gerald! he thought. *Why didn't you say there were no brakes?!*

For lack of another option, Wade turned the key to cut the engine. Immediately the propeller spun down, but the boat continued to glide forward.

For a foolish moment, Wade imagined that if the elephant-croc tried to bite the boat, he could try shooting into its mouth. But then he realized that he would have only a microsecond to make the attempt, so he discarded the idea.

His only hope was that the 'brid would fixate on the airboat itself, rather than on him personally. In that case, as soon as it attacked, he could jump clear and swim to the shore unnoticed.

Looking ahead, Wade could distinguish two bulging eyes skimming the water's surface. Standing up on the pilot's seat, he holstered his gun and grabbed the hat off his head. Holding it tightly by the brim with his right hand, he bent at the knees and anticipated the seconds to impact: 3... 2... 1...

In a rush, the deadly jaws opened, and the elephant-croc took the bow of the airboat full in its mouth.

At the same time, Wade leaped, soaring in a graceful arc and landing with a splash off to one side. Then, without so much as a backwards glance, he swam for his life.

Upon colliding with the boat, the elephant-croc experienced a few seconds of sensory overload, so that it neither saw nor heard Wade's entry into the water. It gave a series of vicious bites to the boat's hull and then clamped down hard and executed a death roll.

Unlike Wade's truck, the top-heavy airboat was easily flipped over.

However, once its flat bottom was turned up to the sky and its engine and propeller were submerged, the craft could be rolled no more.

Even so, the elephant-croc was finally feeling good about itself, and it kept on biting until at last Gerald Nolan's pride and joy sank into the murky depths.

Still clutching his hat, Wade worked the crawl stroke for all he was worth. With each passing second, he grew more hopeful: he was twenty feet away from land and closing...

But unfortunately for him, once the airboat had sunk to the bottom of the channel, there was nothing to mask the sound of his splashing. The elephant-croc detected the disturbance, and with a swish of its tail, it turned to investigate.

With a feeling of elation, Wade finally reached terra firma — only to discover that it was not so firm after all. Rather, what had appeared to be land turned out to be little more than a mucky quagmire, packed with cypress trees.

Wade now realized that he wouldn't be running anywhere fast. Then again, he couldn't very well stay where he was, either.

Slapping his waterlogged hat back on his head, he grabbed some cypress roots and pulled himself out of the water and into the mire. He was relieved to find that he could stand, but the putrid soup came up to his knees and exerted a good deal of suction on his costume boots.

As the elephant-croc swam at Wade from behind, it had only the foggiest sense that he was in some way to blame for its recent troubles. But whatever the case, he appeared defenseless enough now, and that made him prime breakfast material.

With a loud and terrifying SWOOSH, the elephant-croc launched itself out of the water with its mouth stretched wide as if to swallow Wade with one gulp.

Wade dove sideways for the cover of the nearest cypress tree, which handily deflected the snapping mouth. After landing face-first in the muck, he scrambled for distance.

The elephant-croc gave chase, but as with the rhino-bear, its size proved to be a liability among the trees — only much more so. It could barely squeeze between the bulging trunks to begin with, and the faster it tried to move, the more painfully it beat itself against them.

After a minute of feverish exertion, Wade risked a backwards glance. Perceiving the monster's plight, it occurred to him that if he charted a more convoluted course, he would render any pursuit ten times more difficult.

Straining against the suction of the swamp, Wade made a wide U-turn and headed back the way he had come.

He now actually drew closer to the elephant-croc, though they were separated by a wide strip of cypress trees, like two cars approaching each other on opposite sides of a median strip. And whereas moving in a straight line had been frustrating for the 'brid, it found turning to be virtually impossible.

As it contended with the trees, Wade observed that the skin hanging down from its throat was soft and supple, like that of its belly. Finding himself at a fairly decent angle, he took careful aim and popped off three shots.

The first tranquilizer dart struck high and bounced harmlessly off the tougher scales. The second and third, however, stuck into the 'brid's fleshy neck.

Since the TRACER barrel was partially dedicated to the GPS electronics and view screen, three darts were all it contained. Opening one of the pockets on the gun belt's thigh strap, Wade hastily exchanged the empty barrel for a fresh one.

He slogged away until he was midway down the elephant-croc's thirty-foot length with an all-encompassing view of its broad, right side. With total confidence this time, he aimed the gun and pulled the trigger.

But what shot out of the gun was an unwelcome surprise.

A weighted net went hissing through the air, expanding to a diameter of seven feet. It was large enough to ensnare a wolf, or perhaps even a lion, but not a mutant dinosaur the size of a bus.

With a gentle kiss to the elephant-croc's ribs, the net slid noiselessly into the muck. Wade looked down at the gun barrel to see that it was plainly labeled "NET."

"Oh... yeah," he said, remembering back to Joshua Tree, when he had stuck it in the thigh pocket.

In his haste to acquire the airboat, he had neglected to check that all of his tools were mission-appropriate. It was a potentially fatal oversight, but there was no time to dwell on it. The barrel did not have room for much else besides the net, but Wade saw that it did contain a single tranquilizer dart. Promptly he fired it, scoring a direct belly-hit.

He opened the gun belt's second thigh pocket and pulled out his last hope: a five-shot TRANQ / SHOCK / OC SPRAY combo. It held the two remaining darts he would need to incapacitate the elephant-croc, and he quickly swapped it onto the gun's handgrip.

As the 'brid struggled to turn ninety degrees to face him, Wade opened fire. The two darts landed side by side, separated by a mere inch of underbelly.

But whether due to its size or just pure willpower, the beast was resisting the effects of the drug. Not only that, but its rage had finally reached such an intensity that, as it wheeled to the right, it snapped the trunks of the trees that were hemming it in.

As the timber came crashing down, Wade found himself face to face with a very angry, still-conscious elephant-croc that had just found its wiggle room.

In his overconfidence, he had gotten too close to the creature. Now, it had a straight shot at him, and even the closest cypress trees were not near enough to afford him any cover.

The elephant-croc charged, and Wade staggered back. Since all of his darts were spent, he unleashed the only remaining tools in his arsenal.

POP, POP! went the two SHOCK capsules, as they shot out of the gun. The first one struck the 'brid below its left eye, and the other landed right in its open mouth. Due to its sheer mass, the animal was protected against paralysis. But the shocks still hurt like the dickens, and elicited an ear-splitting trumpet of pain.

At long last, Wade perceived that the elephant-croc was growing sluggish. The elephant-croc perceived it, too. Terrified by its rapid loss of bodily control, it summoned all of its remaining strength and surged forward to destroy Wade once and for all.

But the hybrid hunter had one final sting to give. With an extended pull of his gun's trigger, he gave the 'brid a faceful of OC SPRAY that stopped it cold.

For the next few seconds, the elephant-croc swayed from side to side, blustering in agony. Then, with an anguished moan, it toppled forward, creating a tsunami of muck that knocked Wade off his feet. By the time he sat up and wiped the swamp-matter from his eyes, the elephant-croc was breathing the slow, deep breaths of a narcotic-induced sleep.

For a long time, Wade simply sat and breathed and tried to convince himself that he was alive.

Then, after untold minutes, it finally hit him: he had saved the hybrid. And provided that it could be airlifted out of the bayou, it could go on to live a long and relatively happy life in the care of its benevolent captors.

But for that to happen, Wade knew that he would first have to complete a grueling trek out of the swamp. He did not know how long it would take for the tranquilizer serum to wear off, but he couldn't afford to be optimistic.

If he didn't get moving right away, all of his efforts to capture the animal alive would have been for nothing. Motivated almost exclusively by that thought, he rose to his feet, holstered his gun, and struck out to find a phone.

CHAPTER 14: PERFECT STORM

Gerald Nolan was a patient man, but as he waited in his truck listening to his favorite CD over and over again, he began to tire. He was holding out hope that his airboat might be returned to him in good condition, but those hopes were finally dashed when Wade sloshed out of the swamp like the Creature from the Black Lagoon.

Although Wade would not answer any questions about his misadventures in the bayou, he insisted that, true to his word, he would replace the airboat. But by this point, Gerald required a lot more than just the promise of a stranger. Since his plans for the day had been ruined, he informed Wade that he was not going anywhere until he had been given some more tangible proof that the promise would be honored.

Wade could hardly say him nay. But in order to obtain that proof, he insisted that he be allowed to conduct his business in private. Accordingly, Gerald watched Wade from a distance as he retrieved his cell phone from his wrecked truck and dialed up the Genetic Anomalies Task Center.

Though the Task Center did not have the resources in the New Orleans area to transport the elephant-croc on short notice, the National Guard did. As soon as Wade gave Paul the details of the situation, Paul made a series of calls and then, shortly thereafter, called Wade back to tell him that help was on its way.

Soon, a convoy of National Guard trucks came rolling down the swamp road, accompanied by a tandem rotor Chinook helicopter overhead. Finally satisfied that Wade was on the level, Gerald did not argue when he was told to leave, but drove home confident that he would indeed be compensated for his loss.

The elongated helicopter was held aloft by two separate sets of blades, one at each end, and it was powered by great turbine engines that enabled it to transport tremendously heavy loads. Swaying beneath it from thick cables was an empty steel shipping container large enough to accommodate the anticipated live cargo.

First, the helicopter lowered the container down into the swamp, which was a bit of a trick on account of the cypress trees. Next, a team of able-bodied Guardsmen rappelled down to the ground and tied dozens of strong ropes around the tranquilized elephant-croc. Finally, the beast was pulled into the container by means of motorized winches, and then strapped down according to Wade's instructions so that its limbs would not be crushed under its own weight.

Wade knew that the 'brid would probably struggle against the straps once the serum wore off, but he expected that it would still be too weak to do itself any real harm. Still, he couldn't help but remember the old proverb: *There's many a slip 'twixt the cup and the lip.*

Back on the swamp road once more, Wade watched as the shipping container was airlifted out of the bayou, the cables now as taut as bowstrings. As the helicopter turned towards the setting sun, he said a silent prayer that the flight would pass without incident.

Standing beside Wade in the road was the commander of the extraction team — a career military man a few years his senior, who approached life with a can-do, "happy warrior" attitude.

"Didn't think we'd get it in there even *with* the winches," said the commander. "Craziest thing I ever saw!"

"Yeah," replied Wade, absently. He was taking a moment to privately mourn the swamp-stained hat in his hands, which obviously beyond repair.

"So... how'd you say you got out of the swamp, again?" the commander asked.

"Slogged," answered Wade. Then, after a pause, he added, "Swam a little."

Unsure whether to interpret the information as a sign of bravery or insanity, the commander asked, "You know there's *gators* in that water?"

Wade ignored the question and responded with one of his own. "You said Paul was on his way?" he asked.

"Yes, sir," answered the commander. "I've been informed that Mr. Fairfield's plane will be landing shortly."

"And your men know to keep quiet about all this?"

"Yes, sir," said the commander. "They've been told it's a matter of national security, and they're sworn to secrecy."

Taking the commander at his word, Wade said, "Well — you boys do important work, and if no one's told you 'thank you' today, I'm tellin' you now."

The commander smiled. "I appreciate that, sir. I'll pass it on to my men." Then, after a beat, he said, "Well, my hat is off to you, Mr. Boss. Before I head back, is there anything else you need?"

"I'm gonna need to rent a pickup truck with a ball hitch," said Wade.

The commander smiled again and said, "There's an agency about five minutes from here. I'll give you a lift myself."

* * *

Wade would rather have had to chase another elephant-croc through the bayou than face his next task.

Since there was no point in trying to explain things to his insurance company, he had arranged for his unsalvageable truck to be towed to a local scrap yard. Then, he very slowly drove a forest-green rental truck back to the movie location, wondering all the while what he was going to say when he got there.

He arrived to find the entire crew gone — except for Chet, who was talking on his cell phone and seated on the tow bar of Fred's trailer.

Wade parked the green rental truck behind the trailer and then turned off the engine. He had long-since taken off his gun belt. Reflexively and unconsciously, he had also placed his ruined hat back on his head. His makeup and the powder from the airbag had washed off in the bayou, but his costume clothes — scarcely more than tattered rags to begin with — were now also infused with muck, and only half-dry.

Looking more woeful than a twice-drowned rat, he slowly stepped out of the truck. Then, like a man headed for the gallows, he put one foot in front of the other.

First he checked on Fred, peering through the window of the tiger's temperature-controlled trailer to find the animal contentedly snoozing. Then, having delayed the inevitable for as long as possible, Wade took a deep breath and approached his aggrieved assistant.

Chet's arms were crossed, and his face was expressionless. After a painful silence, Wade opened with less of a question than a statement of the obvious.

"So... it looks like they wrapped?"

Silence.

Wade gulped hard and then said, "You're... prob'ly wonderin' what happened to my truck..."

"Actually, *Wade,*" said Chet, and then he paused, meaningfully. He had never addressed Wade by his first name before, and the pointed use of it now signified a total loss of respect. After letting the verbal slap sink in, he concluded by saying, "I don't even care."

Wade looked wordlessly at the ground.

Eventually, Chet continued. "I figured you wouldn't just abandon

Fred — though I was starting to wonder. I was just about to call for a rental so I could tow him out of this place before dark. Now at least I can make other plans."

"Listen..." began Wade.

"I quit," said Chet, cutting him off. "Now that you're here, I'm going to book myself a room and fly out tomorrow morning. If you don't want to give me a ride, that's fine. I'll just call a cab and have Chandra reimburse me."

Wade felt sick. "Chet, please..."

But with cold finality, Chet said, "There's nothing you can say, so don't bother."

After another long silence, Wade's cell phone rang. He wasn't likely to get a better 'out', so he pulled it from his pocket and said, "I'd better take this."

He turned and walked out to the main road, rounding the house on the corner until he was hidden from Chet's view. As he went, he puzzled over the unfamiliar number on the phone's little backlit screen. Drawing a blank, he finally answered and said, "Hello?"

"I don't even know what to say," came a familiar voice.

"Genevieve?" asked Wade. "Where are you callin' from?"

"A pay-phone, if you can believe it," she said. Her tone was flat and dangerous. "I knew if you saw my name on the caller I.D. you wouldn't answer. So... is it true?"

Feeling smaller than he had in perhaps his whole life, Wade simply said, "Yeah."

"You know..." Genevieve began, but suddenly her voice caught. Then, after a moment of ominous silence, she exploded. "I thought you meant what you said the other day!"

"I did!" Wade insisted. "Look, I know it must seem..."

But he got no further. That he should presume to justify himself in even the slightest way, Genevieve took to be the supreme insult.

Accordingly, she went nuclear.

"I am *humiliated, Wade!* Do you know who just called me? Lucas Stevens! Do you know what he said? He said he just talked to James Blakeman and told him to find someone else for the India picture, because you're the most unprofessional person he's ever met in his entire life! *Lucas Stevens!* Do you know what this is going to do to my reputation?!"

"I'm sorry," said Wade. "Believe me, I didn't have a choice..."

"Didn't have a *choice?!* Were you kidnapped at gunpoint? What in the world could possibly have come up that was worth your entire career?!"

Just then, Wade's phone beeped, alerting him to another incoming call. He glanced at the screen to identify the new caller.

It was Rose.

A wave of relief washed over him. Even as Genevieve continued her tirade, he said, "Listen — I got an emergency call comin' through."

Livid beyond description at the prospect of being put on hold, Genevieve shrieked, *"Wade Boss, don't you dare...!"*

Wade pushed the answer button and switched lines. "Rose!" he exclaimed. "Am I glad to hear from you!"

But when Rose spoke, it sounded like she had been crying. "Is it true?" she asked.

"It's OK!" said Wade. "I'm all right. We got the 'brid packed up, and it's in the air."

"Are you *with* her?" Rose asked him.

Wade was confused. "Am I with who?" he asked.

"I was just at the grocery store," said Rose. "One of the tabloids had a picture of Genevieve Parker on the cover holding hands with her new 'cowboy beau'. *You*, Wade."

Wade felt like he had just been slugged in the gut. A wave of vertigo washed over him, and then he stammered, "L-look Rose... I..."

"Are you in love with her?" she sobbed.

"I... now just hold on..."

"How could I have been so *stupid?!*" Rose cried, and then with a 'click' the line went dead.

Wade froze. In the last few hours, he had nearly been eaten alive, had destroyed his career, had lost his right-hand man and most likely his movie star girlfriend as well.

And yet somehow, up until this moment, he had been able to retain at least a tiny shred of masculine dignity — the smallest that can be left to a man before he snaps.

But Rose's grief was too much.

Wade was done. Spent. Empty. And so completely raw that even the slightest irritation was foredoomed to elicit a volcanic response.

Then Paul drove up.

"Wade!" he shouted out the window of his rental car. Wade made no reply, but slowly lowered his phone.

After screeching to a stop, Paul jumped out of his vehicle. "They told me you'd be here!" he exclaimed, rushing over. "Thank goodness you're all right!" Then, as if needing to prove it to himself, he clapped Wade on the shoulder.

Ka-*boom.*

"DON'T TOUCH ME!" Wade thundered.

Paul staggered back. Then, in a state of shock, he beheld what only a few people had ever been unfortunate enough to witness: the unbridled temper of Wade Boss.

"*My life is RUINED!*" Wade hollered. "Thanks to you, I've just managed to hurt almost every person I know, plus a whole bunch more that before this mornin' I'd never even *met!* Speakin' o' which..."

He pulled a folded scrap of paper from his pocket and thrust it at Paul as if it were a sword.

Timidly, Paul received and unfolded it. Struggling to decode the penciled chicken scratch, he read aloud: "'Gerald Nolan'?"

"You owe him a boat!" Wade declared. "It's no coincidence that that 'brid showed up here today, which makes *twice* now that I've been personally targeted! These sociopaths — whoever they are — somehow know who I am, what I'm doin', and where I'm doin' it almost before I do! I don't know if your building is bugged or if someone just has loose lips, but seein' as how nothin' I do seems to be private anyway..."

Then he threw back his head and shouted to the world, "I QUIT! You hear me?! Whoever you are, I know you're listenin'! I quit! Now *LEAVE ME ALONE!"*

Finally, he looked back at Paul and said, "Don't you ever call me again — stay out of my life! You and your whole stinkin' Genetic Anomalies Task Center! I am done! DONE!"

And so saying, he grabbed the sorry hat off his head and threw it at Paul.

Out of sheer reflex, Paul caught it. Then, in stunned silence, he watched as his number one hybrid hunter turned his back, stormed off, and finally disappeared among the flood-ravaged houses.

CHAPTER 15: DESOLATION

The New Orleans fiasco impacted Chandra almost at once, making for the worst Thursday of her life.

No sooner had Wade begun his pursuit of the elephant-croc than the phone at the ranch office started ringing off the hook. Within the space of an hour, Chandra fielded more than a dozen angry calls from various producers and studio executives, all looking to ream out her employer for some unforgivable sin about which she knew nothing.

After countless failed attempts to reach Wade on his cell phone, she called Chet, who picked up only long enough to tell her that he couldn't talk, and that Wade had left the shoot in a rush and had effectively dropped off the face of the Earth.

Chandra was beside herself with worry for the rest of the afternoon. Then, just as she was about to go and crash in the bunkhouse, Wade called the office. He sounded like a zombie, and in spite of Chandra's desperate pleas for more information, he said only that he would be back a day later than planned.

Early Friday morning, Chet called Chandra on her cell phone to tell her that he would be flying into LAX airport in the afternoon. He said that if she could come pick him up, he would give her the full story.

After his flight landed, the two of them rode back to the ranch in Chandra's maroon Buick, and Chet laid out all the horrible details. Chandra begged him not to quit, but by that point, there was no talking him out of it.

On Saturday morning, Chet showed up at the ranch in his black Jeep. Chandra looked on in despair and disbelief as he first collected his personal belongings and then bade a sorrowful farewell to Ginger, Hank, Roland, and Dolly.

Finally, after many tears on Chandra's part and many mutual promises to keep in touch, the last goodbye was said.

So ended Chet Hubbard's employment at Boss Ranch.

On Monday morning, a forest-green pickup truck pulled up the ranch driveway with Fred's trailer in tow. Without Chet along to take turns with the driving, an already exhausted Wade was now fried to a crisp. Chandra was a little better rested, but just as much of an emotional wreck. She and Wade said hardly a word to each other as they hastily settled Fred back in with Ginger — the only happy reunion of the lot.

Chandra followed Wade to a rental agency where he returned the green truck, and then she gave him a ride back to the ranch. It was a miserable experience, during which Wade divulged nothing new — except to say that, since he was no longer welcome in Hollywood, he would probably be moving back to Texas.

The obvious, unspoken significance of this was that Chandra would either have to relocate or lose her job.

After she dropped Wade off at his house, she drove home and cried almost straight through to the next morning.

* * *

Exactly two weeks after that fateful, black Thursday, a decidedly un-cheerful Chandra pulled a plastic food container from the refrigerator in the ranch office. She was halfway to the microwave when Wade entered from outside.

"Hey, Boss," she said, trying her best to sound upbeat.

"Hey, Chandra!" returned Wade, with a smile too broad.

The recent changes, and those yet to come, had cast a pall over the ranch. In an attempt to combat the oppressive sadness, Wade had been overcompensating with a forced 'positive attitude'. And though he sensed it wasn't working, he didn't know what else to do.

After an awkward silence, Chandra turned away from him and continued to the microwave. Unable to come up with a lighthearted topic of conversation, Wade headed into his private office.

Chandra opened the door of the microwave and set her plastic food container inside. But before she could punch in the cook time, Wade reappeared.

"Say, did the mail come in?" he asked.

"Oh yeah — sorry," replied Chandra, and she walked around to the far side of her desk. Squatting down, she picked up a box with a stack of letters on top. Wade took a few steps towards her and received them.

"Thanks," he said, awkwardly.

"Mm-hmm," replied Chandra, avoiding direct eye contact with him.

As she returned to the microwave, Wade looked down at the letters. The one on top had been sent from the Lone Star Predator Preserve, in Texas. Setting the box on Chandra's desk, Wade opened the letter and began to read.

After pushing the cook-button, Chandra tentatively asked, "Good news?"

Wade smiled over at her. "Oh... they say they're interested — if I'm serious." Then he sighed and said, "I don't know."

"Not gonna go back to the circus?" Chandra asked.

Wade shook his head and said, "Nah — I think I'm done with show business. Besides, I don't want to be on the road so much." Then after a pause, he exclaimed, "Oh! I almost forgot..."

Pulling a folded piece of paper from his jacket pocket, he took a few steps and handed it to Chandra.

"Here's that letter of recommendation," he said. "I uh... I think anyone who reads it will prob'ly offer you a job on the spot!"

Chandra received it with as much relish as if it were an eviction notice — which, in a sense, it was. "Oh," she said, with a lump in her throat. "Thank you."

Wade felt like the biggest heel on the planet. He knew that working at the ranch was Chandra's dream job, and here he was, sending her away.

He knew he would never find a replacement who was her equal, which is why he had offered to cover all of her moving expenses if she would come with him. She had declined, since most of her loved ones lived in Southern California. Still, Wade figured it couldn't hurt to extend the offer one more time.

"You know," he said, "there's a lot to like in Texas."

Chandra forced a smile and said, "Oh — I'm sure. It's just my family... my boyfriend..."

"Sure, sure!" said Wade, quickly backing off. "I understand — completely."

Anxious to change the subject, Chandra said, "I'm sure your folks'll be glad to have you around again."

"Yeah..." said Wade, cringing at the thought of returning in disgrace. "Actually, I haven't told 'em yet — figure I'd better have something more to talk about besides how I burned all my bridges in Hollywood!"

Chandra gave a weak courtesy laugh, and then it grew uncomfortably silent again. After a few seconds, she gestured to the box on her desk and said, "Looks like your new hat came in!"

"Oh — yeah!" said Wade, grateful that she had such a knack for keeping conversations moving. "S'pose I ought to check it out!"

He turned back to the desk, pulled out his pocketknife, and began slicing through the tape on the package.

Wanting to encourage Chandra, over his shoulder Wade said, "You know, it'll prob'ly be a while before I can find a buyer for this place. You'll have plenty of time to find somethin' else."

"Yeah," was all that Chandra replied. From her tone, Wade realized he had only made her feel worse.

At last he opened the box flaps and pulled out a brand new cowboy hat, custom made to the same specs as his old one. He put it on and turned around.

"So — what do you think?" he asked.

Chandra smiled genuinely this time and nodded her approval. "It's identical!" she said.

"Fits just right, too!" Wade informed her.

A 'ding' from the microwave told Chandra that her lunch was ready. She popped open the door and pulled out the container as Wade gathered up the mail.

"Say, that smells good!" he remarked.

"Yeah," said Chandra, "I found this great little Chinese place called *Yum Wang's*. It's orange chicken. You want some?"

Suddenly Wade's mind was flooded with memories of Rose and their wonderful, dreamlike, "non-date" dinner in that very office.

For a moment, he couldn't speak. At last he managed to say, "Uh... no. Thanks."

Then without another word, he turned and walked back into his office, closing the door behind him and leaving Chandra wondering what she had said wrong.

* * *

Metaphorically speaking, if Paul had been on the ropes before, by now he was face down on the mat.

Calling upon the National Guard to extract the elephant-croc from New Orleans had not gone over well with his superiors, and it didn't seem to matter that he had had no real choice. And regardless of the fact that he was doing an amazing job on a very tight budget, he was taking more heat every day.

The real reason, of course, was that the hybrid phenomenon was ballooning into a much bigger problem than anyone had anticipated. Bigger, and more expensive.

Now that the dangerous creatures were turning up in populated areas, the Task Center's oversight committee was running scared. Paul was the obvious dog to kick, and although he tried not to take the criticism of his performance personally, it was steadily wearing him down.

The obvious solution was more manpower — more field agents, especially. And of course that boiled down to money.

Just days after the mutilated 'brid had turned up in Wade's truck, Paul had been granted a special allowance to beef up security for the main office building — to an extent.

The first order of business had been to hire a daytime guard, but the low salary winnowed the field considerably. In the end, the job went to a retired police officer named Maurice, who just wanted something to do and didn't particularly need the money.

Paul also purchased some surveillance cameras to put around the building, but that was as far as the allowance went. He was told that if he wanted to spend any more on security, he would have to draw up a new and detailed budget proposal.

For the last four days, that's just what he had been doing.

Now, at 4:30 on Thursday afternoon, Paul was beat. There had been no new 'brid sightings since the elephant-croc, but after fourteen days of relative calm, he imagined that his luck wouldn't last for much longer. If ever he hoped to catch up on sleep, he figured now was the time.

After packing his briefcase and grabbing his coat, he decided to notify Dr. Jules Krennick, Head of Research, that he was leaving for the night.

In the genetics lab, the brilliant scientist with the wire-rimmed glasses and precisely-sculpted goatee was hunched over his computer. He was too immersed in his work to notice when the white steel door opened and Paul peeked in.

"'Night, Jules!" Paul called from across the room.

Dr. Krennick looked up. "Is it?" he asked, glancing over at the clock on the wall.

"It is for me," said Paul, wearily. "Figure I'd better catch up on some rest before the next calamity hits."

"Probably a good idea," said Dr. Krennick, sympathetically.

"Well — see you tomorrow," said Paul, with a wave.

"Good night, Paul," replied Dr. Krennick.

The door swung shut. For a long moment, Dr. Krennick stared at it in silence. Finally, after his private thought had run its course, he turned back to his work.

* * *

Paul continued on his way out of the building, entering the lobby through the oak door behind Rose's desk. As he passed by the adorable blonde receptionist, he said, "Good night, Rose."

"Good night, Mr. Fairfield!" said Rose. "Skippin' out early?"

"Oh, you know me," Paul said, with a tired smile. "I'm a slacker!"

"Yeah, and I'm a saddle sore!" Rose joked. Then, sincerely, she added, "Hope you're gonna grab some extra shut-eye."

"That's the plan," said Paul. "See you tomorrow."

"Bye, now," said Rose.

Over at the lobby's tiny coffee station, the new security guard, Maurice, was fixing himself a stale cup.

At sixty-five, he still had most of his gray hair, which he combed proudly and often. Forty extra pounds helped to keep his uniform nice and snug, and also suggested that, during his years on the force, he had lived up to the stereotype about cops and donuts.

Whenever he wasn't walking, he stood with his feet slightly apart and his thumbs hooked on his utility belt. In addition to a walkie-talkie that he used to communicate with Rose, he also carried a Glock 9 mm pistol.

The fact that he already owned a gun and knew how to use it had been the deciding factor that convinced Paul to hire him.

As Paul neared the lobby doors, Maurice called out, "Good night, Mr. Fairfield!"

Paul stopped and turned to face him. "Oh — hey Maurice!" he said. "Didn't see you over there. How are you liking the job so far?"

"I'm still getting back into the swing of waking up early," Maurice chuckled, "but it suits me real well. I appreciate the opportunity!"

"Well, we appreciate you," said Paul. "Goodnight now." And with a wave, he exited the building.

Rose swiveled in her chair to face her new workplace buddy. "Maurice," she said, "I don't know why you won't just let me make you a new pot."

"No, no!" said Maurice, holding up a hand. "You've got more important things to do, Miss Rose! Besides, after thirty-five years of drinking battery acid downtown, I'm not all that particular."

"Whatever you say," replied Rose.

Then, on a different note, Maurice told her, "I'm going to make another round outside. Call if you need me!"

Rose picked up the walkie-talkie that was now a fixture on her desk. Pressing the 'talk' button, she said, "Roger, Roger!"

On his way out of the lobby, Maurice paused to hold open one of the glass doors for a deliveryman who was coming up the walkway carrying a large cardboard box.

"Thank you, sir!" said the deliveryman, as he entered.

"You're welcome," replied Maurice, and then he continued outside to patrol the grounds.

The deliveryman smiled at Rose as he approached. "Afternoon, ma'am," he said, setting the box on the half-wall in front of her desk.

"Is that my box of diamonds from Prince Charmin'?" Rose joked.

"Might be!" the deliveryman replied. He then handed her a digital pad to sign and said, "It's not addressed to anyone specific."

"Well, then — I guess it *must* be for me!" said Rose, entering her signature on the touch-screen. "Leastways, I'm the one that gets to open it."

As he received the pad back from her, the deliveryman said, "Well, if it's not those diamonds, you just let me know, and I'll tell that prince he'd better get on the stick."

"That's a service you provide?" asked Rose.

"Straightening out neglectful royalty is standard company practice," the deliveryman informed her.

"Then I'd say your competitors don't stand a chance," said Rose.

"That's the idea!" returned the deliveryman. Then, doffing his cap to her, he said, "Good day, my lady. And may you receive your wish!"

"Thank you, kind sir — and may your every light be green!" said Rose, with a touch of melodrama.

The deliveryman smiled, put his cap back on, and walked out of the lobby feeling twice as clever and handsome as when he came in.

Rose sighed and slid the box onto her desk. As the deliveryman had mentioned, there was no addressee other than the Task Center. This was not unheard of, though it usually happened with the standard mail. By default, it fell to Rose to open such poorly labeled items and then send them on to their intended parties.

She pulled a pair of scissors from her desk and then glanced up at the return address for some clue as to the package's contents.

A jolt of adrenalin made her blood run cold as she read the sender's name.

W. BOSS.

Although her visit to the ranch had not technically been a date, Rose had not bothered about splitting hairs. A few mixed signals from Wade notwithstanding, she had felt confident in her belief that the evening had marked the beginning of a true romance.

But then... the grocery store.

Even though she wasn't one to read the gossip rags, like any person waiting in the checkout line, Rose always took casual note of the juicy covers. Thus it was that, at the most unsuspecting of moments, an arrow pierced her heart.

For what she saw, in full color on the front of the most notorious tabloid of them all, was a picture of Wade — hand in hand with America's sweetheart, Genevieve Parker.

Rose had nearly fainted. The fact that she had only just met Wade was irrelevant, for in matters of the heart, there is no such thing as a 'reasonable' amount of time.

Now, seeing Wade's name printed on the cardboard box that had just been delivered to her desk, Rose felt like she was right back in that checkout line.

It was the pain in her fingers that brought her back to the present. Looking down, she saw that her knuckles were white from squeezing the scissors.

Willfully, she relaxed her hand. Then, feeling like a spectator outside her own body, she mechanically cut through the tape that secured the box flaps.

She set the scissors down and then slowly, slowly, opened the flaps. She recognized the contents of the box at once: a silver case

— or rather, *the* silver case. The very same one over which Wade had tripped while trying to impress her on the day they met.

It was the first time he had made her laugh.

Now, the memory of it crashed down upon Rose like a breaker upon the rocks. Helpless to control herself, and not caring to anyway, she burst into tears.

CHAPTER 16: PENDULUM

There's a line in a song that goes, "Freedom's just another word for 'nothing left to lose'."

What a crock, Wade thought to himself, wondering how the tune had gotten stuck in his head. For in spite of having lost virtually everyone and everything he truly cared about, he had never felt less free in his life.

Yesterday, Chandra's lunch of orange chicken had reminded him of his dinner in the front office with Rose. Then, last night, the Texas sweetheart kept appearing in his dreams with tears in her eyes, asking how he could have so callously led her on.

This morning, after Chandra parked her maroon Buick in front of the hitching rail, she greeted Wade looking as though the sky of her world was as black as her hair. As she performed her various duties in the office, she looked so miserable that Wade finally told her she could go home at 11:00 — which was as much for his sake as for hers.

He moped about the office until supper time and then returned to his house and made himself a waffle, which was the most un-Chinese food he could think of.

After spending an hour cursing stupid politicians on the Friday evening news, and then spending several more cursing his stupid self for all his stupid failures, he felt the need for some unconditional acceptance.

The only earthly relationships he had that still seemed to be intact were those with his parents and his animals. And since the former were hundreds of miles away, at the end of another dismal week, Wade sought comfort in the latter.

Even more than working with his tigers, Wade enjoyed just hanging out with them. Not that his other animals weren't also very dear to him. It was just that Fred and Ginger possessed a certain calming grace, like the dancers for whom they had been named.

Sitting with his back against one of the concrete walls of their habitat, Wade affectionately scratched Fred behind the ears. The regal cat lay on one side, lazily enjoying the attention, while Ginger groomed herself on a nearby log that was her favorite perch.

As he listened to the regular *thrum-thrum* of Fred's purring, Wade was lulled into a dreamy state. After nodding off for the third time, he roused himself enough to head back to the house.

He had only been in bed for about an hour when his ringing cell phone woke him. Grabbing the charger cord that hung down from his nightstand, he swung the phone onto his chest.

The glowing screen was too bright to look at, but even in his groggy condition, Wade reasoned that no one was likely to be calling at 11 p.m. just to yell at him. Therefore, it must either be someone who still loved him — which seemed less likely — or else someone having an emergency.

"Hello?" he answered, in a gravelly voice.

"Hey," came a reply, and that single syllable was enough to tell Wade that it was Genevieve. Strangely, though, she did not sound angry.

"Hey," Wade responded, doubly confused for being only half-awake. When Genevieve said nothing for several seconds, he asked, "Are you OK?"

"I've been better," she replied. Then, in a very subdued tone, she said, "I miss you."

It took Wade a couple of seconds, but finally it dawned on him that she was expressing a change of heart.

"Really?" he asked.

"Really," said Genevieve. Then, with uncharacteristic meekness, she asked him, "Can we talk tomorrow? I mean, in person?"

Wade hardly knew what to think. After Genevieve's last diatribe, he had told himself that she was a vicious harpy, and that he was better off without her. But later, after some reflection, he had finally admitted to himself that he had given her just cause to lambaste him.

And, of course, he himself had been just as nasty to Paul — or rather worse — so he could hardly throw stones.

And the truth was that he missed Genevieve. Not everything about her, to be sure. But much. And in his vulnerable state, at this late hour, the prospect of getting back at least something that he had lost seemed very appealing.

Ignoring the warning bells sounding in his brain, Wade cleared his throat and said, "Sure."

* * *

"No, no, no!" shouted Genevieve, for if there was anything she hated, it was a wardrobe department screw-up. "The *gold* necklace! Does this outfit say 'silver' to you?"

"I'm sorry," said the new girl, who in addition to being inexperienced had also been sick the day before, and thus knew nothing of the costume change. Bordering on tears, she said, "I just thought..."

"Stop right there, honey!" said Genevieve, holding up her palm. "Your job is not to *think,* it is to *fetch*. Now go fetch me the gold necklace and get rid of that atrocity!"

The girl looked down at the silver necklace in her hands which, in spite of being the wrong one, was actually a beautiful piece. With a quivering lower lip, she simply said, "Yes, ma'am," and hurried off to do her sovereign's bidding.

At that moment, Wade walked up dressed in the uniform of a

British Indian Army officer. "Everything OK?" he asked.

"What?" replied Genevieve. Then, realizing that he was referring to her outburst, she smiled and said, "Oh, that! Just some stupid new girl. But don't you look great!"

And he did — against all odds.

His very presence on the studio backlot had significantly loosened his grip on reality. In the space of just one week, his life had flip-flopped yet again: just when he was sure that his career in Hollywood was over, Genevieve had tossed him a lifeline. Using every ounce of her charm and box-office clout, she had actually — unbelievably — talked James Blakeman into keeping him on the India picture.

Hence the uniform, and her compliment.

"Thank you," Wade replied. "And you look beautiful."

"Think so?" asked Genevieve, though it was more of a rhetorical question.

Between her detail-perfect gown and her natural, proud bearing, she looked every inch the wife of a high-ranking colonial officer. The role was serious and dramatic — the kind that defined an actress's career and also won awards.

Wade had no doubt that she was going to be sensational.

Finally, Genevieve noticed that he was holding two cups of coffee. "Oh!" she exclaimed. "Is one of those for me?"

Wade raised one of the cups and announced, "Breakfast!"

Taking it eagerly, Genevieve said, "You're an angel! I hate these 6 a.m. calls."

Just then, a voice called out, "Genevieve! How's my leading lady?" She turned to see the director of the picture, James Blakeman, walking towards them from across the set.

"Oh — James!" she said. As soon as he reached her, she leaned down and gave him a showbiz-kiss on the cheek.

Like his friend Lucas Stevens, James Blakeman was a cultural icon. And though small in stature, he was a titan in the movie business.

A competent director, he was also an innovator of new technologies related to cinema. Though he was difficult to please, cast and crew alike bent over backwards for him, for they knew that his perfectionism always paid off at the box office.

Positively beaming at him with excitement, Genevieve said, "You remember Wade, of course!"

The last time the two men had seen each other, it was to discuss the India picture at a posh restaurant. Given all that had happened since then, James smiled wryly as he offered his hand.

"Hello, Wade," he said with a chuckle. "Seems to me I've heard your name mentioned more than a few times since we met."

Embarrassed, but also relieved to acknowledge the elephant in the room, Wade shook his hand and replied, "Yeah, I guess you have."

"Listen," said James, in an understanding tone. "Of all people, I should know that, sooner or later, everybody needs a second chance. Stuff happens." Then, with the slightest hint of a warning in his voice, he added, "Just not today, OK?"

"No, sir — not today!" said Wade, feeling very self-conscious.

"All right," said James. Then, turning to Genevieve, he said, "We're about ten minutes out, so why don't you take a few more sips of coffee and then mosey on over."

"I'll be right there," said Genevieve, adopting the deferential demeanor she reserved for moguls and power players.

Looking back at Wade, James said, "We'll get to those tiger shots in pretty short order, so whenever you're ready, you can bring the animal on set. Just make sure to give Bobby over there a heads-up before you do."

"Sounds good," answered Wade.

"OK!" said James, and with a parting smile, he walked off.

"I still can't believe this is happening," said Wade, looking dazed. "I don't know who's more excited about it — me or Chandra!"

"Yeah, well, they don't call me the most powerful woman in Hollywood for nothing," said Genevieve, rather immodestly.

"I guess not," said Wade. "Well — I think I'll go get Ginger."

"Hey..." said Genevieve, taking hold of his lapels. She locked eyes with him, and then in all seriousness said, "This is it. One mistake today, and even I won't be able to get you another job."

Feeling put off by the unnecessary reminder, Wade nonetheless swallowed his pride and said, "I know."

The moment passed, and having made her point, Genevieve was all smiles again. "We make a great team, don't we?" she asked, stroking his chest.

Wade smiled and simply replied, "Yeah."

Just then, the wardrobe girl returned with the gold necklace.

"Finally!" said Genevieve, snatching it from the girl's hands.

Wade pretended he hadn't seen, and quietly excused himself.

* * *

Since her breakup with Wade — for she didn't know what else to call it — Rose had valiantly resolved not to let her personal life affect her professional performance. The returned silver case had been a blow, but bringing her Texas defiance to bear, the very next day she was back on the job as if nothing had happened.

Not only that, but she also began requesting whatever menial tasks the staff in the cubicle-office were willing to throw at her. At first, this consisted mostly of photocopying. But when it was discovered that she excelled at data entry as well, her schedule became so full that there was no time left for brooding.

In addition to taking on the extra clerical duties, Rose had made a commitment to herself to be the first person in the building each morning.

At 7:45 a.m., she would unlock the front doors, start the coffee percolating, and then assume her post behind the reception desk. This allowed her to welcome every single employee with a smile and a friendly hello, which she reasoned would set the tone for the entire building for the rest of the day.

When Maurice the security guard had told Paul that he was still getting used to waking up early, it had been the literal truth. Six months of retirement had reset his sleeping patterns, and though he was making gains, he had yet to show up by 8:00.

Then there was Paul himself, whose morning habits were erratic. Sometimes he would turn up for work right after Rose, but just as often, he would show up after Maurice. Rose finally deduced that the determining factor was whether or not he had had a good night's sleep.

Within days of instituting her new schedule, Rose could predict with a fair degree of accuracy the order in which people would arrive. But the one thing of which she could always be certain was that at 7:48 sharp, Charlie Malloy would walk through the glass lobby doors.

Today was no exception. Second only to Dr. Jules Krennick, Charlie was the number-two research scientist at the Task Center, and as brilliant as he was quirky. Now in his early fifties, he had remained a bachelor and lived alone. He always arrived for work with his sparse hair oiled down, but by the time he left each night, it invariably resembled a deep-fried bird's nest.

"Mornin', Charlie!" Rose called out cheerily.

"Good morning, Rose," returned Charlie, in his soft-spoken manner.

As he approached Rose's desk, she wondered how it was that his feet never made any sound. She also wondered anew at the contents of his tattered briefcase, for his right shoulder always hung so low that it seemed on the verge of being dislocated.

It was Charlie's daily custom to furnish Rose with a nugget of scientific knowledge. In a short time, he had considerably deepened her understanding of the natural world, and she had come to look forward to the ritual with eager anticipation.

"Say," Charlie began, "did you know that there are ten times more bacterial cells in your body than human ones?"

"Wow!" replied Rose. "How is that possible?"

"Well, they're smaller than human cells, so they don't take up as much space," explained Charlie. "Still, you could fill a half-gallon milk jug with 'em."

"That's incredible," marveled Rose. "A little gross, but incredible."

"Isn't it?" Charlie asked. Then, without any formal closure, he walked around to the oak door, punched a code into the keypad beside the handle, and disappeared into the cubicle-office.

Amused and better educated, Rose pulled up her "to do" list on the computer.

It was not thirty seconds before she heard Charlie yell.

Fearing that he had slipped and fallen, Rose hit the buzzer beneath her desk and rushed back to the oak door. She yanked it open and then froze, struggling to make sense of what she was seeing.

On the other side of the cubicle office, Charlie was flat on his back — but he had not slipped.

A beast with scaly black skin and tufts of orange hair stood on top of him, pinning his shoulders to the floor with thick, corded forelegs.

Charlie struggled, but the creature's claws were embedded in his flesh. He gave one final scream and then was silenced by a throat-crunching bite.

Rose shrieked, and the beast looked up. They locked eyes, and then Rose turned and ran.

The oak door would have saved her, except that its closing speed was regulated by a hydraulic hinge, and it did not swing shut in time. She had almost reached the lobby doors when the tiger-lizard jumped up onto her desk and sprang at her from behind.

Just at that moment, Paul was coming up the walkway from the front parking lot, looking at the ground and bracing himself for another day of abuse. But as he lifted his eyes to pull open one of the glass doors, he was astonished to see Rose running towards him with a look of terror on her face.

In the next instant, he saw the tiger-lizard land on her full-force, sinking its claws deep into her back. By the time she hit the floor, her white blouse was already stained a deep crimson.

In a flash, Paul dropped his briefcase and burst into the lobby, simultaneously drawing a Colt .45 revolver from beneath his blazer.

Immediately, the tiger-lizard looked up and zeroed in.

Paul didn't even have time to cry out.

* * *

After taking his leave of Genevieve, Wade headed for the studio parking lot to get Ginger. On the way, he was stopped by a fellow British officer coming from the direction of the men's wardrobe tent.

"Hey, dude!" called the actor.

"Oh, hey," said Wade, trying to remember whether or not they had already met.

"It's Wade, right?"

"That's right."

"I'm Mark," said the actor, giving an exaggerated military salute. "Say, as soon as you left the wardrobe tent, your phone started ringing like crazy. Hasn't stopped. Anyway, I don't know if you've got a second, but it sounds like someone might have some kind of emergency."

"Oh — thanks," said Wade, suddenly concerned.

"No problem!" said Mark, and he continued on to the set.

When it came to himself, Wade was not opposed to risk-taking, but where others were concerned, he was something of a Nervous Nelly. Until he found out who was so desperate to reach him, there was no way he could concentrate on his work.

He jogged back to the wardrobe tent and headed straight for the table where he had left his clothes. They sat in a neat, folded pile underneath his brand new hat, which he quickly placed on his head.

Fishing his phone out of his jeans pocket, he saw that he had missed ten separate calls in the last fifteen minutes. And sure enough, they had all been made by the same person: Paul Fairfield.

Wade shook his head. *The guy just doesn't know when to quit,* he thought to himself. Then he mused that Paul was like the clear sap you couldn't get off your hands when you made the mistake of climbing a pine tree.

Wade breathed a sigh of relief, knowing that there was no crisis that affected him personally.

He was mildly startled when his phone rang again. He fully expected to see Paul's name on the screen, but was surprised to see "BOSS BEASTS" instead. Pressing the answer button, he said, "Hey, Chandra. What's up?"

"Oh, hey, Boss!" said Chandra. Her voice was extremely chipper, for she was still riding high on the news that Wade was staying in California, and that she was not going to lose her beloved job.

"Didn't expect you to answer," Chandra continued. "I was just going to leave you a message."

"Yeah, I was just checkin' 'em," said Wade. "Everything OK?"

"I hope so," said Chandra. "You just got a call from a guy named Paul... Fairfield, I think?"

"Yeah," said Wade, "he's been callin' my cell, too. I don't want to talk to him."

"OK, well... he sounded pretty upset," said Chandra. "He said it was an emergency."

"It always is," replied Wade.

Then, just to be conscientious, Chandra added, "He said to tell you that something happened to... Rose Rogers?"

Wade stopped breathing. At the sound of Rose's name and the mere suggestion that some harm might have befallen her, all of Creation suddenly became inconsequential to him.

In a hoarse voice that was barely audible, he asked, "Rose? *What's* happened to Rose?!"

"He didn't say," said Chandra, becoming more serious on account of Wade's reaction. "He just said you needed to call him."

"OK — bye!" said Wade, and he hung up and quickly dialed Paul. After three rings that seemed to last an eternity, Paul answered.

He had obviously checked his caller I.D., for his first word was, "Wade?"

"Where's Rose?!" Wade demanded.

"Listen, Wade," said Paul. "There's been an accident. Somebody left open the holding cells in the lab last night. The first people in the building this morning were... some people got hurt."

At that last word, Wade's fear became full-blown panic. In a voice that alarmed everyone within earshot, he shouted, *"WHERE'S ROSE?!"*

CHAPTER 17: NEW GROOVE

Five seconds later, Wade was running across the set with his hat on his head and his folded clothes under his arm. Actors, actresses, extras, crew — everyone stopped to watch as he raced on by.

His path to the parking lot took him right past Genevieve's personal beauty station where, at the moment, she was checking her lipstick in the mirror.

As Wade rushed towards her, she at first assumed it was to share some good news, or perhaps to tell her about something funny that had just happened. In a delighted voice, she called out, "Wade!"

But in the next millisecond, she perceived from his expression that something was seriously wrong. "Wade?" she asked, rising from her seat to intercept him.

All Wade wanted to do was to blow on by, to get to Rose and make sure she was all right. He was desperate, terrified, frantic...

And yet, in spite of all that, he knew he had to stop. As he did, Genevieve grabbed him by the shoulders.

"What's wrong?!" she asked.

Then she realized that he was wearing his cowboy hat. She looked down at the bundle of clothes under his arm, and her concern turned to dread.

With an ashen face, she asked, "Why do you have your clothes?"

Wade knew that for this one brief moment, he had no choice but to do the impossible. He had to wall off any and all thoughts of Rose — to pretend that she did not even exist — so that he could attend to what he absolutely could not avoid.

With superhuman effort, he forced his eyes to meet Genevieve's.

He didn't have to say a word.

"No..." gasped Genevieve. "You're not... you can't... you're not *leaving!*"

Of all people, Wade knew that Genevieve Parker had justly earned the title of 'diva'. He had no illusions about how vain she was — how arrogant, how spoiled...

And how empty.

For each and every morning when she awoke, she had to do what he was doing at this very moment. She had to wall off a torrent of overwhelming fear and desperation, and pretend that something she knew to be true was somehow not — namely, that her hopelessly shallow life had some deeper meaning.

Yes, Wade knew her faults all too well. But he also knew — with crystal clarity in this moment — that inside the most beautiful, most powerful woman in Hollywood was a little girl who didn't know who she was. And even though the whole world told her she was a goddess, the only voice she ever heard was the one inside her head telling her she was nothing.

"NO!" she screamed, and the set came to a standstill.

At once, Genevieve realized that everyone was staring at her — not adoringly, but aghast.

She was caught. Caught between her rage on the one hand and her need to appear invincible on the other. Wade could see the conflict in her eyes, and he knew that it was tearing her apart.

Ever so gently, he laid his hands on her arms. Then, in a soft voice full of genuine compassion, he said, "I know you won't believe me when I say I'm grateful to you, but with all my heart, I am. Not many people have stuck out their necks for me the way you have. You're a special woman, Genevieve. You deserve someone who can give you what I can't. I thought maybe I could, but I was wrong. And I'm so sorry."

Then, very tenderly, as if she was the only person in the world, he leaned forward and kissed her on the cheek. One last time, he looked in her tear-filled eyes... and then he left.

They say that when all you've got is a hammer, every problem looks like a nail. So it was that Genevieve pulled out the only tool she had — the one weapon that all her life she had relied upon to stave off shame, fear, loneliness, and confusion.

She called upon anger — faithful, comforting anger — and feeling as though she had already made a fool of herself, she saw no point in acting anymore.

"DON'T BE!" she screamed, and though half of Tinseltown heard her, Wade did not.

* * *

Some people find hospitals scary, but generally speaking, Wade was not among their number. His own past surgeries, of which there had been several, had all gone very smoothly. For him, hospitals had always been a place one went to get better, and from which one returned safely home.

But he was scared now.

The dripping tubes, the beeping monitors — all the medical equipment that surrounded Rose seemed thoroughly sinister, even though he knew it was for her good. Every click of the hallway intercom sounded to him like a gunshot, and he had to will his startle response into submission.

The doctors had pronounced Rose's condition to be stable, but given her appearance, Wade found that difficult to believe. She lay asleep on her right side, for her back was covered with deep lacerations that had required hundreds of stitches to sew shut.

She had lost a tremendous quantity of blood, but now that her body had been replenished, her prognosis was good. Other than embarrassment at the scars, her injuries would not result in long-term residual suffering.

Still dressed in the British officer's uniform, Wade sat on the edge of a wooden chair with his cowboy hat in his hands. As Rose breathed oxygen from a tube, he stared at her intently, as if by concentrating hard enough he could somehow speed up the healing process.

Just to Wade's left, Paul stood against the wall with crossed arms and a somber expression.

Poor Charlie Malloy had been pronounced dead at the scene. His only surviving relative, his mother, was quite old. Paul wondered how he was going to break the news without killing her, too.

At last Rose stirred. Wade hoped that she might be waking up, but after a tiny sigh, her body relaxed again, and she slept on.

For a man whose strongest emotion was his desire to protect the weak, her condition was overwhelming enough. But coupled with the fact that this was the woman who had won his heart almost at first sight, Wade was on the verge of coming undone.

Paul looked down at the floor, finding it too hard to see a grown man so distraught.

Except for the hospital noise leaking in through the half-open door, the room was quiet. Finally, not taking his eyes off Rose, Wade asked Paul, "You're sure it was Jules Krennick?"

Paul gave a sorrowful sigh and said, "Yes. He stayed late yesterday — all the cameras show that he was the last person to leave the building. Besides, only three people have the codes to unlock the holding cells: Me, Jules... and poor Charlie."

Wade digested the information and then asked, "So where do things stand?"

"We were able to tranquilize two of the 'brids," said Paul, "but the rest had to be shot — the ones that hadn't already been eaten. At least none of them got out of the building. The lab is trashed, and Jules uploaded some kind of virus to the computers that wiped out all of our data. And he left this..."

Paul held out a folded piece of paper. Wade took and opened it, and then read aloud a message typed all in capitals:

"ART CANNOT BE CONTAINED."

Below the text was a symbol like an Egyptian hieroglyph: eight circles, evenly spaced around a central one that served as a hub. Each of the outer eight was connected to the hub by a line, creating the overall impression of an eight-spoked wheel.

Inside the hub-circle was the symbol of a keyhole, and each of the surrounding circles contained a unique icon of its own: a feathered wing, a clawed foot, a fanged mouth...

But Wade was not able to study them all, for Rose had opened her eyes. She blinked a few times, and then Wade softly spoke her name.

"Rose?"

She turned her head towards the sound of his voice. Gradually, his face came into focus, and she recognized him.

It suddenly occurred to Wade that, after their last conversation, he was probably the last person in the world she wanted to see. But to his relief, the corners of her mouth turned up in a weak smile, and she sighed as though a great burden had just been lifted from her.

Gently clasping her tiny hand and with tears standing in his eyes, Wade said, "I never meant to hurt you, Rose. In the last few weeks, my whole life's been turned upside down. I haven't known what I'm about or who I'm supposed to be — let alone who I should be with. But I know now. And I'm just hopin' you can find it in your heart to give me a second chance, because more than anything in the world, I want to find out what you and I could be together."

Even in her weakened condition, Rose was still up for playing coy. Hearkening back to the corny joke Wade had told her at the ranch, she whispered, "Swear you ain't *'lion'?"*

Wade wanted to laugh and cry at the same time. Choking back his emotions, he said, "I swear."

For a long moment, Rose simply basked in the warmth of his affection. Then she looked over his uniform and asked, "So where's the rest of your regiment?"

Wade glanced down at the costume and said, "Oh... I guess I'm kind of AWOL. They'll just have to manage without me."

Rose smiled again and then said, "I had a rough mornin'."

"I can see that," replied Wade. "Thank God that new security guard had a gun."

Rose shook her head and whispered, "Not the guard. *Him.*"

"Him who?" asked Wade.

Rose tilted her head to the side and looked up at Paul.

Being a genuinely humble man, Paul was looking at his shoes. In telling Wade of Rose's rescue, he had neglected to name himself as her rescuer.

Wade was dumbstruck. As it happened, he didn't have to say anything, for just then a nurse entered with a snack on a tray.

Wade stood up, and Paul pulled away from the wall.

"Well, look who's having a party!" said the brassy, red-headed nurse. "Hello, gentlemen."

"Ma'am," said Wade and Paul in unison.

She squeezed her squat, amorphous body past the two of them to stand at Rose's head.

"And you, young lady," the nurse continued, "you're looking mighty spry for someone who's just been mauled by a mountain lion! I can't believe there's any still left up in those hills, but I guess they find a way to survive."

Rose kept silent, and Paul flashed Wade a quick glance. Wade returned a subtle nod to show that he had picked up on the cover story.

The nurse set the snack tray on the bedside table and said, "Well, boys, I need to give things a look-see, which means you'll have to step out of the room."

Wade nodded, and Paul said, "Of course."

Looking at Rose once more, Wade told her, "There's only you."

It was one of the happiest moments of her life so far, and everyone in the room could tell.

"OK, then," said Rose.

"OK, then," echoed Wade, and he stepped out into the hall a new man.

* * *

Wade and Paul stood facing each other outside Rose's door for a long, awkward moment. Finally, in a tone that showed he was both surprised and impressed, Wade asked, "You carry a gun?"

Paul gave a little laugh and replied, "Well... it was beginning to seem like a good idea."

What Wade had to say next couldn't be summed up in words. Even so, he couldn't say nothing.

"Paul, I... I can't thank you enough."

Immediately self-conscious, Paul held up a hand and dropped his eyes.

After letting the sentiment hang in the air for a few seconds, Wade followed it up with another, which was long overdue: "And... I'm sorry."

In expressing his repentance, Wade had shifted the focus of the conversation onto himself. Relieved to be out of the spotlight, Paul raised his head.

It takes a big man to stoop low, and Paul was not one for spite. To make it a little easier on Wade, he graciously replied, "You had a bad day. Anyone would've felt the same."

"Maybe so," said Wade. "But you didn't deserve that. And I apologize."

"Well..." said Paul, "I forgive you."

And he sincerely did. In that moment, a bond of true friendship was formed — one that would endure in spite of all the many trials that would soon follow.

Now that the business of first importance had been taken care of, Wade moved on.

"I want you to know," he told Paul, "that as soon as I get a spare second, I'm gonna give a call to my assistant, Chet — the one I drove away. And if he's interested, I'm gonna sign my business over to him."

Paul was stunned, and he stared at Wade with bug-eyes. Wade sighed pensively, as if the full weight of the decision had not hit him until he heard it from his own mouth.

But as he remembered his reasons, his resolve solidified like concrete. "Whoever did this to Rose has to be stopped," he said. "And I reckon that, in order to do that, you're gonna need your 'Number One'. What I'm sayin' is: As long as these monsters are out there, I'm all in."

Paul's expression was a mixture of relief, gratitude, and hope — the first he had felt in longer than he could remember. He said nothing, but nodded in silent acceptance of Wade's pledge.

Then, as if on cue, Paul's cell phone rang.

"Hello?" he answered. After a few seconds, he said, "You're *kidding!*"

He flashed Wade a look that spoke of disaster. After a few more seconds, he said into the phone, "OK, listen — I want you to send a truck down there right away with two field kits and an extra badge, got it? Call me if anything changes!"

He hung up and looked at Wade.

"Well?" asked Wade.

Paul shook his head and said, "You're not going to believe this."

* * *

They took Paul's car so that Wade could change back into his regular clothes on the way. He was only halfway through the process when Chandra called his cell phone in hysterics.

"Boss! What the heck is going on?!" she cried. "I've gotten a hundred calls in the last half-hour, and everyone in Hollywood wants your head! We're finished! You told me everything was going to be fine from now on, so I went and renewed the lease on my apartment, but now I'm going to have to pay a five-hundred-dollar early-termination fee *and* lose my security deposit! I don't know what you did, but this time you've *done* it, and what am I supposed to do?!"

"SHUT UP, CHANDRA!" Wade yelled. Then, having stunned her into silence, he tried to allay her fears as quickly as possible.

"I know this is gonna sound hard to believe," he said, "but I swear you're not gonna lose your job, and business is gonna go right on as usual!"

"How?!" cried Chandra.

"I can't explain right now, so you'll just have to trust me! Now listen good: my new truck's at the general hospital with the trailer hitched behind. I left the key under the mat, and you need to go get Ginger and bring 'er home. Then just sit tight at the office, and we'll pick up your car when I get back. And for heaven's sake, don't answer the phone for anybody but me! You got all that?"

"I... I think so," Chandra stammered.

"All right! I gotta go — bye!" said Wade, and he hung up.

Two minutes later, just as Wade was pulling on his boots, Paul turned onto the busy downtown street where, moments ago, their worst fears had been realized.

A huge crowd had gathered on the sidewalk to their right, and in the street just ahead, a policeman was trying to keep traffic moving.

A little further away, a second policeman stood at the entrance to an underground parking garage. With the help of a bullhorn, he was repeating a set of instructions to anyone and everyone inside.

"Attention!" he said. "This is the L.A.P.D. A big cat of some kind — a lion or a tiger — has escaped from captivity and is loose in the garage. Animal Control is on the way. So that we may resolve this matter quickly and safely, we ask that you remain in your vehicles with your engines off. Please DO NOT DRIVE, as this may startle the cat and cause it to run out into the street."

Then he began the message all over again.

As Paul pulled over to the curb, he asked Wade, "Where are our guys?"

Looking around, Wade said, "Don't see 'em."

"Great!" said Paul, and they both hopped out of the car.

Their one lucky break in the entire affair was that the citizens of Los Angeles were all well armed — not with guns, but with cell phones capable of taking high-resolution pictures and video.

On the sidewalk, people had gathered in clusters around those individuals who had been quick enough on the draw to capture still or moving images of the unbelievable event that had just transpired.

Every second or two, a cry of shock and amazement would go up from one of the clusters. Wade and Paul joined the group that seemed the loudest, which happened to be huddled around the phone of a young businessman in a navy-blue suit.

"Where did it come from?" asked a slender young woman wrapped in multi-colored scarves.

The businessman was more than happy to recount the tale. "This moving van was stopped at the light," he said, "and then suddenly the back doors flew open and the thing just jumped out! The van took off, and then the thing started running around in the middle of traffic!"

"Play it again!" shouted a boy with a skateboard, pointing to the cell phone.

"Hang on, hang on!" said the businessman. He cued the video to replay from the beginning and then said, "OK — here we go!"

All attention was now fixed on the tiny phone screen, and the group held its collective breath...

The amateur video opened with a view of the street as seen from the sidewalk. A line of cars was backed up at a red light, but aside from an excessive amount of honking, nothing appeared to be out of the ordinary.

Then, suddenly, a creature leaped into view from behind a mid-sized sedan and landed on its roof...

The phone-watching audience gasped in astonishment — all except for Wade and Paul, who silently scrutinized the image for every possible detail...

As the video played on, the beast crouched down on all fours atop the sedan. Frightened and confused, it gnashed its teeth and twitched its tail.

Even from forty feet away, the phone-cam footage plainly showed that this was no ordinary animal, but something profoundly unnatural.

Wade's initial assessment was that the hybrid was not much larger than his cougar, Dolly. It was covered with short, tawny hair, except for its neck and shoulders, which were shrouded in dark, shaggy fur.

Its movements struck Wade as being distinctly feline, yet at the same time ungainly. Malformed and emaciated, the creature seemed almost to be a prisoner in its own skin — not unlike the tiger-lizard that Paul had shot dead just hours before.

Then, before Wade could analyze the video image any further, the 'brid jumped to the ground and disappeared in traffic.

On the recording, the businessman's voice kept asking, "What the heck is that? What *is* that thing?!" Then the picture got shaky for a few seconds before becoming altogether scrambled.

"This is where I tripped," the businessman explained to his audience. Then quickly, he added, "There's more..."

When the picture stabilized, the perspective had changed. The phone-cam was no longer aimed across the street, but down it.

On the left side of the screen was a line of cars extending to the horizon. On the right was the sidewalk, filled with people looking anxiously about.

Without warning, the 'brid shot out from amongst the cars and skidded to a halt on the sidewalk.

The businessman was braver than the other pedestrians, for as they cried out in terror and ran for their lives, he continued to take video. Despite being repeatedly bumped, for the space of a few critical seconds, he was able to hold the camera steady.

The video showed the beast crouching on the sidewalk and snarling this way and that. Then, from somewhere off-screen, the siren of a police cruiser blared to life, giving the animal a sudden start.

Its surprise quickly turned to anger, and jutting its chin forward, it let loose a mighty roar that touched off a new round of screams all up and down the street.

After expressing its extreme annoyance, the creature bolted down the sidewalk, away from the phone-cam. Upon reaching the entrance to the underground parking garage, the beast darted under the gate and disappeared into the darkness.

Thus ended the video.

"That's all there is!" pronounced the businessman.

"Play it again!" demanded the boy with the skateboard. While the businessman cued the video back to the beginning, spontaneous commentary filled the gap.

"What *was* that thing?"

"Looked like a lion or something!"

"That wasn't a lion — haven't you ever been to the zoo?"

"It was some kind of monster — like out of a movie!"

As the debate continued, Wade and Paul withdrew from the group. Just then, the white delivery-style truck from the Genetic Anomalies Task Center pulled up behind Paul's car.

"Here they are!" said Paul, and he and Wade hurried on over.

The cab doors opened and out jumped tall Kent and squat Irving, from Research.

"Kent, Irving," Paul greeted them.

"Got here as fast as we could, sir!" said Irving, who had done the driving. "Things are still pretty chaotic at the office!" As soon as he noticed Wade, he asked quizzically, "Mr. Boss?"

"He's back on board," explained Paul.

On a day of almost exclusively bad news, this came as a major encouragement, and Kent and Irving exchanged a glance as if to say, "All *right!*"

The four men walked quickly around to the back of the truck, where tall Kent opened the doors and yanked two field kits to the edge of the bay. He stood aside, and then Wade stepped forward and opened one of the silver cases.

He had to smile in spite of himself, for the gleaming *FLEXCALIBER* seemed to him like an old friend. With a chuckle, he pulled out the gun belt and strapped it on.

To his left, his movements were mirrored by Paul, who had

requested the second field kit for himself. Though less practiced than Wade, he seemed reasonably familiar with the gear.

Wade was moved by his bravery, but even so, he said, "Paul — you don't have to do this."

With grim determination in his eyes, Paul replied, "We just lost Charlie, and darn near lost Rose, too. If somebody else has to die today, I'd prefer it be me."

Wade marveled to himself that you just can't tell what's inside a man until the chips are down.

Then, to keep the mood from getting too serious, Paul poked himself in the chest and said, "Besides which — *I'm* the boss!"

"Yes, sir," replied Wade, with a grin.

Then they were all business.

After stuffing two backup barrels into the thigh pockets of his gun belt, Paul drew his *FLEXCALIBER*.

"What do you guess?" he asked Wade. "About a hundred and fifty pounds?"

"Sounds about right," answered Wade, and they both took a moment to adjust the thumb-sliders on their TRANQ darts.

As he re-holstered his gun, Paul turned to Irving and said, "Badge?"

"Yes!" replied Irving. He dug into his pocket and pulled out a silver, palm-sized badge featuring the Task Center seal. He handed it to Paul, who then passed it on to Wade.

Paul pulled his own badge from his pocket, and then without another word, the two brothers in arms headed for the parking garage.

The policeman with the bullhorn was a broad-shouldered gentleman in his early forties, who had made a lifelong commitment to the principle that "bald-is-beautiful." At present, he was fairly sure that the message he had been repeating over and over at the garage would be revisiting him in his dreams that night.

He was just about to reprise the announcement yet again, when he was suddenly alarmed to see a pair of gunslingers headed right for him. His hand was halfway to his own gun when Paul and Wade held up their badges.

"It's all right, Officer!" called Paul. "We're federal agents."

"Federal agents?" asked the officer.

"That's right," said Paul. "We're here to apprehend the animal that's loose in that garage."

Once they were close enough to speak in a conversational tone, Wade and Paul stopped. Wade kept his badge held aloft, and the officer squinted to read the fine letters. "Genetic *what?*" he asked.

"We're a division of Homeland Security," explained Paul.

The officer seemed unconvinced. Shaking his head, he asked, "Why would Homeland Security be concerned about an *animal?*"

"Listen," Wade cut in, "how many ways are there in and out of this garage?" He spoke like a man who knew what he was about, and though the officer was still perplexed, he recognized the ring of authority when he heard it.

"For cars?" asked the officer. "There's this entrance here and one over on the other side."

"Is that one blocked off?" asked Wade.

"Yeah," said the officer, "but there's gotta be a dozen staircases and elevators all leading up into the building. Help's on the way, but there's a bad pile-up on the 405. Half the cruisers in the area are tied up, so right now there's just a few of us, plus Mall Security..."

"Mall?" interrupted Wade.

"Yeah," said the officer, "that's what's inside: a shopping mall. Anyway, we can't really lock things down, but hopefully between the P.A. system inside and me on this bullhorn out here, anyone within earshot will keep out."

Nodding at the garage, Paul asked, "You have men in there right now?"

"Two," answered the officer. "They're trying to find the thing and corner it, but if there's any chance it might get out, they've got orders to shoot."

"Thank you, Officer," said Wade, and he boldly walked on past.

Paul wasn't used to being so assertive, and it took him a second to realize that the conversation was over. Once he did, he repeated, "Thank you, Officer!" and hurried to catch up to Wade.

Still not sure what to make of the agents with the jumbo sidearms, the officer drew his radio and called his fellows inside the garage.

"Jansen! Fiedler!" he said. "You've got two feds in plain-clothes coming in to help."

Then, clipping the radio back onto his belt, he raised the bullhorn to his lips and continued to broadcast the official police instructions.

* * *

Even though four men had been assigned to the White Mountains mission, the capture of the rhino-bear had for all intents and purposes wound up a solo affair. And although being a "Lone Ranger" held a certain appeal for Wade, today he had no objections to working with a partner.

He knew that if hybrids continued to appear in heavily populated areas, hunting them down would henceforth be a team sport. But provided that his teammates were all as courageous as Paul, he thought that wouldn't necessarily be a bad thing.

The gate attendant had long since left his post, and no one was to be seen walking about inside the parking garage. Apart from the reverberating voice of Officer Bullhorn, all was quiet.

"You see those two cops anywhere?" asked Wade.

"No," said Paul. "They must be way down — this place is huge."

Indeed it was, despite being only one level. Not only was it vast, but it was also packed with cars, which, in addition to a forest of concrete support columns, made it impossible to see very far.

They had entered the garage at one corner, and on their right was a solid wall extending for hundreds of feet. To their left, the vehicles were parked in rows, and a through-lane zig-zagged between them all the way to the far side.

"OK — I may be the boss," said Paul, "but you're the man. Tell me how we should do this."

"Well," began Wade, "I expect it's prob'ly scared to death and hunkered down behind one of these cars. I don't figure there's anything else to do except take it slow, one row at a time."

"Right," said Paul.

Seeing that the lighting conditions deteriorated the further one got from the entrance, Wade turned on both the flashlight and laser sight of his *FLEXCALIBER*. Paul followed his example, and then they approached the cars.

Wade took the first row to the right and Paul took the first on the left, such that they were back-to-back across the empty through-lane. Without any formal signal, they commenced their search.

What they did not know was that, just a few rows away, a green mini-van was abuzz with activity...

Molly Paulson, mother of five, could feel the onset of a migraine as her three boys and two girls competed for her attention.

"I bet it's a lion!" said Matthew, her eleven-year-old son. "Mom, do you think a lion could break through these windows?"

Nine-year-old Christie, the whiner of the bunch, called out, "Mommy, I just dropped my earring, and I can't find it..."

Soccer star Andrew, age eight, declared, "If we don't leave now, we're gonna miss my game!"

Rachel, who at seven years old still could not sleep with the lights off, fretfully asked, "Mommy? Do lions eat people?"

And last of all, fuzzy-headed Danny of only five tender years announced, "Mommy, I have to go to the bathroom really bad!"

Molly put her fingers to her temples and performed the stress-management technique she had seen on T.V. that morning: "You're on the beach, the sand is warm, the water is blue... You're on the beach, the sand is warm, the water is blue..."

.She repeated this to herself many times, but in spite of a commendable effort, her temper was beginning to boil.

Meanwhile, Wade and Paul made slow progress. The fluorescent ceiling lights did little to illuminate the spaces between and under the cars, which significantly increased the danger of a surprise attack.

Furthermore, Wade was not willing to endanger his less experienced friend by getting too far ahead of him, and so they progressed together at rookie-speed.

As Wade passed behind a red Jetta with a bumper held on by duct tape, the newly-licensed teenager behind the wheel rolled down his window. "Hey, Mister!" he said in a loud whisper. "When can I get out of here?"

"Workin' on it!" Wade whispered back, irritably.

"Well, could you hurry it up?" the teenager asked impatiently. "I got things to do!"

Wade flashed him an angry glare, and the teenager gulped and closed his window.

Soon the two partners reached the end of the row, which was at the southeast corner of the garage. Here the only means of entrance or exit were two elevators, which of course were useless to an animal.

Wade looked at Paul, who returned a subtle nod to show that he was ready to continue. They then followed the through-lane around the bend.

Meanwhile, over in the mini-van, Molly struggled to suppress her anger. She had made some important growth-steps over the previous few weeks, having technically yelled on only two occasions. But unless she got some relief soon, the tally would go up to three.

"Mom," said Matthew, "do you think it escaped from the zoo? Or do you think it was somebody's pet?"

"Mommy," whined Christie, "I found the earring, but it's broken!"

"Come on, Mom!" shouted Andrew. "The coach promised I could play center today!"

Rachel, on the verge of tears, said, "Mommy, I'm scared — are you scared?"

Then, above them all, little Danny cried, "I have to go *potty!*"

Two days before, Danny had mortified his mother in the grocery store with a spontaneous, pant-soaking bladder release, and the last thing she needed now was a booster seat that reeked of urine.

Taking a deep breath, she told him, "Danny, you're just going to have to hold it."

"I can't!" protested Danny, straining his seatbelt to its test limit with a Category 5 potty-dance.

Molly looked around for anything that might be able to catch pee. Grabbing an old milkshake cup, she pulled off the lid and handed it back.

"Here!" she said. "Go in this!"

"No!" cried Danny. "I have to go *poop!*"

"Honey, you'll just have to..."

"I have to go poop NOW!" Danny hollered, and there was no arguing the point.

"ALL RIGHT!" yelled Molly, and the mini-van fell silent. "EVERYBODY BUCKLE!"

It was Molly's practice to back into parking spaces, because with five children, she was always having to dash off to her next destination. Consequently, as she turned on the ignition and the mini-van's automatic headlights blazed forth, she had an unobstructed view of the parking space across the through-lane.

As it happened, the space was empty — or more accurately, it was not occupied by a car.

The rogue hybrid had been creeping stealthily through the semi-darkness, and had chosen just the wrong moment to pass by the mini-van. Caught in mid-stride and now literally in the spotlight, it arched its back and glared over at Molly.

"AAAAAAHHHHHH!" screamed Molly.

"GRRRRRRRRRRRR!" growled the beast.

"AAAAAAHHHHHH!" screamed the five children, in high-fidelity surround-sound.

The cries reached Wade and Paul, who were still several rows away. Thanks to its shining headlights, the mini-van was easy to find.

The 'brid shot off in the direction of the southeast corner, cutting across the zigs and zags of the through-lane and hurdling the vehicles in its path.

"There!" yelled Wade. Paul caught sight of it too, and they engaged pursuit.

Wade now saw that his suspicions were correct: the animal was definitely part lion — though running up and over the cars, it reminded him more of a dolphin jumping waves in the ocean.

"The elevators!" he cried. "Corner it!"

Paul hadn't run so hard since high school, but even though his chest was heaving, he could not help exclaiming, "Man, it's *fast!*"

When it reached the southeast corner, the lion-'brid was confronted with the closed doors of the two elevators. With no open route of escape, it whipped around to defend itself...

Between the bullhorn outside and the mall P.A. system inside, the parking garage had by now been effectively quarantined. The decree that it was off-limits, resounding from within and without, was simply impossible to miss.

That is, unless you were deaf, as college sophomore Seth Cranston had been since birth.

Now a strapping young man of nineteen, Seth had gone to the mall to do a bit of shopping with the birthday money his parents had sent him in the mail. When he was finally through making his purchases, he found himself at the northwest corner of the mall.

Since he had left his bike chained to a rack down in the parking garage at the southeast corner, he consolidated his goods into one bag and began the long trek back.

Rather than waste the minutes by simply walking, he pulled out his phone to do a little multitasking on the way.

In anticipation of his upcoming political science class, he looked up a lecture on YouTube that his professor had told him about — a lecture delivered all in sign language. He began watching it right away, relying upon his peripheral vision to navigate as he walked.

When he finally arrived at the southeast corner elevators on the first floor of the mall, Seth was too engrossed in the lecture to give any thought to the dozens of other shoppers who were aimlessly milling about.

Those shoppers were, of course, anxiously awaiting some kind of announcement that the animal in the garage had been captured, and that they could finally return to their cars. Since most of them were busy griping, they hardly noticed when Seth boarded the right-hand elevator.

When he pressed the button for the garage level, the other shoppers finally realized what he was doing and called out for him to stop. But only after the doors had closed did they understand that he could not hear them.

Down below, Wade and Paul were converging on the lion-'brid, when, to their horror, the doors of the right-hand elevator opened with a "ding."

The lion-'brid spun around to face the sound.

"NO! NO!" cried Paul.

"LOOK OUT!" shouted Wade.

Seth took two steps into the garage and then perceived that there was an obstacle in his path. He looked up expecting to see a fellow mall patron. What he got instead was the shock of his life.

All at once he screamed, dropped his phone and shopping bag, covered his face with his arms, and shrank into a defensive posture.

In the next instant, the lion-'brid leapt over him and sailed through the open doors of the elevator car.

Wade temporarily lost sight of the beast, since he was approaching the elevator at an oblique angle. Paul was coming at it more directly and would have had a decent shot, except that Seth was in his line of fire.

"Get out of the way!" Paul yelled.

As if the hideous monster was not startling enough, Seth now saw that he was being descended upon by two men with space-blasters. Then, when the red dot of a laser sight started dancing on his chest, he threw his hands up into the air.

Wade reached the right-hand elevator just after the doors closed shut. In the next instant, the situation went from bad to catastrophic as the green arrow above the doors lit up, announcing that the elevator was in motion.

"Somebody called it back up!" yelled Wade, and he punched the button for the left-hand elevator. Mercifully, its car was already on the garage level, and the doors immediately sprang open.

Wade rushed inside and was joined a second later by a huffing, puffing Paul. Turning to face outward, the two men saw Seth staring at them with wild eyes, his hands still raised.

"Are you crazy?!" Wade shouted at him.

Seth, who was adept at reading lips, simultaneously signed and gave utterance as best he could: "I'M DEAF, STUPID!"

Feeling like a fool and not believing his bad luck, Wade simply hung his head. Then the doors closed, and the elevator began its ascent.

In between gasps, Paul asked, "A shopping mall?"

"Yep," said Wade.

Over the hum of the elevator, they detected a new sound that quickly grew louder as their altitude increased.

"You hear that?" asked Paul.

"Yep," said Wade again, thinking to himself that screams of terror were apparently going to be the soundtrack to his new life.

CHAPTER 19: THE UNTHINKABLE

As the elevator doors opened, two things happened at once.

First, the decibel level of the screaming increased tenfold. Second, Wade and Paul were knocked backwards by a wave of frantic humanity.

The elevator had only been designed to accommodate fifteen people, but within seconds, it was packed to nearly twice its legal capacity.

The lion-'brid, of course, was to blame. At the conclusion of its own brief ride, the doors of its elevator had opened automatically onto the first floor of the mall. Those same shoppers who had failed to stop young Seth got one look at the beast and then ran for their lives.

Excited by the delicious smells wafting down from the second-floor food court, the famished lion-'brid had followed its nose. As it went, it created mass hysteria, as well as a general consensus among the shoppers to exit the mall — *fast*.

As soon as the creature took off for the food court, the southeast elevators were again seen as an expedient means of escape — hence the stampede that slammed into Wade and Paul when the doors of the left-hand elevator opened.

"Let us out! Outta the way!" yelled Wade.

"Move! Let us through!" shouted Paul.

Realizing that they could not muscle their way through, Wade called out, "Paul! Drop down! Down!"

With some difficulty, the two of them wriggled down below belly-level and onto the floor where there was less flesh to contend with.

As Paul relied upon his arm strength to pull his way through the forest of legs, Wade adopted the more efficient method of pushing off the back wall with his feet. By keeping his hands close together, he was able to separate the legs as a wedge splits a log.

Being packed in like sardines, the evacuees did not topple over as their legs were swept out from under them. But even though they were held upright by the jiggling bodies of their neighbors, the alarming sensation inspired a number of exclamations:

"Hey! Who's knocking me over?!"

"Help! It's got my leg!"

"What's going on down there?!"

And so on.

After pushing off the rear wall to the fullest extent, Wade was stretched out on the floor in a diving position. He continued to crawl forward until at last his hands were almost out the elevator doors.

Which were closing.

Thrusting his right arm forward, Wade managed to get the muzzle of his *FLEXCALIBER* across the threshold so that it stuck out into the mall. The sliding doors closed upon the gun, which in turn triggered the safety mechanism. Immediately, the doors sprang open, touching off another round of outbursts:

"Who opened the doors?!"

"It's some psycho on the floor!"

"Knock it off, fool, before I step on your head!"

And so forth.

While Wade and Paul wormed and squirmed, a smallish man dressed all in tweed kept zealously pressing the button to close the doors. By the time they responded, Wade's right arm was completely out into the mall.

His head, however, was only halfway out. As the doors came together, one smacked against his right shoulder while the other rammed him in the face. Yet again, they sprang open, and the reaction from the evacuees was instantaneous.

Acting as one, they began kicking at Wade and Paul. Those who were too squished to kick made effective use of their knees. The unanimous opinion seemed to be that the work was best facilitated by a steady stream of expletives.

When at last Wade had dragged his bruised body out onto the cold, hard tile of the mall, a cry of relief went up — but only from half of the group.

Since no one could actually see below belt level, everyone had just assumed that there was a single, insane individual crawling around, who for reasons unknown was hellbent on getting out of the elevator.

But as Paul continued to struggle, it became apparent to the passengers that there was a *second* lunatic on the floor with the same agenda as the first. At this realization, they went absolutely nuts.

"WHO'S DOWN THERE NOW?!"

"YOU MEAN THERE'S *ANOTHER* ONE?!"

"KICK HIM OUT! KICK HIM OUT!"

Any brutality the mob might have been holding in reserve, it now unleashed, and things might have ended very differently for Paul had Wade not been able to grab his wrists and pull him to safety.

For the third time, the doors came together and, at long last, closed completely shut. As the elevator descended to the garage, a muffled, quickly-fading cheer assured Wade and Paul that they would not be missed.

Wade was somewhat worse for the wear, and would have benefited from a few ice packs and some aspirin. Paul, however, looked more like he had just fallen down three flights of cement stairs.

Blood trickled down in distinct streams from the top of his head, his left eyebrow, and his lower lip. The injuries were nothing compared to Rose's, however, and today of all days, Paul wouldn't have dreamt of complaining.

The mall consisted of two levels and was hundreds of yards long. The main walking area between the stores was open all the way up to a ceiling of glass skylights, and from the second level, one could peer over a bannister to see the ground floor.

Rock-walled gardens were spaced at regular intervals of about thirty yards. Some of these encompassed miniature waterfalls, while others featured palm trees that reached nearly up to the skylights.

Like a big neon arrow, the cries of terror told Wade exactly where to look for the lion-'brid. In a matter of seconds he spotted it, a hundred yards off and heading up to the second level by way of an escalator.

The unlucky passengers who could not race to the top fast enough cleared a path for the animal by jumping overboard, suffering a hard landing on the floor below.

"Escalator!" yelled Wade, and the chase was back on.

As he watched the lion-'brid progress up the moving stairs, he was struck by something that had eluded him since viewing the business man's phone-cam video, out on the sidewalk.

Arriving at a hyphenated classification for this particular hybrid was proving to be rather a challenge. Clearly it was half lion, as evidenced by its mane and overall body mechanics. But as for the other half, it was harder to say.

But now, all at once, everything clicked. Even from a distance, its telltale scamper up the escalator proclaimed the truth — so loudly that Wade felt stupid for not having figured it out sooner.

Chimpanzee. The lion-'brid's other half was chimpanzee.

When Wade was a boy, one of the privileges he had enjoyed as the tiger-trainer's kid was having special access to the other circus animals. Of these, his favorite by far was Willy the Chimp, whom he had regarded almost as another boy.

Willy epitomized the popular image of the chimpanzee, being cute, hilarious, and affectionate. But from Willy's trainer, Wade had learned that there was a dark side to the species as well.

Chimps are not generally thought of as being dangerous, but in fact they are capable of shocking savagery. Willy's trainer had recounted to Wade more than one story of a chimp that had turned on its owner, and the details were always gruesome.

The favored fighting technique of the chimpanzee is the bite. Those who have found themselves victims of a chimp's wrath have lost fingers, hands, noses, ears, eyes, and even life itself.

As a boy, Wade could never quite believe that Willy was capable of such malevolence. But as a man, he knew that *any* tamed animal could unexpectedly snap and revert to its jungle nature.

Oh, yes — chimps were dangerous.

And smart.

Willy had been able to read and sign dozens of words. Heck, for all Wade knew, the lion-chimp could have pressed the up-button in the elevator all by itself.

By the time Wade and Paul reached the stairs of the escalator, they had lost sight of their quarry. But as they ran up to the mall's second level, a mass exodus from the food court put them back on track.

After a free-for-all of jumping, falling, shoving, and running, the court was empty of people. Wade and Paul arrived to find what looked like the aftermath of the biggest food-fight in history. And though they could not see the lion-chimp, they knew it was close.

The court dining area was proportionate to a football field, with fast food vendors on either side and a carousel at the far end.

"Must be behind one of the counters," said Wade, in a low voice. Paul nodded, and they split up as they had done in the parking garage: Wade to the right, Paul to the left.

Even the burger-flippers had wasted no time in clearing out, and

Wade could smell the abandoned beef patties already overcooking on the grills. He only hoped a grease fire would not break out.

Scuttling forward in a half-squat and peering over one order counter after another quickly took a toll on Wade's knees. He was just about to sit on the floor to stretch out his legs when his acute hearing told him that the creature was just ahead.

Finding the aroma of assorted cold cuts to be especially enticing, the lion-chimp had leapt behind the counter of the sub shop, where it proceeded to gorge itself.

From its noisy chewing and satisfied grunting, Wade calculated that the 'brid was crouched down where the sandwich-makers would normally stand. Now sure of its location, he knelt down at the payment end of the counter and waved at Paul until he got his attention.

As soon as Paul saw that he was being flagged, he embarked upon the perilous journey across the court. Wending his way between overturned chairs and tables, he stepped over slippery piles of spilled food as if they were booby-traps.

He had nearly completed the crossing when a Philly cheese-steak finally got him. As the edge of his shoe came down on it, he found himself suddenly dropping into a split.

With a move that sent his inner thighs into spasm, he managed to raise and then re-plant his foot, but only after the sole of his shoe made a loud SQUEAK on the tile floor. He froze, clenching his jaw and shaking his head at his own ineptitude.

The eating-noises from behind the counter suddenly stopped. Wade held up a finger for Paul to remain still and then listened hard for about fifteen seconds. When he heard nothing, he realized that the lion-chimp had detected their presence.

Paul was understandably demoralized, but since the mistake could not be unmade, Wade's priority was to get his friend's head back in the game.

Adopting an unbothered expression, Wade held up a hand as if to say, "No big deal." Then he gestured for Paul to continue the rest of the way.

With the utmost care, Paul completed the crossing and knelt down at the order-placing end of the counter. He closed his eyes, refocused his mind, and then looked up at Wade to show that he was ready.

Wade nodded and then silently mouthed the words, *"On three. One... two... three!"*

Like mirror images of each other, the two men stood up and swung their weapons around the sneeze-shield.

But even with the advantage of the opening move, they could not outmatch the lion-chimp's lightning reflexes. As luck would have it, Paul took the hit.

With the force of a locomotive, the lion-chimp slammed into his chest, knocking him all the way out into the dining area and landing on top of him.

Paul's gun went flying, leaving him no defense other than to grab two handfuls of shaggy mane and push against the beast with all his might.

"PAUL!" cried Wade. He could not very well shoot, since the tranquilizer dart was just as likely to strike his friend as the lion-chimp. Besides which, even in the five seconds that it would take for the serum to work, the 'brid could easily tear out Paul's throat.

Without any thought for himself, Wade jumped over the chairs in his path, tucked his chin against his left shoulder, and hit the lion-chimp with a flying tackle.

Since it still had a tight grip on Paul, the three of them went rolling until they ended up in a pile with Paul on the bottom, the 'brid in the middle, and Wade on top.

Finding himself in a piggy-back position, Wade swung his right arm around the lion-chimp's neck and put it in a rear-choke.

It let go of Paul, but Wade soon discovered that strangling the beast was an impossible proposition, for its neck was far thicker and stronger than a man's. By the time Wade realized his mistake, there was nothing for him to do but hold on for dear life.

The lion-chimp began jumping and twisting like a crazed bucking bronco. In its frenzy, it slammed Wade so hard against an overturned table that he lost his grip and slid to the floor.

The instant it was free, the beast took off. Paul by now had recovered his wits, and had salvaged his gun from a pile of Chinese noodles. He took a wild shot at the fleeing 'brid, but the tranquilizer dart merely ricocheted off a metal chair.

Realizing that a second shot was pointless, Paul ran over to his fallen partner. Wade was still reeling from his collision with the table, but nonetheless, he sat up shouting, "Gun! My gun!"

After a few seconds of searching, Paul fished the weapon out of a bowl of chili. Giving it a quick wipe on his shirt, he tossed it to Wade.

The two of them raced back out to the shopping area, hardly believing their eyes as the lion-chimp jumped up onto the bannister and leaped into thin air.

But instead of falling to the ground floor with a splat, the 'brid landed neatly in the top of a two-story palm tree. After a bit of wild oscillation, the tree stabilized and the lion-chimp clambered down, head-first.

Wade reached the bannister before Paul, and leaned over it just in time to see the animal disappear into a camping supply store below.

Since he couldn't pull off the death-defying leap to the palm tree, he sprinted over to the escalator and bounded down the stairs, taking them three at a time.

Once he arrived at the store's entrance, he stopped to wait for Paul, who joined him a few seconds later, completely out of breath.

"You OK?" asked Wade. Paul was too winded to make a verbal response, but he gave a nod.

Then they heard a new sound: voices, coming at them from behind, from the other end of the mall. It was the police, storming the building with weapons drawn.

"We'd better finish this fast," said Wade.

Paul nodded again. Then, half-wheezing, he said, "Wade! Thanks... for saving my life!"

"I owed you," Wade replied with a smile, and then they rushed into the camping store.

At once, they were dismayed.

They found themselves in less of a store than a self-contained universe of outdoor recreational equipment.

Every imaginable type of gear was on display: tents, sleeping bags, skis, canoes, fishing rods, guns, bows, arrows, water bottles, etc. In addition to the merchandise, fake boulders and trees were everywhere, some of which contained hidden speakers that filled the air with recorded forest sounds.

But what posed the greatest problem to Wade and Paul was the wildlife.

Bears, cougars, wolves, coyotes, badgers, beavers, ferrets, owls, eagles — all creatures great and small were peeking out from behind clothing racks, climbing up the walls, and even hanging from the ceiling.

In a magnificent exhibition of taxidermy, the store featured a full spectrum of North American animals, all stuffed and posed so that customers could enjoy an immersive wilderness experience free of mosquitos and never more than ten paces away from a sanitized bathroom.

All the lion-chimp had to do to keep from being discovered was remain still.

"Great," said Wade, under his breath. Not knowing where to begin, he pointed Paul towards a section of camouflage outerwear, while he himself ventured into a collection of display tents.

In his immediate field of view were a moose, a black bear, a family of foxes, and a twelve-point buck. He had the distinct feeling that at any moment the whole lot might suddenly come to life and descend upon him.

It was not ten seconds before Paul signaled to him and pointed to a spot deeper in the store. Wade looked and saw a pyramid of ice coolers stacked three high in the middle. He nodded to Paul, and they quickly converged on the spot.

Wade was a mere five feet away when he saw the dark, shaggy mane rise above the tops of the coolers.

He leveled his gun, but held his fire until he could be sure that he was aiming at flesh, and not just hair. As it turned out, the opportunity passed, for the mane sank back down just as slowly as it had risen.

Wade's heart was beating double-time. He looked at Paul and once again mouthed the words, *"One... two... three!"*

In perfect sync, they swung around the pyramid from opposite sides and opened fire. Both of them scored direct hits and then jumped back to escape swift retaliation.

But instead of lashing back at them, the lion-chimp remained where it was — utterly unperturbed by the two hypodermic needles that had just pierced its hide.

Wade was just about to pull the trigger for a second time when he realized what he was looking at.

It was not the lion-chimp at all, but only an ordinary lion, a bit larger than his own Roland. And though its mouth was stretched wide, the king of beasts remained silent and still — all except for its head, which bobbed up and down in a slow, mechanical rhythm.

Then Wade looked *behind* the lion, and the mystery was explained. Hanging from the front of the cooler-pyramid was a banner with a picture of the African Savannah, at sunset. Across the top of the banner in big yellow letters were the words: "WIN AN AFRICAN SAFARI FOR TWO!"

What had at first appeared to be the lion-chimp was in fact an animatronic lion, put on display to advertise a sweepstakes being sponsored by the cooler manufacturer. Wade and Paul looked at each other in disbelief.

FOOM!

One of the stuffed animals over by the cross-country skis suddenly proved to be not-so-stuffed, and bolted from its place.

Wade was quicker to recuperate from the shock than Paul. In a mad scramble to acquire his speeding target, he knocked over camping stoves, kayaks, collapsible chairs, and everything else in his way.

The chase led him to the very heart of the store, which was a vast atrium constructed around a towering artificial mountain. From its peak, a crystal waterfall cascaded down to an emerald pool stocked with live fish.

Fine examples of taxidermy had been set upon the numerous ledges, but the only animal that interested Wade was the one scaling up the rock face by leaps and bounds.

The prospect of hitting the lion-chimp with a dart was poor at best. But as Wade's boots skidded up against the knee-high rock wall that encircled the fish pool, he had a flash of inspiration.

Fingers flying, he ejected the barrel that was attached to his *FLEXCALIBER* and replaced it with one of his two backups.

The lion-chimp was nearly at the mountain's summit when the

tiny red dot of the laser sight appeared between its shoulder blades. Wade pulled the trigger, and then the next several seconds unfolded as though predestined.

Out of the gun shot forth a net, which expanded in flight and unfurled to a diameter of seven feet before engulfing the lion-chimp.

The 'brid lost its footing, fell backwards, and plummeted to the pool below, landing with a splash that left Wade half-soaked.

To Wade's relief, he saw that he had guessed correctly, and that the shallow water had been just deep enough to protect the creature from serious injury. Wet and tangled but still very much alive, it floundered about, gnashing its teeth in helpless rage.

Paul finally arrived at Wade's side, and for a moment, the two of them watched the pathetic struggle in silence.

The grappling match in the food court had confirmed for Wade that the lion-chimp weighed just about a hundred and fifty pounds. The NET barrel contained the single tranquilizer dart he would need, and he adjusted the thumb-slider to set the dosage.

Stepping up onto the knee-high wall of the pool, Wade stared down at the 'brid.

As it cast about in the water, it slowly worked its way to the base of the mountain and up onto a pebbly strip of simulated beach. There, just to the right of the waterfall, it leaned against the artificial rock to keep from falling over.

With crooked, hand-like paws it pulled at the net, groaning in misery all the while. Although Wade was relieved to be able to draw the crisis to a close, now that he had prevailed, his characteristic pity welled up inside him.

It was with a heavy sigh that he raised his gun. Training the laser dot on the animal's left quadricep, he applied gradual pressure to the trigger.

Suddenly, the captive beast pulled itself erect. Then, looking Wade straight in the eyes, in a voice full of despair and anguish, it said, *"LEAVE ME ALONE!"*

Time stood still as Wade and Paul stared at the creature, stupefied. What they had just seen — or rather heard — had no place within the framework of their reality.

But as the hybrid redoubled its efforts to tear free of the net, Wade began to perceive the truth.

He had been wrong. Since watching it clamber up the escalator, he had assumed that the 'brid's primate features and mannerisms must be simian. He had not even considered the possibility that they might be sapien.

Homo sapien.

The elusive second half of the lion-chimp's dual-identity was not chimp.

It was man.

A loud clatter of shoes announced that the police were entering the store. Robotically, Wade pulled the trigger the rest of the way.

The tranquilizer dart sailed straight and true. Five seconds later, the impossible anomaly collapsed beside the waterfall and slipped into unconsciousness.

CHAPTER 20: GAME ON

Wade walked beside Kent and Irving as they wheeled a loaded gurney out of the parking garage.

On their way to the white Task Center truck, they passed scores of on-lookers and several news crews who were all eager to catch a glimpse of the notorious Terror of the Shopping Mall.

But in this, the people were disappointed, for the tranquilized creature was covered over with a sheet, just as if it were a corpse. Mercifully for Wade and company, the police reinforcements held back the pressing throng.

Wade jogged ahead and opened the back doors of the Task Center truck. While Kent and Irving loaded the gurney, he cast a glance back at Paul, who was talking in earnest on his cell phone just outside the garage entrance.

All this time, the reporters kept shouting questions at Wade:

"Sir! Is the creature dead?"

"Could you give us a look at the body?"

"Do you work for the police?"

"Is it true that the beast is some kind of mutant?"

Then, over the clamor of the reporters, the crowd began chanting, "SHOW — THE — BEAST! SHOW — THE — BEAST!"

Wade just ignored them, wishing that Paul would hurry up and get off the phone.

Then he heard his name being called by a gruff voice that sounded strangely familiar: "Mr. Boss! Over here, Mr. Boss!"

Turning around, Wade was pleasantly surprised to see the mustached Officer O'Connor striding towards him.

"Officer O'Connor!" he exclaimed.

It seemed like forever and a day since together they had lugged the tiger-lizard out of Marjorie's canary-colored house. The last thing Wade could have imagined on that day was that they would be meeting again soon, and under similar circumstances.

Officer O'Connor gave him a firm handshake, and then with a wry smile said, "So! You've decided to make a career out of chasing monsters, have you?"

Wade chuckled and replied, "I guess it kinda looks that way, don't it?"

"Kind of does," said Officer O'Connor. "Listen, I've got orders to escort you and your people back to wherever it is you're going, and as quickly as possible."

"Of course. And thank you!" replied Wade, feeling that they could not get out of there soon enough.

In the back of the white truck, Kent attended the sedated patient, checking vital signs and performing a cursory physical. Irving jumped back down to the ground and looked to Wade for further instructions.

"All set?" asked Wade

"All set," said Irving.

"As soon as Paul gets over here, we'll take off," said Wade. Gesturing to his friend in blue, he told Irving, "Why don't you tell Officer O'Connor here what route you want to take."

As Irving proceeded to do just that, Wade saw to his relief that Paul was finally on his way over.

"Yes, sir!" said Paul, wrapping up his phone conversation. "Thank you, sir! Good-bye." With that, he pressed the call-end button and walked up to Wade with a curious grin on his face.

"Looks like somebody's got some news," said Wade, wondering what on earth could account for Paul's expression, given all that had just happened.

"When it rains, it pours," said Paul, cryptically.

Wade turned to Officer O'Connor and said, "All right, Officer —

we're ready to go."

With a nod, Officer O'Connor turned and walked over to his cruiser.

As Paul climbed into the back of the white truck, Irving asked him, "What about your car, sir?"

"I'll come back for it after all these reporters are gone," answered Paul.

"Yes, sir," said Irving. He waited for Wade to climb into the truck as well, and then closed the rear doors.

Wade improvised seats for Paul and himself by standing the silver field kits on end. The two men sat down facing each other, and then the truck lurched forward.

From the look on Paul's face, he was clearly bursting with news.

"Well?" asked Wade.

Paul took a deep breath and then said, "After the New Orleans debacle, I submitted three new budget proposals — one that was bare bones, one that would give us a little breathing room, and one that was pie-in-the-sky."

He paused dramatically, and then with something close to giddiness, he said, "I just got off the phone with the Chairman of the oversight committee. In light of everything that's happened this morning, they've opened the floodgates. We've got a blank check."

"You're kidding!" said Wade.

"New offices, field agents, equipment!" Paul elaborated. "Anything we want, and as much as we need. They just told me to start drawing up plans for a new containment facility — secure, state of the art, the whole nine yards!"

It gladdened Wade's soul to see this good man finally relieved of his crushing burden, for even though more crises were sure to come his way, at least now he would not have to face them with his hands tied.

After savoring the good news for a moment, Wade looked over at the gurney. Paul followed his gaze, and the two of them became very grave.

"Kent?" asked Wade.

"Vitals are stable. Seems healthy," said Kent. His tone was cold and clinical — much more so than usual, for he was finding it difficult to complete the exam.

After carefully inspecting the patient's eyes with a pen light, Kent sank down onto a metal stool. Looking at Wade and Paul over the body, he opened his mouth to speak.

Then he hesitated, as if by keeping silent he might be able to keep the lid on a Pandora's box. But of course it was too late now, and there was nothing he or anyone else could do except face the horrible truth.

Finally, with a heavy heart, Kent told Wade and Paul what they already knew: "This hybrid is half human."

For a long moment, the words just hung in the air.

It was Wade who broke the silence. With his eyes fixed upon the hybrid, he said, "If I had to make a guess, I'd say this is just the tip of the iceberg."

Paul and Kent soberly nodded their agreement.

"There might be a silver lining, though," Wade continued. "If this... *lion-man*... can talk, then maybe he can give us some information about who's behind all this."

The thought had not yet occurred to Paul or Kent, and they realized immediately that it was a key insight.

Next, Wade looked directly at Paul and said, "Listen, Paul — I told you before that I'm all in, and that's unconditional..."

"But?" said Paul.

"But," Wade continued, "I'd like to ask you for two things."

Paul nodded, and then Wade said, "Whether or not these

creatures *should* exist, the fact is, they *do*. And half-human or otherwise, they need to be treated with respect. You said we'll be getting the money to build a new facility?"

"That's right," said Paul.

"Then I want to be in on the planning, the construction — everything. There's a hundred things that go into makin' a proper habitat, and I want to make sure the job gets done right."

"Sounds good," said Paul. "And second?"

Wade looked back over at the gurney and said, "This poor soul — I want to be the one in charge of his care, and the care of any others like him that turn up. When it comes to decisions that affect them, I want my voice to be heard first, and loudest."

In spite of the seriousness of the subject matter, Paul had to smile, for everything Wade had just said confirmed that he was indeed the indispensable man.

Gratefully and without reservation, Paul replied, "Done."

* * *

A week later, the midday sun was bright and the sky a perfect blue — though the wind was up, making for a choppy ride.

The speedboat driver took the whitecaps head-on without any concern for the comfort of his solitary passenger, so that by now, Dr. Jules Krennick was quite green.

The yacht with which they were to rendezvous was floating only a mile or so out from San Francisco Bay. Still, the brief ride could not be short enough for Krennick, who was much relieved when they finally pulled alongside the floating palace.

Gritting his teeth, he reminded himself that he must maintain his composure.

Normally, he was able to keep his insecurities at bay with thoughts of his own astounding brilliance. Whenever he felt inadequate in a social setting, he always took comfort in the knowledge that he was the smartest person in the room.

But in just a moment, that would not be true — not by a long shot.

He was helped onboard the yacht by a muscular bodyguard in an expensive suit, who was formidable enough even without the submachine gun slung around his neck. The automatic weapon made it all the more difficult for Krennick to suppress his anxiety.

The bodyguard escorted him to the yacht's upper deck, and by the time they arrived at the opulent dining lounge, the doctor felt seasick, flustered, intimidated — in a word, *vulnerable*.

And that was a thing he could not abide.

The armed guard remained silent and opened a glass door framed with brass. Krennick entered the lounge, and as the door closed behind him, he was seized by a now-familiar dread that conjured with it visions of ancient tyrants and lions' dens.

Enjoying a surf-and-turf lunch at the end of a rich mahogany table was a man who cut a handsome figure for someone presumed by the world to be long dead.

At forty-five years of age, his long hair was streaked with gray — or would have been, if he did not bleach it. It was also feathered back to look as though it were being perpetually blown by gentle tropical breezes.

His expensive clothing was worn with a calculated casualness — especially his shirt, which was buttoned low to reveal a good deal of his bronzed, waxed chest. His face was tanned and clean-shaven, but it was his brilliant white teeth that made him truly look like a men's fashion model.

As always, Krennick wanted to punch him in the mouth.

The man smiled, pushed back from the dining table, and stood.

Nothing in the world brought him as much delight as entertaining, and Krennick always seemed to need extra help loosening up.

"Jules! At last!" said the Entertainer. He approached the doctor with arms wide open, as if to give him a big, welcoming hug.

To preclude an embrace, Krennick extended his hand.

The Entertainer wagged his head and downgraded his reception to a two-handed clasp — though even this was a little too familiar for Krennick's comfort.

"Sir," said Krennick, through a forced smile.

"'Sir'?" the Entertainer chided. "Jules, aren't we friends yet?" Then, after an awkward silence, he broke off the handshake and gestured to the mahogany table. "Lunch?" he offered.

"No, thank you," Krennick declined — not because he wasn't hungry, but because he was preoccupied. He was busy searching the room for someone — someone who had a preference for the shadows, who as a world-class poacher and smuggler had made a career out of stealth.

Because the lounge was flooded with daylight, Krennick found it easier than usual to locate the subject of his concern. As soon as he did, his blood turned to ice.

He saw the man standing in the corner off to his right. As always, the man was dressed in black, from his button-down shirt and designer jeans to his cattleman's hat and cowboy boots. The sun streaming in through the windows glinted brightly off his sterling cufflinks, custom belt buckle, expensive sunglasses, and hat band of silver links.

But even more striking than the man's flawless ensemble were the deep scars on the left side of his face that suggested that, once upon a time, it had been raked by terrible claws.

The last time the man had seen Krennick, it was to be informed of Wade's plans to go to New Orleans. But while the Task Center's former Head of Research had committed the betrayal, the inspiration to set loose the elephant-croc had come from the poacher himself.

The Dangerous Man.

Standing with his arms folded across his chest, he was fully aware of the fear he instilled in Krennick. Smiling a cruel smile, in a rasping voice, he said, "Doctor."

At the sound, Krennick flinched. Mustering what little courage he possessed, he returned the greeting with a slight nod.

By now, the Entertainer had resumed his lunch. "So!" he said, clapping his hands together. He gestured for Krennick to sit at the other end of the table, and the doctor stiffly complied.

The Entertainer dipped a lobster tail in some melted butter and took a bite. Then, with a full mouth, he said to Krennick, "Here's the part where you tell me we've over-played our hand."

Though the billionaire-genius had a disarming persona, Krennick knew that he had to frame his reply very carefully. Once he had done so, he said, "We're no longer dealing with a small, under-funded agency."

With an overdramatic sigh, the Entertainer conceded, "Yes. In retrospect I suppose it was a fool's errand, trying to dissuade them. But, as they appear resolute, we shall simply revise our strategy. Where intimidation has failed, sheer numbers will prevail."

Krennick leaned forward. "Accelerate the release schedule?" he asked.

As if to check Krennick's apparent eagerness, the Entertainer held up a hand. "Slightly!" he replied. "But not without regard for theatricality. As I was just telling our friend Mr. Stone, here: a crescendo rushed is a crescendo wasted. A deluge is artless where a rippling brook will suffice. We must simply determine how much the camel can carry, and then add a single straw!"

So saying, the Entertainer stood and walked over to the panoramic window facing the harbor. Again, he spread his arms wide, this time as if to embrace the entire city of San Francisco — or perhaps the country itself.

"Ah, Krennick!" he said grandiosely. "Life is a show — and my public awaits!"

TO BE CONTINUED IN...

AGENT OF MERCY